The woman threw away her useless blaster

"Macahuitl!" she screamed. *"Macahuitl!"*

Ryan wondered if it was a prayer or a curse. It was neither. One of the handful of Chichimecs still on their feet tossed her one of the obsidian-edged clubs.

The female marauder fielded the club deftly. She hacked it savagely into the tentacle that gripped her. The volcanic glass, sharper than a surgeon's scalpel, half severed the leg-thick member.

Holding the SIG-Sauer in both hands, Ryan backed cautiously away from the rail. He looked around quickly, trying to take stock of the tactical situation.

It was, basically, battle over.

**Other titles in the
Deathlands saga:**

JAMES AXLER

DEATH LANDS®

Shaking Earth

A GOLD EAGLE BOOK FROM
WORLDWIDE®

TORONTO • NEW YORK • LONDON
AMSTERDAM • PARIS • SYDNEY • HAMBURG
STOCKHOLM • ATHENS • TOKYO • MILAN
MADRID • WARSAW • BUDAPEST • AUCKLAND

First edition December 2004

ISBN 0-373-62578-2

SHAKING EARTH

Printed in U.S.A.

A conquering army on the border will not
be halted by the power of eloquence.

—Otto von Bismarck
1815–1898

THE DEATHLANDS SAGA

This world is their legacy, a world born in the violent nuclear spasm of 2001 that was the bitter outcome of a struggle for global dominance.

There is no real escape from this shockscape where life always hangs in the balance, vulnerable to newly demonic nature, barbarism, lawlessness.

But they are the warrior survivalists, and they endure—in the way of the lion, the hawk and the tiger, true to nature's heart despite its ruination.

Ryan Cawdor: The privileged son of an East Coast baron. Acquainted with betrayal from a tender age, he is a master of the hard realities.

Krysty Wroth: Harmony ville's own Titian-haired beauty, a woman with the strength of tempered steel. Her premonitions and Gaia powers have been fostered by her Mother Sonja.

J. B. Dix, the Armorer: Weapons master and Ryan's close ally, he, too, honed his skills traversing the Deathlands with the legendary Trader.

Doctor Theophilus Tanner: Torn from his family and a gentler life in 1896, Doc has been thrown into a future he couldn't have imagined.

Dr. Mildred Wyeth: Her father was killed by the Ku Klux Klan, but her fate is not much lighter. Restored from predark cryogenic suspension, she brings twentieth-century healing skills to a nightmare.

Jak Lauren: A true child of the wastelands, reared on adversity, loss and danger, the albino teenager is a fierce fighter and loyal friend.

Dean Cawdor: Ryan's young son by Sharona accepts the only world he knows, and yet he is the seedling bearing the promise of tomorrow.

In a world where all was lost, they are humanity's last hope....

Prologue

Away across the night the great paired mountains spewed arcs of orange fire. Their fury could be felt as well as heard, a continual mutter of thunder, punctuated by blasts that pained Raven's ears. If the fury of the old gods wasn't soon appeased with the blood and souls of the evildoers, so the priest Howling Wolf said, that pillar would grow to hide the heavens, choke sun and moon and stars, plunging all beneath into gloom. It had happened once before, during the time legend called the Great Skydark.

Only this time, Howling Wolf said, the dark would never end.

Reflected hoops of orange, distorted and wavering, were the only hints that a great lake lay like a discarded obsidian mirror between the fire mountains and the hogsback ridge behind which the horde was camped. Although the eyes of the man named Raven were no longer so keen close up as they had been in his youth, his far vision remained to justify his name. If he didn't gaze toward the flame fountains for a time, he could just make out tiny fugitive glimmers of light closer at hand, here and there down in the valley, and even in the rotted corpse of the dead city itself, which lay in the lake like a broken giant sprawled facedown in the pond that had drowned him.

Dead no more. Men once more crawled like maggots among the great bones of metal and stone and pale glass.

Screams beat like the buffets of the wind at Raven's bare bronzed back. In the great encampment captives were being cut and burned in sacrifice to the ancient gods. When the wind blew one way, it stank of sulfur; another way, and it reeked of blood and fear and charred flesh.

At such times Raven chose to walk away from the camp when he could. He was a hunter, a warrior, living in a land devoid of mercy; had he ever shrunk from the most brutal necessity he would never have lived long enough to take a man's name. It was the necessity of such cruelty he questioned.

His absences from the rituals of offering didn't please the priest or his acolytes. They had dropped hints that Raven, of all people, should display more piety. He ignored their threats. For he of all people they dared not harm—not the flesh and blood of the very one whom Howling Wolf said the old forgotten gods, so thirsty for blood and pain, had sent to save the people and all the world.

Over the cries of terrible anguish, he could hear the priest's voice, knew the sense of the words even though he was not close enough to actually hear them: once more the wicked seek to probe the lost evil secrets, to wake the dark powers that once devastated the world. They would revive the city, which forsook the gods and mocked the sky with its haughty towers. If we the chosen do not stop them, the wickedness they unleash this time will destroy the world utterly.

And so it might be, he thought. It was certainly true that the valley in which the lake lay was green and fertile despite the frequent shaking of the earth and the lethal clouds that sometimes flowed over it from the fire mountains. Likewise was it true that the high country where the people had dwelt time out of memory was becoming uninhabitable, racked by alternating drought and terrible storms that blew down from the lands of death to the north, with their strange hissing rains that could melt the skin from a man's bones. The people and the dwellers in the valley had coexisted, not always in peace: sometimes they traded, as often they raided one another. It didn't escape Raven that in exterminating the people of the valley for their presumption and wickedness, the true folk could insure their own survival. Indeed, Howling Wolf's preachings made sure the fact escaped no one.

So this great endeavor, so great that it joined not only true folk and witches but the very beasts of the wasteland, wasn't just good: it was necessary. But as he leaned on his flintlock, in the night between fires, Raven's spirit was troubled.

He glanced back at the camp. Not all the shapes dancing black against firelight were fully human. It was strange to see true men and witches together, except linked in deadly combat. But in many ways that was one of the least strange of the changes that had come.

And maybe the strangest of all was the boy.

He had been different from the first: no child of the people had ever been so pale. He was different, and so by ancient immutable tradition he should have been taken into the desert and left beneath the spines of a maguey. There either the coyotes and vultures would take him, or the witches would find him and take him in, raise him as one of their own, for indeed that was where the witches sprang from, the sons and daughters of true men who had been born tainted with difference and so had to be cast out.

But no one could bring himself to do the ancient duty: expose the boy to his fate. For anyone who looked upon him, unnatural though his appearance was, was instantly filled with a vast sense of well-being and love. Those at whom he smiled would sooner hurl themselves into a live lava flow than allow the least harm to befall him. He had such power, though never spoke a word.

As time passed the child grew larger, although his form altered little: he maintained the proportions of an infant. It became obvious that he could somehow control the very feelings of those around him. In time they would learn that this power extended not only to true men but to witches and even wild beasts.

By not exiling him as a newborn the people had in effect judged that his difference wasn't a taint, wasn't a mark of evil, as it was with witches. Therefore he had to be holy. He was a gift of the heavens, that much was sure. But to what purpose? None could say.

None until the boy was ten summers old and the tall,

gaunt man who covered his head and shoulders in the skin of a great wolf had appeared out of the south. He had taught the people the meaning of the gift. When he spoke in his deep, compelling voice, with the blood of sacrificial victims glistening on his cheeks in the fire-light, few could doubt the truth of what he said.

But Raven was among those few.

The boy's father, Two Whirlwinds, had never recovered from the shock of seeing what he had sired. Despite the people's judgment that the child was holy, he had felt shamed, tainted himself. He had begun to drink too much maguey wine, and when the child was two summers old had been surprised, dismembered and devoured by a pack of giant javelinas. Raven, elder brother to the boy's mother, had assumed the role of father. It was a role he welcomed. From the very first, it seemed, there had been a special bond between the two. It took no mystic power to make him love the child as if he were his own.

And so, though he was little given to fruitless questioning, he wondered.

If it were all true, if the boy had been sent by forgotten gods to restore to the people their ancient glory—a glory that not even the eldest of the people had witnessed, nor even heard tales of, but that Howling Wolf assured them was their birthright—why hadn't Raven, who raised the boy as a father, known of it before the strange priest came?

Chapter One

Long white hair streaming behind him, the young man ran through the woods. On the matlike floor of dead needles his combat moccasin boots made little more sound than morning mist flowing between the straight boles of spruce and fir. He was short and slight of build, and expertly dodged around potentially noisy patches of scrub oak, dry-leaved and prone to rattle in the early spring, nor did he brush against low-hanging tree boughs. Yet the fact he moved so quietly, despite the fact he ran flat-out, and even when he vaulted a low snaggle-toothed arch of dead fallen tree, seemed somehow almost supernatural.

That the skin of his face was as white as his hair did nothing to dispel the ghostly illusion. Nor did his eyes, narrowed with exertion, that gleamed red as shards of ruby. But ectoplasm wouldn't take scars like the ones that seamed his narrow feral face and pulled the right-hand corner of his mouth upward in a hint of perpetual grin. Nor was there anything the least bit insubstantial about the chrome-plated steel of the .357 Magnum Colt Python blaster he clutched in his right hand.

As swift as a deer he moved and as silent as a

thought. But his hunter's heart, virtual stranger to fear, felt it now. Because as fast as he was, he was whipped by the dread certainty he couldn't move fast enough to save his friends.

"THE BOY STOOD on the burning deck," the gaunt old man declaimed in a voice of brass.

"How come," asked the stocky black woman clad in an olive-drab T-shirt and baggy camou pants, "I'm the one who usually winds up elbow-deep in deer guts whenever we get lucky hunting?"

J. B. Dix, known otherwise as the Armorer, grinned at her around the carcass of the young whitetail buck that had been strung from a sturdy tree limb by its hind legs. Morning sunlight glinted off the round lenses of his steel-framed spectacles. "'Cause you're the doctor, Millie. You wield a mean scalpel."

She flipped him a gory bird.

"The boy stood on the burning deck," the old man said, even more loudly. He had the air of a man trying to jar something loose from memory's grasp. He was tall, with lank gray-white hair that fell to his shoulders. He wore a calf-length frock coat that had seen better days and cradled a Smith & Wesson M-4000 shotgun in his twig-skinny arms.

"I was a cryogenics researcher, for God's sake, John, not a surgeon," the black woman said. "Much less a veterinary pathologist."

J.B. smiled. "Well, I reckon you know what you're doing."

"You might as well make that crazy old coot you're trusting with your shotgun there do the gutting, since he's entitled to call himself 'doctor,' too," the woman said, ignoring the gibe.

J.B. doffed his fedora and scratched at his scalp. "You got training in cutting up folks. You told me so yourself. Everybody in med school did back in the day. Mebbe you just missed your calling."

Mildred Wyeth, M.D., glared at the little narrow-faced man. "Yeah. Maybe I should have become a cutter instead of a researcher. Then I could have been rich, had a big house in the 'burbs, a nice docile hubby, two-point-five kids, a shiny new Caddy every year." She looked thoughtful, scratched at her cheek with the very tip of her thumb, as if maybe if she did it gingerly enough she wouldn't get gore on her cheek. She failed. "And then of course I'd've died while at the operating table instead of having a nice experimental cold-sleep pod on hand, to get slipped into for a snug century or so."

"I'm glad you pulled through, Millie," J.B. said quietly.

"Yeah, well at times like this I'm almost glad, too, even if I am stuck on shit detail. A little peace and quiet is doing us all a world of good. And bagging some good game without any taint of mutie doesn't hurt, either. Sometimes it seems we're in danger of getting too dependent on what we can scavenge from the redoubts or scam out of the villes. Woman does not live by century-old MREs alone. Or at least this woman doesn't."

"The boy stood on the burning deck!" the old man almost shouted.

"'Eating peanuts by the peck,'" Mildred said.

The old man blinked at her.

"That's the next line, Doc," she said. "Trust me."

"Quoth the raven," Professor Theophilus Algernon Tanner said in a deflating kind of way, "nevermore."

"And here I thought he was okay these days," Mildred muttered, shaking her head as she returned to her grisly work.

"Doc," the Armorer said with gentle firmness, "don't go wandering off into neverland, now. We need you to keep a sharp lookout. Not had a whiff of anything menacing, two-legged or more, norm or mutie, in three whole days. And that very fact itself makes me uneasy."

The old man nodded. His eyes seemed to have gained focus. "You are quite correct, John Barrymore. It's when the illusion of peace and safety seems most perfect that danger draws nigh."

"Yeah," Mildred said bitterly. "Any state less than constant screaming terror just isn't natural."

J.B. nodded. "They don't call these the Deathlands for nothing."

RYAN CAWDOR LAY on the ground, with his bare feet planted in a lush mat of fallen Ponderosa pine needles, long and gracefully curved as sabers, held together at the bases in clusters of three. The freedom afforded by temporary safety, to take his boots off and feel untainted nature beneath his soles, was an almost erotic pleasure.

Krysty Wroth, the most beautiful woman of the Deathlands—and not just in her mate's single prejudiced eye—lay on the ground beside him. Both were gloriously nude, enjoying a moment of closeness and solitude after an hour of lovemaking.

He marveled in the sight of her, her white skin given a faint golden luster by the sunlight filtering through the trees. He would never tire of her, could never imagine tiring of her beauty, her vitality, her untamable spirit.

Both of them were alert to their surroundings, knew from the soft forest sounds that no immediate danger threatened. Both also knew the interlude could last but moments, that they would need to pick themselves up and square themselves away too soon, because as Mildred had just observed, unheard by them, peace and safety were unnatural states in the Deathlands, unstable as an isotope of plutonium.

All the same, the Deathlands had taught them to make the most of any and all such moments they could tear out of the grim, potentially lethal fabric of their daily lives. He stroked her cheek. They kissed. "Time to go, lover."

With a sigh of regret the lovers stood.

Ryan picked up his Steyr sniper rifle and stood guard, unself-conscious of being buck-ass naked, while Krysty dressed without either hurrying or dawdling. Then she took temporary possession of the longblaster while he got his clothes on.

When he was ready she handed him back the rifle with a smile. "Better get back to camp, lover," she said. "Don't want the others to think we're ducking the dirty work…"

Her voice trailed off. Ryan had cranked the bolt on

reflex on getting the blaster back, pulling it back so as to lay an eyeball on a comforting gleam of brass in the chamber, just a sliver, because he knew from bitter experience that an unexamined blaster was always in the worst possible condition.

Because the forest sounds around them—the squirrel cussing them out from up the tree and the Steller's jays yammering at each other from the scrub—had gone as still as the grave.

Chapter Two

"Coldhearts!" Jak Lauren yelled as he burst through the scrub oak at the foot of the clearing where Mildred worked and the others watched. "Mebbe thirty, riding hard!"

"Shit!" Mildred said.

Instantly, Doc tossed her J.B.'s Smith & Wesson longblaster and unleathered his cumbersome LeMat percussion pistol.

Mildred's hands were still encased in gloves of gore when she fielded the M-4000. She winced. J.B. was going have a fit when this was done. She preferred her own target-grade ZKR 551 .38-caliber handblaster, but unlike Doc Tanner, she wasn't nutty enough to waste time swapping for it when the hammer came down.

Instead she threw the shotgun to her shoulder just as three riders burst out of the patch of mountain oak hard on Jak's tail. One of them swung a club that looked like a baseball bat with nails driven into it, the heads snipped off at a bias to create a bristle of lethal spikes. The albino youth dived facedown into the tan grass and the horses thundered past him.

"Bastards!" Mildred yelled. She aimed the front sight

right for the middle of the fleshy black-bearded face of the man who'd dropped Jak and pulled the trigger. The blaster bucked and roared; the face disappeared in a spray of red blood and white bone chips.

But the physician's pang of grief was wasted. As canny and feral as a wolf, Jak had gauged the swing and dived to avoid it. He reared up to one knee and blasted off three shots from his Colt Python. A brown-haired coldheart with ochre stripes painted across his hatchet face threw up his arms in a spasm as one of the 158-grain Magnum rounds blew one of his vertebrae into powder, then carried on with the aid of bone-splinter shrapnel to pulp his heart and lights. A remade Mini-14 with a broken stock went spinning away as his horse reared and dumped him over its croup.

The third rider charged straight for J.B., a long black queue of hair with finger bones braided into it flapping like a pennon behind and blazing away with some kind of booming revolver. He had no more luck firing from a galloping horse than most did who tried such a double-stupe stunt. The Armorer coolly reached down, picked up his Uzi and held down the trigger one-handed. Copper-jacketed 9 mm slugs punched holes in the rider at the buckskin-clad thigh, walked their way up his filthy plaid flannel shirt, tore out one side of his jaw and poked a hole through one cheekbone. That rider went down, the horse screaming and veering off into the brush to get away from the terrible flame and noise that had gone off in its face.

Jak pelted upslope, stepping on the still-writhing

body of the man he'd shot. "Ryan! Krysty!" he shouted. "Where?"

J.B. and Mildred looked blankly at each other.

RYAN STOOD with his rifle butt against his shoulder but the barrel depressed, seeking targets. The telescopic sight severely restricted the shooter's field of vision. He didn't want to be lost in the scope when an attacker appeared from a whole different angle. Krysty was beside him, her .38 Smith & Wesson model 640 in hand. It wasn't an ideal weapon for a fight in the woods, even with undergrowth cutting down engagement range. Still, it beat a knife to hell.

The clearing they were in was much smaller than the one a hundred paces or so away, not far downslope from the entry to the redoubt where they had left their comrades to butcher the carcass of the deer Ryan had shot that morning. They heard crackling in the brush, glimpsed large shapes between the trees. Horsemen, Krysty mouthed to Ryan.

He nodded. Neither fired. Against a known enemy, ambush was mere good sense. But unless you were a stone coldheart yourself you didn't shoot at strangers on sight. Enemies were plentiful enough as it was without going out of your way to manufacture more in the persons of vengeful survivors.

From the direction of the camp came shouts, shots, which changed everything. With Krysty ghosting along at his side, Ryan moved fast and crouched, not directly back to where the others were but at an angle down the mountainside. That way they might either take a force attacking their friends in the flank or possibly intercept enemies attempting a flanking maneuver of their own.

The forest had come alive again with sounds of a different sort: yells, the thudding of hooves, the crack of branches breaking. Apparently a substantial band of mounted raiders had stumbled upon their camp. Ryan had time to be thankful his group had camped so near the redoubt entrance. There were too many attackers to stand off and even in these woods a party of six would have had a hard time evading them.

The possibility of negotiation never entered his mind.

A warning cry from Krysty brought his head around. Three horsemen had appeared not twenty yards downhill, heading directly for them, trying to outflank J.B. and the others. One carried a dilapidated lever-action carbine with brass tacks hammered into stock and foregrip for decoration; one, a slab-sided 1911-model .45 autopistol; the third, a steel-headed lance decorated with feathers and what seemed to be scalps. Both riders and mounts were painted in fanciful patterns.

The horsemen faltered in surprise at encountering the pair. The carbine man threw his weapon to his shoulder. Ryan already had his Steyr up, cheek welded to stock. He laid the crosshairs just below the wrist of the coldheart's left hand, which supported the carbine's fore end. He squeezed the trigger. The rifle cracked and slammed his shoulder. The 180-grain, boat-tailed bullet, painstakingly loaded into the cartridge a hundred years before at the Rock City Arsenal in Illinois, passed through meat between radius and ulna without slowing, drilled a neat hole through a rib, began to yaw as it tore through his heart, knocking a huge plate of his right scapula out along with a bloody chunk of trapezius muscle as it exited his back. His horse, a buckskin with a blue ring painted around one eye, reared. He toppled right over the rump without firing.

The spearman uttered a blood-curdling scream and kicked his horse into a charge. Krysty crouched, holding her blaster at full reach of both arms, coolly waiting with her hair stirring around her shoulders. When the rider got within ten yards she began squeezing off shots. The rider screamed as a bullet entered his belly. Another smashed his shoulder. He fell and screamed more as his horse, sheering away from the redheaded woman, dragged him off through the trees at a panicky run.

The third rider had hesitated when the man with the carbine was hit. Then he turned his pinto away and booted its sides. He was just about to vanish among the trees when Ryan, having thrown the bolt and brought the Steyr SSG back online as quickly as he could, broke his spine just above the level of his heart with a shot. Ryan had no qualms about blasting an enemy in the back. It was just a way to make sure he didn't circle around once out of sight to try his luck again, hopefully when your guard was down.

He looked at Krysty. She had the cylinder open, had spilled both empties and whatever unfired cartridges remained into her hand and transferred them to her pocket, and was feeding in reloads quick as she could.

She could sort the spent casings from the live rounds later; what counted now was a full handblaster.

"You okay?" he asked.

She nodded and snapped the cylinder shut. "Let's go," she said.

AT THE CAMP J.B., Mildred, Doc and Jak had fanned out and taken cover. They didn't have long to wait before more coldhearts arrived, eight riders charging them across the thirty-yard-wide clearing.

J.B. sprayed them with one long burst from his Uzi. A 9 mm slug was unlikely to drop a horse, at least right away. But back in the Trader days the Armorer had noticed something about horses: they had minds of their own and they didn't like getting hurt, and they especially didn't like the smell of equine blood. Also their legs, skinny by comparison to their big muscular bodies, were relatively fragile. So he deliberately fired low, hoping to cripple or wound as many mounts as possible as fast as possible.

Horses screamed, reared. Two went down, one pinning its rider's leg. One began bucking uncontrollably, and a fourth simply turned and ran away despite its rider's cursing and hauling back on the reins.

Like most late-twentieth-century people, at least from Western cultures, Mildred hated seeing animals suffer. She was actually fighting tears when she unloaded a charge of buckshot from J.B.'s M-4000 into the glossy brown chest of a bay. It reared, shrieking in an almost human voice. Its rider calmly aimed a sawed-off double gun at her. She fired at him rapidly and had to have hit him because he fell before his horse did.

Jak blazed away at a rider charging him. Scarlet bloomed against the horse's white neck but the animal only stumbled, then came on. The rider was returning fire with a handblaster but only throwing up clumps of pine needles near the albino. Jak rolled to the side as the injured horse ran right through the place where he'd lain prone. Its rider reined it in, pivoted in the saddle, trying to turn his blaster to bear on the albino youth.

Then the coldheart dropped the handblaster and clapped his hand to his neck just below his ear. It wasn't quite enough to stem the violent spray of blood from the carotid artery, severed by the leaf-bladed knife Jak had thrown.

A wiry rider armed with a machete, to which some enterprising postnuke weaponsmith had added a spiked knuckle-duster by way of a handguard, rode a black horse with a white blaze straight for Doc, who was kneeling with his LeMat in one hand and his swordstick in the other. Doc had already fired several shots at other targets, but he emptied the remaining .44 rounds into the horse before the beast collapsed. The rider rolled over his mount's neck, somersaulted, came up on his feet running right at Doc. He raised his machete over his head for the deathstroke.

Then he looked down at his chest. A slim length of steel had transfixed it, right through the heart. Doc had unsheathed a rapier from his swordstick, and the cold-heart's run had forced him to impale himself. The marauder looked at Doc with an expression of complete surprise and collapsed.

One of the coldhearts whose mount had been downed was kneeling, firing wildly with a .22-caliber Ruger autoloading rifle. Abruptly the right side of his head opened up in a cloud of pink spray. Ryan and Krysty had arrived in some brush at the edge of the clearing. The one-eyed man had popped a 7.62 mm round through the raider's temple.

There was a rustle and swirl of motion farther down the slope as the other coldhearts withdrew. From the shouting it sounded as if there were plenty of them left.

"Go!" Ryan yelled, breaking from cover. Shots cracked from the trees, knocking out chunks of bark and raising little sprays of fallen needles from the ground. "We've gotta clear out while we got the chance. They won't hold back for long!"

Mildred looked toward the deer carcass she'd been gutting. A bullet cut the rope that suspended it from the branch. It fell into the dirt. Not even she had enough twentieth-century squeamishness left to care much about that—it'd wash off—but the damned thing was simply too heavy to try to pick up and haul off under fire.

"Son of a *bitch*," she said. She grabbed her pack and, still clutching J.B.'s shotgun, ran toward the redoubt entrance.

With a running start Ryan reached the entryway first. Instead of ducking behind the granite protrusion that sheltered the entrance from view, he spun, knelt and began firing to cover the others. They came—Doc Tanner first, running with surprising alacrity, his elbows out to the sides and pumping; Jak, hair trailing like a cloud of white smoke; J.B. crab-walking alongside Mildred to make sure she made it while spurting quick bursts from his Uzi toward the unseen foe.

Realizing their quarry was somehow getting away, the coldhearts raised an outcry of cheated fury. Riders burst from the trees and scrub like steel marbles from a Claymore mine, hurtling toward the redoubt entrance.

Ryan dropped them as fast as he could throw the Steyr's butter-smooth bolt. Krysty was beside him, knowing he'd insist on her getting to safety before he would, but wanting to stand by him as long as she could. "Go!" he told her. She turned to dart inside the entrance they'd left open as he fired the last shot in the SSG's detachable magazine.

A quick blur of motion, a sound like an ax hitting wood, a gasp, more of surprise than pain. Ryan took his eye from the scope to see Krysty slumped against the granite face with a crossbow bolt protruding from her back, just inward of the left shoulder.

"*Krysty!*" he shouted. The word seemed torn from him like skin from his back.

The woman came around. With her right hand she raised her blaster. The crossbowman was closing fast, dropping his spent weapon to reach for a Bowie-type knife in a beaded sheath under his arm. With cool deliberation Krysty aimed and shot him through his thick, dirty throat. He roared, the noise drowning in a gurgle of his own blood.

As he fell, Krysty turned at last and stumbled into the redoubt. A rider loomed above Ryan. He was a big man with flying blond braids and an eagle feather at the back of his skull, grinning all over his bearded, painted face as he raised a battered CAR-4, a 9 mm submachinegun version of the venerable M-16. Ryan knew at once he was the coldhearts' leader.

"You lose, fucker," the blond man said.

But Ryan had already released the empty rifle with his right hand, still holding it in his left. His panga whispered from its sheath. With a thunk, the heavy blade severed the coldheart's gunhand right above the wrist.

The raider boss stared in gape-mouthed amazement at his own hand lying on the bare dirt, spinning as random dying neural impulses spasmed the finger on the subgun's trigger. Blood sprayed from his arm like a hose.

Ryan followed his injured woman into the redoubt, then keyed the blastproof door shut.

Chapter Three

Hardness against his cheek. Pulsing warm—or was he only feeling the heat being drawn out of his face into a floor cold as a baron's heart?

Ryan lay on his belly. He was unaware of having fallen. The world, slowly, ceased to spin around him.

The groans of his companions made their way through the fog that wrapped his brain. It had been a bad jump, the kind that reached down your gullet and yanked your guts out your mouth.

Krysty!

His eye felt as if it were glued shut. He forced it open. The upper lid came away from the lower with a sick gummy sensation. His empty socket throbbed with scarlet pulses of ache.

Krysty at least had begun the jump on her back, carefully laid down by Mildred and Ryan. She remained pretty much as they had left her, left arm strapped across her sternum to immobilize it. The right, which had been crossed over her stomach, now lay by her side. A thin trickle of blood ran to the floor of the gateway where she had clenched her fist so hard during the jump that her nails had pierced her palm. Her face was unnaturally pale, almost blue, contrasting harshly with her hair, which lay limp around her head like a tangle of red seaweed.

Ryan crawled to her, more lizard than man, feeling as if a mutie the size of a mountain were squatting on his back jeering at his misery. He grabbed her right arm, felt for pulse inside her wrist. It was there and strong.

Now that he knew his woman lived, Ryan allowed himself cautiously to become aware of more of his surroundings. The chamber had walls of orange-red arma-glass that passed the dim illumination of the room beyond, which had automatically come on when the gateway powered up to materialize them, like the glow of a fire. There were bad smells, not the bland sterile smell of a long-unused chamber. There were sounds, too: dull distant thumps like giant stone fists being slammed together; pops and cracks like the fire of heavy blasters, the kind needed to be toted with a big war wag; and under everything a deep-note noise that wasn't quite a moan and wasn't quite a roar, with a bit of crackle and sort of a seethe. A sound you could hear through your bones if both eardrums were shot.

Ryan braced himself on one elbow and looked around. J.B. had hauled himself to a sitting position and was helping Mildred do likewise. Jak already sat with his knees drawn up and his crimson eyes sunk in his face like blood spots in a sheet. A dribble of puke, semidried, still trailed from the corner of his mouth.

"Shit," the albino said. "Look like Doc croaked."

Doc lay on his back, arms outstretched, mouth agape, rheumy eyes staring unblinking at the top of the mat-trans chamber. Seeing him like that made Mildred shift to rise up and tend to him. Then she settled back down on her haunches, gazing sorrowfully at him and shaking her head. There was obviously no point.

"I never thought one of us would go like this," Mildred said, shaking her head. "Dean, now Doc."

Ryan's mouth was a thin line. "Doc looks about as peaceful as he ever gets," Ryan said. His heart weighed down his rib cage. Seeing Doc lying there stark and dead was like losing another part of his body.

He lifted Krysty's hand, kissed the back of it, laid it across her other arm. Then he got up, wobbled, fought for and regained his balance, and walked staunchly upright the few steps to where his comrade lay. He knelt, reached down and, with thumb and forefinger of his right hand, started to close the lids of Doc's eyes.

The old man jerked and blinked. "By the Three Kennedys!" he exclaimed. "What are you trying to do, my dear boy? Blind me?"

Ryan recoiled as if the old man had transformed into a coiled diamondback. "Fireblast!"

Doc sat up with an almost audible creak of joints. "Indeed. One might think you had never seen a man in repose."

"Doc, you was the deadest-looking article I ever hope to see," the Armorer said with a chuckle. The old man stood, shot his cuffs and dusted off his frock coat.

"Lover."

Ryan's head snapped around. Krysty was sitting up. The color had returned to her cheeks. Before he or

Mildred, who had at last gained her own feet, could move to assist her, she stood.

BARE FROM THE WAIST UP, Krysty Wroth had sat in the infirmary of the Rocky Mountain redoubt, teeth locked on Ryan's scuffed old leather belt. Mildred Wyeth had a pair of channel-lock pliers from J.B.'s armorer's kit clamped on the head of the crossbow quarrel. The cold-heart missile had a barbed iron head that reached halfway down the shaft to make it hard for the recipient to tear it out of the wound. However, a crossbow quarrel had enormous penetrating power. The bolt had actually gone all the way through Krysty's left shoulder to tent out the fabric of her jumpsuit with two inches of gory tip.

"Hold on, Krysty," Mildred said. She pulled hard. Krysty closed her eyes, her fingers dug deep as talons into Ryan's hand. She made no sound.

The quarrel came free with a sucking sound. Blood gushed out, flowing down into towels they'd discovered inside an old laundry storage bin and heaped around the redhead's middle. Mildred had told the others they'd need to let the wound bleed freely for a short time to flush the channel. The benefit would offset the minor additional blood loss.

But even before she nodded to Ryan and J.B. to start pressing gauze compresses over the holes, entrance and exit, Mildred's broad dark face was wrinkled in a gesture of disgust. Ryan frowned.

"The smell," Mildred said, holding the grisly trophy away from her. "Not much question what it is."

"Not gangrene, surely?" Doc Tanner asked.

"Way too soon. No, it's feces, probably human. Those coldheart mothers didn't miss a beat."

"Want to guarantee nobody gets away from them," J.B. said, sharing a grim look with Ryan. They were well familiar with that particular trick from their time with Trader, years before. Smearing a penetrating weapon, like a missile or a punji stick, with human feces all but guaranteed infection, deep-seated and virulent, in anyone unlucky enough to be punctured by it.

"There's still alcohol and gauze left in the redoubt stores, and even some packets of antibiotic powder," Mildred said. "I can make a lick and a promise at cleaning out the filth. I can make a pass at debriding the wound, cutting out the dead and tainted flesh with a scalpel, to minimize the infection. But one thing we don't have is anesthetics."

Krysty sat, pallid and swaying, with Ryan's arm around her. "Do what you need to do, Mildred. I can take it."

"Do you need to?" Ryan asked. "What about Krysty's natural ability to heal?"

"It has its limits," Mildred said, "like everything else. As a doctor and a friend, I can't in conscience let it go without getting some of that crap out of there. I think we can pass on debriding, since that would add to the existing trauma, and nothing in my power is going to prevent infection totally. On the other hand, cleaning the wound channel will help keep the infection down while doing minimal extra damage. But…it'll be rough."

It was. Mildred had borrowed both a segmented screw-together aluminum cleaning rod from J.B.'s kit and the concept of another gun-cleaning implement, the pull-through bore scrubber. She used the rod to poke a string through the wound, back to front, and then used it to pull through some thicker cord braided first with alcohol-soaked gauze patches, then dry ones, and finally patches liberally coated in broad-spectrum antibiotic powder. Krysty had endured all in the same stoic silence with which she had taken Mildred's pulling out the bolt. But by the end her eyes were tightly shut and Ryan had to hang on to her to prevent her toppling from the steel table as she passed out.

SHE'D STRUCK IT lucky one way, anyway: she'd been out for the jump. Now she was standing unassisted.

"Careful, there," Ryan began, eyeing Krysty carefully in case she started to sway.

Krysty shook her head, smiling. Her hair continued to stir around her shoulders after the motion was done.

"I'm fine," she said. "Well, not fine. I'm okay for the moment. The power of Gaia is strong right here and now. Can't you feel it?"

"I can sure hear it," Ryan said. The colossal groans and creaks and thuds reverberating in the very marrow of his bones could only originate within the Earth itself, he knew.

"The infection's working in me," Krysty said. "Gaia's power will help me fight it, but I'll need time."

"Time, fair lady, is one commodity we might not be

vouchsafed," Doc said. "Judging from the prevalence of mephitic vapors, if we have not actually attained the infernal regions, we may have found ourselves in surroundings scarcely more salubrious."

"From the smell of sulfur and the sound effects," J.B. said, looking up and around the mat-trans chamber as if judging how likely it was to hold up, "I reckon we might just have jumped in the belly of a live smoky." He shrugged. "Out of the frying pan—"

"But these redoubts were built to withstand nuclear explosions," Mildred protested. "What can a volcanic eruption do to them?"

Doc shook his head, his face set in a look of bloodhound mournfulness. "Much, it is to be feared, dear lady. When I was the involuntary guest of the Totality Concept and Operation Chronos in your own charming time, I read studies to the effect that a single large eruption discharged the force of many, many multimegaton warheads. The illusion of safety afforded by our surroundings may be precisely that."

"A live volcano? What imbecile would've decided to build a redoubt inside a volcano?" Mildred asked.

"It might not've been live back before skydark," Ryan said. "Mebbe they reckoned on it staying dormant."

"And how much do you trust whitecoat judgment?" J.B. asked. "They did such a swell job with the good Doc here."

"Talk fills no empty bellies or water bottles," Ryan said. "We better take a look-see, find out what's actually going on."

He glanced around the chamber with its flame-colored walls, now sinister and suggestive. Had the builders intended it as some kind of ironic commentary on their own arrogance in building their shelter in the gut of a volcano? Or was it a sign of their obliviousness?

He didn't bother to shrug. Only bigger waste of time than reckoning men's motives, he thought, was trying to reckon dead men's motives.

"Let's move," he said. "Krysty keeps to the rear, with Mildred to guard her." Ryan stepped forward and opened the door to the chamber.

Mildred nodded, her ZKR already in hand. Krysty, he noted with approval, hadn't drawn her own weapon. Last thing anybody headed into potential danger—and the unknown was always dangerous—was somebody at his back with a blaster who wasn't in complete control of himself. Or herself. Normally, Krysty pulled her weight and more without being asked. Now she did her part by keeping out of the way, because Gaia or not, she wasn't fit to fight, and had sense to know and accept it.

He nodded to J.B., who with scattergun ready moved swiftly out the open door of the mat-trans chamber. He stepped left to clear the doorway. Ryan followed, holding his 9 mm SIG-Sauer in both hands, through the antechamber and right, to hunker down behind a control console. Each scanned half of the large room beyond, all senses stretched to greatest sensitivity, not just vision.

This room was pretty standard, if darker than usual. Black walls and ceiling seemed to soak up the dim white light that had come on automatically when the transfer completed. The room was circular, perhaps ten yards across. The only visible doors were closed.

Except for the groans and bangs of the Earth itself, shivering up through the floor and Ryan's boots and the bones of his legs, the place gave off a pervasive feel of emptiness, of deadness.

"Clear," J.B. said.

"Clear," Ryan echoed.

Jak came out next as if shot from a coldheart crossbow, hitting the far wall with his big Python a dull metallic gleam in both hands, covering the room either side of the mat-trans. Doc came next, LeMat held out at full extent of one arm as if probing like an insect's feeler.

Jak's nose was twitching like a wild animal's and his lip was curled. "Stinks," he said. "But dead. Nobody here."

"Reckon you're right," Ryan said. "But we make sure. Mildred, you and Krysty stay here and stay sharp. The rest of us will secure the place."

THE REDOUBT WAS EMPTY, all right. Its automatic life-support systems seemed to function properly. As the four men moved with swift caution through the corridors and up and down stairs the stench of brimstone, which had infiltrated the vast subterranean structure over a century or more, was replaced by cooler, cleaner-smelling air scrubbed by the filters. "Cleaner-smelling" was a relative term; the redoubt was full of a musty smell no HVAC system could exorcise, of dust and mildew and disuse—and, faintly but unmistakably, of

death. They found several corpses, shrunk and mummi-
fied in the dry sterilized air, bundled in ancient U.S.
army uniforms. Unusual.

When the group came back to the gateway control
room Ryan was alarmed to find Krysty lying apparently unconscious on a pallet composed of their coats
and jackets. "She's just resting," Mildred said, moving
away and lowering her voice so as not to disturb her patient. "Letting Gaia get a head start on healing her. They
and me got a job of work ahead of us." She studied the
four. "Especially if we need to move right away."

"You called the shot," J.B. said. "Place is cleaned out
pretty good. No food, no weps, no meds. There's all the
water we could want. We can get cleaned up and drink
until our skins are swollen out like three-day-old dead-
ers. But that's all she wrote for resupply."

Mildred sucked in her lower lip. The mountain retreat
had been good to them. The abundance of game and natural food to gather had left them with a few days' MREs
and self-heats in all their packs. But all that really
granted them was a little time to forage for more food
in whatever terrain lay beyond the redoubt—and the
erupting volcano.

"And to think," Mildred said sourly, "right about now
those bastard coldhearts are stuffing their faces with
that nice juicy deer I gutted. Well, we can't stay here,
even if the roof doesn't open up and pour lava on our
heads."

She looked around at the scouting party. "You guys
must have some *good* news," she said, "'cause you're

bouncing around like schoolkids who got to pee. So spill it. I'm not in a mood for games."

J.B. looked to Ryan, who shrugged. "Well, we do have to get out of here," the small man said, "but we don't have to walk."

"PRETTY, ISN'T SHE?" J.B. asked, words echoing in the vastness of the underground garage. "She's a Hummer."

"I know what a Hummer is, J.B.," Mildred said. "A Humvee, too. It's not like it's the first one we ever found."

"Got a nuke battery, so we don't need to worry about fuel," Ryan said. "It's all there and good to go."

"Wonder why they left it," Mildred said.

Ryan shrugged. "I suspect everyone used the gateway. Who knows?"

Mildred eyed the circular hole in the vehicle's roof. "Too bad they dismounted whatever the pintle gun was and took it with them."

"But then, should danger rear its ugly head," Doc said, "we simply rely on flight rather than fight."

"We do both," Ryan said, "if we need to. We can always shoot through the windows. Right now, let's get cleaned up and get a good sleep. Whatever's waiting outside, at least we can be rested, strong and squared-away to face it."

Chapter Four

The giant fans of the redoubt's HVAC system produced a slight overpressure. Air gusted outward as the great doors began to slide apart noiselessly—or at least with no noise that could be heard over the horrific bomb-blast concerto playing nonstop outside.

Night waited. But no stars. A roof of cloud or maybe smoke, lit by pulsing hell-glows of yellow and orange from below, from within by blue-white lightning novas.

As the doors opened wider, the air from outside eddied back in, stinging hot, bringing a swirl of gray ash soft as the finest fur. Ryan choked and gagged on the stink of sulfur and his eye watered. He staggered back, coughing.

After a moment he got the coughing fit under control and looked around at his friends. They were covering their mouths and noses with their hands to filter out the ash and dabbing at their eyes. "What's the verdict, Mildred?" Ryan croaked.

"Just smells bad," came the physician's muffled voice. "If that was hydrogen sulfide we were breathing, we'd be in our death throes already with our lungs full of sulfuric acid."

Ryan looked back outside. The brightest and most persistent glow seemed to come from his left. He guessed the main vent was off that way. Relief: they weren't staring down the hellbore muzzle of the mountain, at any rate.

Then a handful of blazing light balls like giant meteors arced across his vision to spatter the slopes below and to his right with brief pulses of yellow fire, just to keep him from getting cocky. But the doors themselves were clear and the ground outside seemed unobstructed by rockslide or lava flow.

"Looks like we got us a road outta here, anyway," the Armorer muttered from behind. Ryan nodded.

Doc stretched out an arm, long finger pointing. "By Jove! Look there!"

By the underlighting of the clouds they could tell they were looking out over a bowl-shaped valley many miles wide. Way, way off lay a sheet of something like black glass, with a jagged trail of crimson stretching out across it—a lake, it seemed, reflecting the fire plume of the erupting vent. Out in the middle of that black glass sheet, reflecting in it, was visible a scatter of faint lights.

"A ville," Ryan said.

"Villes," Jak said.

"He's right," J.B. agreed. There were at least half a dozen other small clumps of lights scattered across the valley, shimmering slightly in the ground effect.

"Pretty dense habitation, comparatively speaking," Mildred said. She hovered protectively near Krysty, who stood on her own power but seemed at least halfway in a trance, from the infection that had taken root in her shoulder despite Mildred's best efforts—just as Mildred had predicted—or from the forces of Gaia surging so mightily around them, or both. "There's food here. And safety."

"How you reckon that?" J.B. asked.

"Number of villes. Way they're spread out, rather than all clumped up together in one big defensive perimeter. You wouldn't get that kind of population in that kind of distribution without at least comparative peace."

The Armorer grunted noncommittally. "Likely you're right. But still, mebbe you aren't. No guarantees in this life."

"Things change," Jak said.

"Tell me something new," Ryan said with a winter smile.

GETTING TO THE CENTERS of habitation proved to be more than difficult.

With the Hummer's independently suspended tires bouncing over lava rocks head-size or better and his partners, including the sorely injured Krysty, bouncing around in the cab like badly stowed luggage, Ryan wondered if he would even be able to drive them off the fire mountain. It would have been vicious enough going in the dark with nothing but the jagged terrain to cope with.

The mountain was spewing. Away off to their left fountains of fire arced red across the sky. The one thing to be thankful for was that their path, such as it was, led steadily away from the eruption.

A scarlet glow shone on the hood in front of him. He leaned forward, eye straining up, trying to figure out where it came from. Suddenly a fang of rock not thirty yards to their left seemed to explode in a yellow flash. The wag rocked. The cab filled with voices crying out in surprised alarm. Impacts thunked off the Hummer's steel and Kevlar carapace like hail. J.B., standing upright with his Uzi in lieu of the missing mount-gun, ducked into the cab with a yelp as a handful of glowing yellow embers spattered across the hood.

"Fireblast!" Ryan exclaimed. "What the fuck was that?"

"Bomb," Doc said. Since the coldhearts had chased them off their idyllic mountain camp into the redoubt, he had been totally lucid, showing no sign of the madness that sometimes overtook him. Somewhat to Ryan's surprise, he remained entirely calm in the face of whatever had just happened.

"You're kidding, Doc," Mildred said, hunching down in back, looking up and out, trying to fathom what had happened. "Somebody's attacking?"

"Only the gods in their wrath," Doc replied blithely. He rode in the back seat with Jak, who sat clutching one of his leaf-bladed throwing knives like a talisman in both hands. Mildred was in the aft cargo compartment tending to Krysty, who lay on a mat laid on top of their baggage, such as it was. "That was a lava bomb. A bubble, if you will, of molten rock, filled with lethal gas. If one lands too close to us we are undone, to say nothing of what should eventuate were one to strike us directly."

"Dark night," J.B. muttered. He straightened reluctantly, poking his head beyond the dubious protection of the cab. Almost at once he yelled, "Right, Ryan! Crank hard right!"

Ryan obeyed. The Hummer heeled over alarmingly to the left as the wag turned sharply. The one-eyed man almost left his teeth in the steering wheel as the front bucked up. And then the engine was straining, whining in anguish as it struggled to push them over a boulder in their path. The wag climbed, almost stalled, then pitched forward. Ryan gritted his teeth as the wag's belly scraped over the sharp-toothed lava rock. But the rugged vehicle neither dropped its guts nor hung. It ground over the top and down. Mildred cursed as the top of her head hit the ceiling.

Ryan cranked his head around to see a yellow glowing worm of lava force its way over a dam of rock and slop down in a shower of sparks, right where the wag had been before the Armorer had shouted his warning.

A long breath escaped Ryan's lungs. J.B. shoved his face back down the well of the blaster-mount. "At least we've shown we can take the bastard best the mountain has to throw at us!" the Armorer called.

The Hummer rocked to an impact that sank it on its springs. Two curving white blades, spaced a hand span apart, suddenly protruded downward from the Kevlar roof.

"By the Three Kennedys!" Doc exclaimed. A dark jet suddenly spewed from each curved blade. Jak and Doc cried out in alarm and flattened themselves against the doors.

"What—" Ryan began.

From almost directly overhead came the ripping roar of J.B.'s Uzi, loud even over the ceaseless bellow of the volcano. With a rending, wrenching sound, the curved blades were yanked out of the vehicle's roof.

"Snake…" the Armorer shouted, a sudden crackle of noise like skyscraper-size firecrackers going off drowned most of his words.

"What?"

"I said, it's a bastard rattlesnake, the biggest bastard snake I ever saw!"

Ryan stuck his head out the window and craned his neck around. Silhouetted against a demonic sky, a head as wide across as Ryan's own shoulders reared up ten or a dozen feet above the Hummer on an impossibly thick body. Ryan wondered for an endless interval between one heartbeat and the next whether the creature was actually that huge or whether its size was an illusion produced by the glaring, ever-shifting light.

The head split open into a vast flame-yellow mouth. Its fangs, each as long as one of Ryan's arms, unfolded like the blades of a lock-back knife. As Ryan slammed the accelerator home, the head darted forward with dizzying speed, fangs thrusting ahead of it like spears.

Mildred screamed in fury more than terror as the fangs stabbed down through the roof, one gleaming ivory scimitar missing her head by inches. Gathering the now semiconscious Krysty into her strong arms, Mildred rolled herself and the redhead to the side of the cargo compartment, away from the reeking, fuming venom that spurted in pulses from the fangs. Then she turned back to hammer at the nearest fang with the heel of her fist. It had no effect.

"A fascinating adaptation," Doc remarked in as calmly conversational a voice as the others had ever heard him use. "Clearly the serpent soaks up heat from the ambient rocks, allowing it to move and hunt as freely at night as in the daytime."

"That's great, Doc," Ryan said, "but how do we kill the nuke-blasted thing?"

Despite the wag's wild bucking, J.B. popped back up through the vacant gun mount with his Uzi. He emptied the magazine at the creature in three long ragged bursts as it coiled yet again to strike.

Ryan saw a relatively clear stretch of slope, if steep, and sent the wag bucketing down it amid a baby avalanche of loose rubble. The impacts slammed his lower jaw into the upper and threatened to shake his joints apart.

"We're getting away!" Mildred shouted.

"We better," J.B. said, dropping back down into the passenger seat to change mags. "I might as well be pissing at the bastard. I'm not sure any of my rounds even penetrated."

The monstrous snake launched itself, not in a strike but slithering down the slope parallel to them, flowing sinuously over jagged steaming black rock and gray boulders like a living avalanche. It caught up with them, lunged again, this time as if trying to bring its terrible mass crushing down on the wag. Ryan spun the wheel right. For a terrifying fraction of a second the vehicle slewed sideways in the scree, heeling way over toward the bottom of the slope, threatening to break away at any instant and go rolling down the smoky like a loose boulder, battering itself to pieces and churning its occupants to lumpy red puree. Then the vast cleated run-flat tires bit and thrust the wag forward across the slope, no longer in danger of tipping over but still not clear of the snake.

Ryan heard loud reports from close behind, dared a look over his shoulder. From one window Jak was cranking shots from his Python handblaster, from the other, Doc was booming away with his venerable LeMat. The pistol rounds, like the 9 mm bullets fired by J.B.'s Uzi, were almost certainly as futile as spitting at the rattlesnake, but Ryan had to grin approval of his comrades' fighting spirit.

The thing was right after them, writhing with incredible speed. On a flat, on anything like a decent surface, the Hummer would've left the horror in its dust. On this evil broken slope, the snake had every advantage.

"I can't even slow the bastard, Ryan," J.B. yelled, blitzing off another magazine. "Dunno if even your Steyr could hurt it."

"Nor, it seems, can we outrun it, had we Hermes's wings to speed our heels," Doc Tanner murmured.

"Then, like Trader used to say, when all else fails—cheat," Ryan said grimly.

"I thought that was Samantha the Panther," J.B. said.

"Whoever." Ryan spun the wheel left. His companions yelled in alarm as the wag bounced right and cut across the giant snake's path. The rattler, surprised by its prey apparently turning on it, reared up hissing. It struck. Anticipating the attack, Ryan had cranked the wheel and taken off at a tangent. The Hummer still rocked as the monster's head glanced off the wag's rear bumper.

Ryan was hammering the wag right across the mountainside, back toward the spewing vent—back upward toward the river of living fire that had almost trapped them before.

"Ryan," J.B. said from the gun mount. "Ryan, lava—"

Lava it was, yes, running down the mountain at them in a racing flow of glow, red and fast as water. For his part Ryan was racing to meet the stream. It spurted out over a shelf of rock as if reaching out for the puny skittering thing. The snake raced after them, blunt nose almost prodding their tailgate. The fires of Hell danced in its slit-pupilled eyes.

The liquid rock-stream splashed down behind a boulder in a shower of glowing gobbets. J.B. cried out in pain as a droplet of yellow-glowing lava brushed his cheek. Another burned right through the roof and struck, hissing by Ryan's right boot as the Hummer jounced across the lava stream's path with the rattler in mad pursuit.

A vast, fiery wave of lava broke over the boulder and thundered down onto the snake. The monster reared back, emitting a shriek that threatened to rupture the companions' eardrums. A huge cloud of steam bellowed out as the molten rock flash-boiled the snake's body fluids. A terrible stench, like burning hair magnified a millionfold, enveloped the wag. Mildred puked noisily in the back.

"Dark night!" J.B. yelled.

The rattler's head reared out of the lava. The molten rock fell away from it in burning rivulets. For a terrifying moment it seemed as if the monster would continue its hellhound pursuit, shedding the lava like a duck's wing shedding water.

Then it collapsed, to sink steaming and reeking into the already crusting lava pool.

Chapter Five

The wag sat creaking and popping as it cooled off in the long grass beside a stream. Ryan squatted on a roof blistered and discolored by embers, hot gases and blobs of lava, and torn in several places by the giant snake's fangs. He cradled his Steyr across his lean-muscled thighs. Between thumb and forefinger of his right hand he absently rolled the stem of a blue-white wildflower he'd picked before climbing to the top of the Hummer. Patches of them and differently hued blossoms dotted the fertile zone they were in now like pigment spills.

He was keeping watch while his comrades cleaned themselves and the wag. Mildred had insisted on the cleanup, and she wasn't just being predark fastidious.

"We need to clear out every last trace of that venom," she'd said. "Even assuming its potency and characteristics are those of normal rattlesnake poison, and don't carry any kind of nasty mutie kicker, if any of it gets into an open wound, even a scratch, you'll be in a world of hurt. Rattler venom's primarily a hematotoxin. It makes your red blood cells explode. And we're fresh out of antivenin."

So they were taking a pause, down in the surprisingly green and fertile valley that stretched away north from the mountain into whose bowels they had jumped, and a similar volcanic peak a few miles away that didn't seem to be erupting as enthusiastically. They still seemed to be a good twenty miles from the wide lake. In the bright sunlight they could make out the shapes of skyscrapers rising from the middle of it.

J.B. tucked his minisextant into his kit and glanced at his old map. "Latitude's right for Mexland," he announced. "Right about Mex City, truth to tell."

"I could've told you that," Mildred said. She was redressing Krysty's shoulder. The giant rattler's venom had splashed her bandages. Thinking fast, Mildred had clawed them away before the poison could come into contact with Krysty's wounds.

"Air thin," Jak said.

"Yeah. Good thing we've been up in the mountains getting acclimated for a few days. This whole valley's pretty high. Don't remember just how high that is exactly. I came down here for vacation once, couple years before the balloon went up. I recognize those mountains. Big one we popped out of is Popocatépetl . The shorter one's Iztaccíhuatl."

"What's that mean?" J.B. asked, blinking owlishly through his spectacles, which he had just cleaned on his shirttail.

"How should I know? I can't even spell 'em. I don't even know why it looks as if the ruins of Mexico City are out in the middle of a great big lake."

"They were lovers," Doc intoned. He was wringing out his shirt. His thin, shrunken chest was fishbelly pale. In comparison his hands and face looked deeply tanned.

"Say what?" J.B. asked. "You're not losing your grip again, are you, Doc?"

The old man didn't deign to respond. "She was the emperor's daughter. A most beauteous maid. He was a mighty young warrior. They fell in love. Her father disapproved. He sent the young man off to war, then told his daughter he had fallen in battle. Whereupon the girl expired from grief. Then the warrior returned home to find his beloved dead, and *he* died of grief, as well. The gods, taking pity on them, transformed them into the mountains we have just quit. Iztaccíhuatl means 'Sleeping Woman.' Popocatépetl is 'Smoking Mountain.'"

Jak was squatting by the stream, ignoring the fact his feet were sunk in cold muck. He turned his ruby gaze over his shoulder on Doc.

"Gods turned to mountains?" he asked. "What good that do?"

Doc shrugged delicately. "The ways of gods, the theologians assure us, are not the ways of men. Though in sooth, the gods and goddesses of most of the globe's mythologies seem to manifest a decidedly puckish sense of humor."

Ryan checked the rad counter clipped to his coat for maybe the dozenth time. "Anybody getting any kind of a reading?"

"Nope," J.B. said. "Background's mebbe a little high. That's it."

"So no nukes went off in the vicinity." Ryan shook his head. "Something did some damage."

"No kidding," Mildred said. "In my day this was the most populous city on Earth. We should be in the suburbs now. Something didn't just damage them, it made them disappear."

"Mebbe the smokies?" J.B. asked. Ryan shrugged.

J.B. had begun to load the few supplies they'd managed to scavenge from the Popocatépetl redoubt back into the wag. He noticed that Jak was staring out across the little stream again, seemingly morose.

"What's eating at your innards, Jak?" he asked.

"Snake," the youth said.

"You're thinking about that bastard snake?"

Jak shrugged. "Big," he said. "Caught, eat like kings."

As if to emphasize his words, he suddenly lunged into the stream in a great splash. He grabbed, then he straightened, holding a squirming leopard frog. He bit off the head, spat it into the weeds, then began to eat the still-kicking amphibian.

Mildred winced. "I hate it when he does stuff like that."

Ryan gave a last look around. Their immediate surroundings were broken enough with jagged ridges and obvious cooled-lava flows that any ill-intentioned strangers could work their way to well within longblaster range of the party and he'd never see them. He tossed away the flower and jumped to the ground. The soil was black, rich and springy beneath the soles of his boots.

"How's Krysty?" he asked Mildred, walking to where the woman was laid out by the stream.

"Pretty much out of it. The infection's taking hold and she's obviously weakened some since we got away from the eruption, with all that raw Earth energy exploding all over the damn landscape."

Ryan thought he kept his feelings from his face. He had long years of practice at that. But Mildred said, "Don't worry. It's not so bad as it sounds. I think it's a good sign she's out. Her body is fighting to repel the infection and start healing. Her mind has shut down so that she can concentrate her resources on the task at hand. At this point, other than trying to avoid any more exciting encounters with the local wildlife, which was something else I didn't see when I was down here as a *turista,* it's most important to make sure she wakes up regularly to eat. Keep her strength up."

She stood. "Speaking of which, I'm not so concerned about the food thing as I was, for any of us. There's some real fertile-looking land out here, interspersed with all the lava flows and ash falls. So I don't think we'll have to settle for feeding her raw frog. But since it looks as if there's likely to be better on tap, it's probably not too soon to start looking out for it."

"I think there's a ville a couple miles ahead," Ryan said. "We'll make for that."

THEY CAME AROUND one of the omnipresent saw-toothed hogsbacks and found themselves on the outskirts of a ville. At first glance it appeared almost painfully neat, compared to the devastation and decay they were used to: sturdy, square adobe-brick houses, washed in white and pink and shades of tan and brown, with heavy ceiling beams projecting from the fronts. Not a whole lot different than they'd seen in New Mexico north of the Jornada del Muerte, if better kept-up. But worlds different from the urban sprawl that had occupied this area a hundred years before, according to the recollections of Doc as well as Mildred.

The Hummer had rolled in among the first few houses. The companions realized with a sort of shared shock that they'd allowed the ville's appearance at a distance of tidiness momentarily to deceive them. Obviously the place had been built with care since skydark and tended with love throughout however many years it had stood.

It had, however, been trashed quite recently, by the looks of things.

Many houses sported windows of glass, flat, clear, manufactured panes, not ripply and murky from being made in some postnuke glassblower's shop and not purple from a century's exposure to the sun's ultraviolet radiation, either. Sure signs that the residents traded with scavvies working a big city where warehouses and shops still contained unbroken sheets of glass. They were also sure signs of prosperity, since such salvage didn't come cheap.

Many of the panes were broken, which was a sign bad trouble had come to the ville. The modern world was no haven of law and order, likely no more so here than in the most nuke-scarred regions of North America, but one thing about it: people who built their homes by hand and kept the trim painted and paid to put in nice, salvaged windows didn't tolerate casual vandalism. You tagged, they slagged. You busted a window, they busted you. In pieces. That simple.

Doors neatly painted dark red or blue—many hardly faded at all by the intense high-altitude sun—hung askew from their frames. Mismatched curtains of scavvied cloth flapped freely over glass fangs in the quickening afternoon breeze. The travelers saw no flames but smelled smoke—and floating on the wind the unmistakable stink of fresh death.

From the gloomy depths of a hut with its front door gone altogether lurched a mound of horror. It had no head. Rather its right shoulder came to a point perhaps seven feet tall, so that it had to squat down on thin bandy legs to clear the doorway. Its left shoulder was a good foot and a half lower. Normal-appearing arms hung from both shoulders. Another arm sprouted halfway down the mutie's right side. It had a single saucer-size eye in the middle of its lesion-covered torso, that wept constant yellow pus toward a slack-lipped, jag-toothed mouth.

Jak stuck his hand out the window past Ryan's head and shot the mutie with his Python.

Chapter Six

The 158-grain semijacketed slug hit the mutie in its single eye. A spray of fluid that looked more maroon than norm blood and some clotted pale chunks of what had to have been brains erupted from the creature's back. Clear ichor gushing from its collapsed ocular, the mutie emitted a whistling shriek from its mouth and collapsed.

Despite his case-hardened constitution, Ryan winced. The .357 Magnum round had maybe the nastiest muzzle-blast of any handblaster he'd encountered, sharper and more painful to the ear than even the louder but lower-pitched report of a .44 Magnum. Primer fragments blasted out between the rear of the cylinder and the frame stung his cheek and spattered like rain on his eyepatch.

He frowned, not just at the ringing in his ears. A hunter born and bred, as much feral predatory animal as human, Jak was hard even by the standards of his time and place. The word *mercy* was in his vocabulary only because Doc had taught it to him. But the ruby-eyed albino boy had always accepted Ryan's rules, which were pretty much the same as vanished Trader's had been. And one of the foremost was: No chilling for chilling's sake.

Then he saw Mildred, right in front of him, thrust her Czech-made .38 target revolver out her window and fire a solo shot at a figure looming behind the busted-out window next to the door. At the same time the hideous mutie Jak had chilled dropped what it had been holding concealed behind its back with its two right hands: a crude musket or shotgun made out of heavy-gauge pipe and wire.

"Fireblast!" Belatedly, Ryan was becoming aware of movement all around them, seething out of the houses like maggots from so many beast skulls. "Mildred, get us out of here!"

The stocky physician had tucked her blaster away and was doing just that. Both hands death-gripping the wheel, she goosed the beefy wag along the narrow rutted-earth street. The way the Hummer was jouncing over the ruts, Ryan had no chance of acquiring any targets through the variable-powered scope mounted on his SSG. Nor would he have been able to hold on any target long enough to take a half decent shot. Cursing to himself, he hauled out his 9 mm handblaster with the built-in silencer.

The wag was armored, if lightly. The Kevlar and steel of its roof and sides and its Lexan windows should have been more than adequate to keep off the arrows, stones and bullets the suddenly swarming muties showered down on them, especially since the blasters they were loosing off, with hollow booms and big puffs of dirty-white smoke seemed mostly to be crude homemade muzzle-loaders like the one the first mutie had carried, firing big soft blobs of lead or maybe even fist-fuls of nails, busted glass and pebbles. But the Hummer wasn't designed to be an armored personnel carrier, whose occupants were meant to do serious fighting from inside it. It was a utility vehicle, a scout car; the heavy weapon, machine gun or grenade launcher, which had once occupied its pintle mount had been intended to lay down a base of fire from a distance in support of dis-mounted infantry, and also to give it a sting and enable it to scoot out of any trouble it happened to roll into. It didn't have fancy firing ports. It had windows that had to be rolled down to allow the passengers to fire out. Which of course let all kinds of missiles in.

Nor were the muties totally limited to rocks and mu-seum-piece projectile weapons. Mildred yet out a yelp of alarm as fire blossomed yellow-orange right in their path. Flames and dense black smoke rolled in a tide up the hood to break against the windshield. Everybody ducked as a dragon's belch of flame-heated air and choking smoke rushed in at the windows to fill the pas-senger compartment. Then they were through the flame pond created by the Molotov cocktail.

A crowd of screaming muties had rolled a battered stakebed truck into their path fifty yards ahead. "Hang on, everybody," Mildred shouted, and cranked the wheel left, toward a gap between houses just large enough to pass the Hummer.

The wag heeled way over to the right as the occu-pants grabbed for whatever purchase they could. Jak dropped his Python inside the cargo compartment to grab a tie-down with one hand and the out-cold Krysty with the other. Their tires were still spinning off tongues of fire. Then the bow wave of dust they threw up doused the burning mixture.

Almost at once the Hummer went nose-down and tail-up like an angry stinkbug as Mildred hammered down the brakes. A pile of rubble, khaki-colored adobe blocks obstructed the alley. "Crap!" Mildred exclaimed. "Crap, crap, crap!"

"Drive on," J.B. shouted, holding his fedora on his head with one hand and brandishing his stamped-steel machine pistol with the other. "This baby'll plow through."

"Not on your tintype," Mildred shouted back, throwing the wag into reverse and cranking her head around on her neck. "Can't even chance getting high-centered with these hoodoos swarming around like yellowjackets."

The alley behind had filled instantly with ambushers, waving spears and clubs and at least one modern firearm— an M-1 carbine to Ryan's quick glimpse. They stopped and stared with comical surprise as the wag chunked through a gear change and came hurtling straight back at them like a multiton rocket. Most of them were muties, although none in this clot of a half dozen or so was either as huge or grotesquely malformed as the first creature they had seen. Most were downright small. In fact, the one closest behind the Hummer, whose wide anthracite eyes locked on Ryan's for a fraction of a second before the Hummer's rear bumper took him in the thighs and body-slammed him to the ground, looked as human as Ryan himself.

The wag bucked, and screams, along with crunching and squelching sounds, came from beneath the vehicle as the huge cleated tires rolled over several ambushers unfortunate enough not to be able to spin around and clear the alleyway in time. One mutie, a being reminiscent of a stickie in shape but with a dry-looking tan skin covered with reddish-brown camouflage rosettes, clung to the side of the house on Ryan's side with toe and fingers pads. Instead of knocking him free, the Hummer's bulk spun him, pinned him and then rotated his body, crushing and grinding simultaneously as it roared backward down the alley. The creature screamed in a shrill but wholly-human voice. A blast of horrid carrion-eater breath blew in the window as the creature rolled by between the brown-stuccoed wall and the wag's steel flank.

Then the Hummer was back on what passed for the ville's main street. It had flooded with marauders, half a hundred or more. Mildred just kept the wag grinding in reverse, squashing a couple more of their less-agile ambushers, turning the wheel slightly to angle the Hummer into another alley catty-corner across the way behind them. For a moment they passed between mud houses, with more clearance this time. Then they were out and backing at a brisk clip across another street, right at an opening into darkness.

The structure was larger than most of the houses and had double wooden doors open wide. Muties were issuing from the interior with crates and boxes in their arms: looters. They scattered. A taller than average one who looked normal aside from having a mouth that stretched clear to the back of the jawbone on either side was caught standing right in the middle of the entry, clutching a box of what looked like hand tools. He stared at the onrushing wag as if jacklighted. The rear bumper hit him and bore him screaming back to smash him squalling against a set of wooden shelves.

Five muties cringed against the walls to either side of the wag. J.B. popped up out the top of the vehicle. "Afternoon," he said, and chopped down the three to the right with two scything back-and-forth bursts from his Uzi.

The one nearer the door on Ryan's side dropped what he was carrying and ran right out into the sunlit street. The other, who had long tufts of dark hair sprouting at random from face and body, raised a foot-long wrench over his head and lunged screaming at Ryan.

Ryan opened the door into him with a slam. The mutie staggered back gushing blood from a split forehead. The one-eyed man poked his SIG-Sauer through the door's still-open window, shot him twice in the chest. Then, because he didn't go down fast enough, he shot him again through the forehead.

The remaining mutie seemed to be making good his escape. But panicked or plain stupid, he failed to dodge to one side or the other, where a few steps would have taken him out of the line of fire. Instead he raced straight away from the door, across the street.

Unhurriedly, Doc opened his door, unfolded himself. Laying his heavy LeMat across his upraised left forearm he aimed, fired through his own open window. The ancient pistol boomed like an immense drum and spit out a four-foot-long tongue of flame, bright pink in the shaded interior. Dust puffed up from the middle of the back of the hide vest the fleeing mutie wore. The creature threw up taloned hands and went facedown on the hardpan.

The doctor lowered his smoking handblaster. He shook his head regretfully. "Ah, well," he said, "he who turns and runs away, lives to slit our bellies later in the day."

Jak did a roll over the rear seat of the Hummer, piled out Doc's door with his Python in his snow-white fist. Ryan was already racing along the wall toward the gaping entryway. He darted out into the sunlight, firing his 9 mm blaster with sounds like explosively exhaled breaths. The bullets made loud cracks as they passed objects; he wasn't wasting his precious remaining stock of subsonic rounds that made no more noise at any point than a muffled sneeze. Nor was he bothering to aim, merely trying to keep the muties who had fled the Hummer's charge heading in the right direction long enough for him to grab hold of the open wooden door. Loud cracks from behind him told him the albino youth was doing the same thing.

The doors were heavy and their hinges protested with loud squeals against being moved. But the two men had adrenaline on their side; even the slight Jak was able to get his door into motion. Both halves swung back into place well before the marauders outside could get themselves sorted out enough to interfere. Ryan swung a hefty plank down into waiting brackets to bar the doors shut.

A smaller doorway opened in the wall on the driver's side. Mildred got out with her ZKR in hand. J.B.

eeled out the top of the pintle mount, scrambled across the Hummer's torn and blistered Kevlar roof to drop down beside her, Uzi in hand. She nodded to him.

"Cover me," she said, then darted through the door. She had to duck down to get through. J.B. hit the door-jamb with his Uzi up and ready.

From inside the next room two yellow flashes, two echoing cracks. Then a slow, sad, sliding sound.

"Clear," the others heard Mildred call. "Just one mutie who wasn't hid near as well as he thought."

"Damn, Ryan," J.B. said, taking in their surroundings, "nuke me till I glow and shoot me in the dark, but I think this is a garage."

Ryan had popped out his partially empty mag from his handblaster, dropped it in a pocket, brought out a fresh magazine from another. He weighed it in his hand, eyeing it ruefully. Not many left.

He jammed it decisively home in the well. "Think mebbe you're right, J.B.," he said. "Even got a grease pit dug in the middle of the floor."

Jak whipped out one of his throwing knives, stuck it in his teeth, dropped to the packed-earth floor and slithered under the rear of the Hummer. "No muties hide," he reported, voice muffled by the wag's mass. He slithered back out.

"Ryan, John Barrymore," Doc said. "Come take a look at this.

"A hatchway to the roof," he announced when his companions joined him. "It would appear the erstwhile occupants of this ville built with defense in mind."

Ryan had already noted that the adobe walls were a good half-yard thick, enough to stop even a 7.62 mm round from his Steyr. The windows were potential vulnerabilities, but also served as firing ports. Apparently they constituted a compromise between comfort of living and defensibility. That the residents had enjoyed the luxury of making such a compromise spoke volumes for the relative stability they'd enjoyed.

Until today, anyway. "Yeah," Ryan said. "Too bad they didn't stay alert enough."

"Ville like this is used to trading, Ryan," J.B. observed. "My bet is they got took by some kind of trick like that Trojan horse Doc told us about."

"Actually that was me," the one-eyed man said. "My mother read *The Iliad* to me when I was young."

"Whatever. It sounded like the kinda thing that'd come out of Doc's head, anyway."

"'Is this the face that launched a thousand ships,'" Doc quoted, "'and topped the topless towers of Ilium?'" His drawn old face had gone pallid under grime and suntan, and sweat stood out around his hairline. Reaction was setting in. He swayed. "Emily, my Emily, why hast thou forsaken me..." he whispered.

Mildred, who had climbed back into the Hummer to check on Krysty, jumped out with a water bottle in hand. "Here, old man," she said, holding the bottle to Doc's lips. He drank greedily, drooling water out the right side of his mouth. "You just sit down here a minute. Rest yourself."

She led him to a stool by the wall, sat him down.

"Actually, the ville looks deserted to me, not like it

was fought over," Ryan said. "I wonder if the people didn't just bug when the raiders turned up."

He accepted a bottle from Mildred, drank. "How's Krysty?"

Mildred shrugged. "Coming around. Still feverish. I hope she doesn't try to get up, but— Hey!"

She pointed toward the double doors. The bottom line of sunglare was interrupted at several point by shadows. *Feet.*

The muties were gathering right outside.

Chapter Seven

Holding up his Uzi with one hand, J.B. strode toward the front of the garage. Muzzle-flash vomited from the stub barrel. The massive walls seemed to bulge from its yammer. Weighing not much less than Ryan's sniper rifle, the machine pistol was heavy enough to be fired one-handed without climbing uncontrollably. The Armorer walked a long burst from right to left across the double doors. Little points of brightness appeared. Pencils of sunlight stabbed into the gloom like yellow laser beams.

The echo of the shuddering muzzle-blasts seemed to continue for heartbeats after the flame flicker died away, or maybe it was the ringing in the companions' ears. When they were able to hear anything else again they could hear moaning and thrashing from outside.

"Let them writhe," the Armorer said, pulling the spent magazine from the Uzi. "Help keep the bastards' minds right."

As Ryan had just moments before, he hefted the empty magazine in his hand. "Running low. Can't be doing that shit much more."

Jak looked at Mildred. "Any weps? Ammo?"

She shook her head. "No trace. If any were here they were the first thing the muties cleared out."

J.B. walked around the wag to the sprawled bodies of the looters he'd shot when they first rolled into the garage, knelt to inspect them.

"We're a little bit lucky," he said, pulling something gingerly from the waistband of the loincloth one wore. "We got a Colt .45 ACP, Government Model of 1911, or reasonable facsimile, in not too bad a shape, all cocked and locked."

He held up a hefty blaster with checkered wooden grips pinched between thumb and forefinger. "This chill's even got a couple spare mags on him."

He straightened and prodded the corpse with the toe of his boot. "And you know what? He ain't even a mutie."

"Seen a couple of what looked like norms," Mildred said. "That first dude I ran over was one."

"We'll sort out the mystery later." Ryan strode over to Doc, who was sitting slumped, his head lolling to the side. He took a pinch of the old man's cheek, which hung slack, pulled his head up.

"Doc," he said. He patted the old man's other cheek. "Doc, you can't zone out on us now. We're already down Krysty. We need everybody else to hold the fort until we can figure a way to get out of here with all our parts."

The old man moaned. Then he blinked twice, shook himself, and sat upright. "No need to take on so, my dear boy," he said, standing and shooting his cuffs. "Just resting my eyes."

Ryan slapped him on the shoulder. "Good enough. Welcome back."

"We got an exit strategy?" Mildred asked, backing out of the Hummer holding J.B.'s M-4000 shotgun.

"Our best defense is still driving real fast," J.B. pointed out.

Ryan nodded, rubbing his long chin. "Yeah. Mebbe we can hold them off until dark, thin them out some. Then try to bust out."

"They strike me as raiders, like the Scythians of yore, albeit lacking horses," Doc said. "They will naturally incline toward a transient strategy, rather than a persisting one."

"Which translates as hit-and-run's their style, rather than sticking around to keep us under siege," J.B. noted. "Probably even true. Mebbe we get out of this crack after all."

"If they don't burn us out," Mildred muttered.

"Likely a last resort," Ryan said. "They'll want our wag and blasters. All the same, we better get set to discourage that sort of behavior. Mildred, is there a back way out?"

She nodded, making her beaded plaits rattle softly. "Rear of the little office. Big water jug in there, too, while I think of it. Seems clean."

"That's something, anyway. You and Jak hold in there, watch the front and back doors. J.B. and Doc can hold in here."

"What about you?" J.B. asked.

"I'll take the rifle up top, see if I can do a little street-cleaning."

"I'd better check on Krysty first, real quick," Mildred said, ducking into the office.

"Make quick," Jak called from the other room. "Muties coming."

Ryan entered the Hummer. Krysty lay on her pallet in the cargo compartment with her green eyes open. "Lover," she whispered in a cracked voice.

Ryan leaned over to extend a water bottle to her. She reached for it. "Uh-uh," he said. "Just lie back. You need to conserve your strength."

Reluctantly she let him tilt the bottle to her lips. "Gaia's with me," she said more clearly when he pulled the bottle back. "But it's hard."

"You just lie back, try to sleep. Let your mind and body concentrate on healing."

"Outside—?"

He shook his head. "We'll handle it. If we can't, having another body on the line too shaky to hold up a blaster wouldn't do us any good. *This* is your fight, Krysty. Stay with it."

He capped the bottle and laid it beside her. Her hand gripped his with feverish strength; he felt the heat of the battle against infection raging inside her body. She pulled the back of his hand to her lips and kissed it. Then she laid her head back down and closed her eyes.

Ryan placed her hand on her chest and made himself let go. There wasn't any more that he could do for her in the best of circumstances. She was young and strong and healthy, as tough as they came, and she had that Gaia-aided gift of healing. She'd pull through.

He wouldn't even think of the alternative.

A bang from outside. A hole appeared in one of the doors, knocking a slatlike splinter loose to stick out at a crazy angle from beneath it. J.B. ripped a short burst in response, blind through the wood.

Ryan ducked quickly out of the Hummer, slung his Steyr. J.B. handed him the .45, square butt foremost. "Take this and the extras. Don't want to burn out that SIG."

The one-eyed man accepted the heavy handblaster and tucked the two full reloads into his waistband. The SIG-Sauer was a wonderful weapon for stealthy chilling, but the integral suppressor, aside from making the weapon heavier and less wieldy, tended to hold in heat. It had a tendency to lock in a firefight, and too much sustained firing would burn out the barrel. The .45 would spare the SIG for a while, not to mention their dwindling stocks of 9 mm rounds.

A wooden ladder hung on hooks by the wall, so that a person could scramble right up it to the hatch—and pull it up after, an old Indian trick from Pueblo days long before the twentieth century that Doc had told them about. Ryan climbed up to the hatch, carefully slid aside the iron bolt. He sucked in a deep breath, snicked off the big Colt's safety and slammed open the hatch.

Sunlight fell against his face like scalding water. He thrust the .45 up into it and swarmed after.

To find himself staring along the rounded black top

of the weapon into a pair of huge black eyes, shot through with veins and flecks of gold.

The face surrounding those eyes wasn't norm, being drawn out into a dark snout with nostrils as convoluted as a bat's. But the surprised expression was unmistakable all the same.

For as long as it took Ryan's forefinger to exert about three pounds of pressure on the trigger.

The eyes and the top part of the head that held them vanished into a dark haze. The mutie's body rolled over flopping, black blood spurting from the lower jaw and stub of neck that remained. Ryan sprang upright on the roof. A norm-looking ambusher was frozen, having just crawled over the tall roof parapet behind the mutie whose head Ryan had just blown apart. He clutched a spear tipped with black volcanic glass. Ryan shot him twice. He went backward over the parapet with arms flailing.

Something struck Ryan in the back beneath his left shoulder blade. He whirled into a crouch, brought the heavy handblaster around in a two-fisted combat grip. A bandy-legged norm stood on the roof of the next house, desperately trying to notch a second dart to the end of his throwing stick. Ryan centered his sights on the white stripe conveniently painted down the front of the norm's ribby chest, pulled the trigger. The 1911 bucked and roared. The man sat, dropping dart and launcher. He felt his chest, looked up reproachfully from the blood on his fingers to Ryan, and fell backward out of sight.

The one-eyed man went flat on his belly. He thumbed on the safety, stuck the .45 inside the waist of his fatigue pants behind his right hip—not an ideal means of carry, but Ryan was seasoned enough to know always to keep his finger *out* of the trigger guard until the weapon was drawn and pointing downrange, which much diminished his chances of becoming abruptly half-assed.

He reached around to probe at his back. He felt nothing from where he'd been struck, not necessarily a good sign in itself. The impact site was impossible to reach and see, but he didn't feel any trace of blood. A quick check of the flat roof, covered with a thick and well-packed layer of the same hard earth that made up the street below and here and there sprouting a clump of weeds, showed no sign of leakage. He caught sight of the dart: a simple shaft of some kind of wood, whittled to a point and probably hardened in a fire. It hadn't been hard thrown enough to penetrate his leather coat, which was one reason he still wore it despite the heat.

He unslung the Steyr, cracked the bolt, turned it and pulled it back enough to glimpse a confirmatory gleam of brass, yellow in the merciless sun. He closed and locked the bolt again. Then he got a knee up to his chest and a boot under him and raised himself cautiously for a look around.

Three houses up the block a couple of manlike figures pointed at the apparition of his head. One of them threw a longblaster to its shoulder. He ducked. The weapon boomed, its report echoing off the flat fronts of houses. Where the shot went, he had no idea; he heard no noise of its passage.

Through the roof Ryan felt a vibration. From down in the street in front of the garage came a dull heavy thump, followed by cheers and shouts in a language he couldn't make out. He guessed it was Spanish. The muties seemed to have contrived a battering ram and were having a go at the doors. They seemed pretty sturdy, and anyway Ryan was going to have to let his friends below deal with the problem, at least until he got the nearby rooftops clean.

He reared, rolled back into a sitting position, knees up. He brought the Steyr to his shoulder, bracing his elbows against the insides of his knees, snugged the buttplate tight to his shoulder's hollow, welded his right cheek to the stock and peered through the scope with his single eye.

The blaster man who had shot at him was fumblingly spilling powder from a horn—an actual cowhorn, by the look of it—down the barrel of his musket. He was shaking so much he was pouring most of the black grains on his hand, which was twined about with strange yellow growths or veins. Ryan lined the crosshairs up on the center of his chest and squeezed.

The Steyr kicked back against his shoulder. He worked the bolt with quick, calm efficiency as the barrel rose. Another round, head-stamped 7.62 mm NATO, was chambered and ready to go when the long slim barrel came back down on line.

The musketeer was nowhere in sight. His companion, whose skin hung loose on his small skinny frame in flaps, was staring down with puzzled bloodhound

eyes at what was probably him. Belatedly he caught
hold of the notion he might be in some danger here. Instead of simply dropping flat, he started to turn to bolt.
Ryan shot him through and through, right side to left,
and dropped him like a deer.

Ryan felt another shiver of vibration through his tailbone, heard a scrape from right behind. As he spun, a
terrific shuddering, crashing sound assailed his ears.
He knew full-auto blasterfire when he heard it. He threw
himself sideways, clumsily bringing the long rifle
around and up, to aim more or less at the Armorer, who
stood grinning down at him through his wire-rimmed
specs from the shade of his hat brim.

"Scraped off a couple muties coming up the wall,"
J.B. said.

"What are you doing up here? You're supposed to
be—"

"You're welcome for saving your lean ass. Figured
you'd need some backup."

He walked to the front of the garage, leaned out
over the parapet and whistled. "Hey, boys," he called,
"up here."

He fired the Uzi down into the street, three, four, five
quick bursts. Ryan heard shouts, screams. J.B. ducked
back down as return shots cracked from the street, then
rocked back over the parapet and let the rest of his magazine go in a long spray.

He sat, out of sight, to wait out the return fire from
the street, waving his stubby machine pistol in the air
with its heavy bolt locked back to cool it.

"Down to three mags," he said. "Way too few to be hosing them blind through the door."

Ryan nodded. The flash of annoyance he'd felt at his old friend was already forgotten. The companions followed Ryan's lead. Not his commands. J.B. had spotted a weakness in their deployment and acted promptly on his own initiative to correct it.

It had been a good call. That meant they all got to live a little longer. They were a team, which had always been their mainstay.

For what it was worth now.

Ryan eased his head back above the parapet, looked through 180 degrees, ducked back, duck-walked a few steps left, raised up, checked the other half circle. The rooftops were clear of marauders, or at least any who happened to be on roofs were keeping out of sight.

"This is mebbe not so good, Ryan," J.B. said quietly. "Street right out in front is clean, but you can bet your last meal the houses around us are swarming with the bastards. And I can see them all over the streets surrounding. There must be a couple hundred of them out there."

Ryan lay on his back, gazed up toward the sun, knowing enough not to look directly at it. It still rode high in the sky. There was plenty of daylight left.

"Think we'll make it until sundown?"

J.B. laughed, took a swig from a canteen, recapped it and tossed it toward Ryan, who caught it.

"Nah. Not that it'd make a spit of difference. These bastards are taking it personal. If they didn't have their black little hearts bent on seeing the color of our insides, they'd have cut stick and pulled out long since from the hurt we've laid on them."

"How about making a run for it?"

The Armorer shrugged. "They blocked us once. They might do it again. Still, it's probably our one and only shot. Even if it likely doesn't mean anything but the difference between getting chilled moving and getting chilled standing still."

He looked at Ryan. "Doc says the muties keep hollering something about a 'holy child.' It's like their war cry. Don't know what damn good that does us, but there it is. Whoa, what's that?"

The flat dirt-covered roof had shaken beneath them. The two men stared at each other. It came again, a quick triple shake that evoked unnerving creaks from the roof timbers beneath their feet.

From somewhere distant there came a groan, a rumble, a dull vibration.

"Earthquake," Ryan said. "That last was a wall coming down, mebbe a whole house."

"Now we know why such a neat little ville has big piles of rubble lying about the bastard alleys," the Armorer said. "Damn tremors must come frequent enough to keep the locals rebuilding and repairing, not leave them much time to worry about cleaning up all the wreckage."

"Former locals." Ryan had stuck his head up again, looking around. He could see nothing. But he could sense movement around them. He could smell the odors of rank and not all human bodies on the heavy moist breeze, hear the scrabbling like a horde of locusts stripping a cornfield: not loud, but ominous. The muties, he knew, were preparing another onslaught.

Then he frowned. "Hold it," he said softly. "J.B., you hear something?"

"Other than my pulse going like a scared horse down a flight of stairs?" Then he frowned, too, and tipped his head to the side.

"Dark night, but I think I hear—"

"Motors." Ryan stood upright, looking off to the northeast. "Wags, mebbe a big bike.

"Coming this way."

Chapter Eight

A heavy thudding sounded from the distance, like a hammer pounding nails. Big hammer, big nails.

J.B. smiled beatifically. "Browning M-2 .50-caliber machine gun. Sweetest music these ears ever did hear. Called a Ma Deuce predark."

From around them came, more than a sound, but rather a sensation of stirring, like rats in walls. "Seems like our friends have gotten tired of playing and are takin' their toys and heading home," J.B. said.

They heard a cracking sound, not quite a gunshot, too sharp for an explosion. "What was that?" Ryan asked.

"You got me."

J.B. walked to the open hatch. "Hey, down there," he shouted. "Looks like our bacon's saved. Cavalry's coming."

"And precisely what—" Mildred's voice came floating back "—makes you think they're on our side?"

J.B. looked at Ryan and shrugged. "There's an old saying, 'the enemy of my enemy is my friend,'" Ryan said helpfully.

"And we know what a steaming load that one is," J.B. said. "Okay, Millie, you win. But the guys we *know* want to cut us up and mebbe eat us are going away, which even a pessimistic cuss such as yourself has to admit is a positive development."

"What was that you called me?" Mildred's voice came again, dangerously low.

"What? 'Cuss.' It was distinctly 'cuss,' and Ryan will back me up on that."

Leave me out of this, mouthed the one-eyed man.

"Besides, you know I never stoop to foul, fucking language, Millie."

"We can always polish our baron's jester routines later, if we happen to live," Ryan said. "Now let's all pipe down, hunker down, get ready to play whatever hand's dealt us next."

Ryan and J.B. crouched behind the roof parapet, watching the streets below and surrounding their hideout. They heard the rattle of small-arms fire—a pretty serious volume; whoever these newcomers were, they didn't seem to have a lot of worries about ammo. The .50 thumped away, growing steadily louder. And intermittently they heard the sharp, loud cracks.

The marauders seemed to have no appetite for hanging around and getting better acquainted with the interlopers. They began streaming openly along the streets away from the approaching gunfire and motor sounds, a ragged, starved-looking band of muties and apparently normal humans mixed together indiscriminately. What might cause the norms and muties to cooperate like this Ryan had no idea. There was nothing impossible about it, of course. It was just that the hostility between norms and muties was usually so bitter and deeply ingrained that it was rare for them to coexist without bloodshed, much less to fight side by side.

He glanced at his old friend. J.B. looked back at him, shook his head, pulling down the corners of his mouth. Neither of them felt a reflex hatred of muties, obviously; Krysty Wroth was a mutie herself, albeit a beautiful one even to norm eyes. But Ryan, having all his life heard the cliché about having an itchy trigger finger, was actually feeling a tingle in that digit here and now, what with a river of potential targets flowing by right under their chins. He could tell the Armorer felt the same way.

But the raiders were headed the right direction—away—and showing no further disposition to bother them. Shooting at them would serve no useful purpose. At best it would waste scarce ammo. At worst it would draw return fire from the retreating raiders. Better to leave well enough alone.

The fugitive flow passed, ended. At the street's far end a very different procession appeared. Men in tan uniforms advanced steadily, longblasters ready in patrol position. They were dark-skinned, dark-haired, not very tall, resembling the human raiders who accompanied the muties, but better clothed, armed and fed. Behind them cruised a heavy truck with a fabric-covered bed and a welded-together looking mount for the big Browning machine gun behind the cab. And out in front of it rolled an outlandish apparition: a tall, copper-skinned youth, wearing a feathered headdress, a green loincloth, an odd sort of golden harness over his broad chest and shoulders, and armor braces on forearms and lower legs, riding a big, blatting, outlaw-style motorcycle.

"What do you make of that?" J.B. asked. Ryan could only shake his head.

From a house across the street from their perch and a couple of doors toward the well-armed column, a skinny mutie with an outsize asymmetric head bolted. He seemed to have no better plan in mind than to get away as quickly as possible, running balls-out right down the middle of the dirt lane, elbows pumping.

It wasn't a good enough plan.

The bizarre feathered rider raised his right forearm. A pale red beam snapped from it with an ear-shattering crack. It struck the fleeing mutie between his churning shoulder blades. His back exploded in a gout of steam. He went sprawling forward, dug a furrow in the dust with his face, lay still.

"Shit!" J.B. exclaimed. "A laser! That shit he's wearing over his shoulders has a power-pack in it, I'll just bet."

"Impressive," Ryan said.

The rider held up his arm. The column halted. The foot soldiers winged out to the building fronts to either side and lay or crouched, covering the street with their weapons.

"Look at that," J.B. said admiringly. "They got a couple BARs with them. Beautiful."

"Serious firepower," Ryan said.

"Let's hope they're friendlier than they look."

"If they're not," the one-eyed man said slowly, "I'm not sure what we can do about it."

Two soldiers came forward, prodding two captives in front of them with the muzzles of their longblasters. The prisoners, a man and a mutie covered all over in curly golden fur, wore only loincloths. Their arms were bound behind them. One of their escorts leaned forward and apparently cut their bonds, because the two immediately brought their hands up in front of them and began massaging their wrists.

The boy in the feathers dropped his kickstand, swung off his bike, stalked up to the prisoners like a leopard. He was carrying a peculiar-looking weapon in his hand, a flat wooden club maybe two feet long that had pieces of obsidian set in either edge, to create a discontinuous double blade of black glass.

He snapped a question. The human captive turned his face away.

The warrior in the feathered headdress lashed out with the obsidian-lined club. The furry mutant's right arm leaped away from its shoulder in a gush of blood. He screamed and dropped to his knees, ineffectually cutting the great wound, blood spurting between his fingers.

"Dark night," J.B. said. "These are some hard bastards."

The human captive said something to the warrior. The warrior danced a couple of steps to the side, struck down with his weapon. The screaming mutie's head fell away from its neck, bounced twice on the road and came to rest facedown in a rut. A fountain of blood shot out of the neck stump, once, twice, three times, soaking the thirsty earth in red. Then the blood-flow ceased. The headless, one-armed body pitched forward to leak slowly into the dust.

The human captive pointed straight at the garage where the travelers and their vehicle were hidden.

The feathered warrior turned to study the structure. Then he lashed out backhand. The human captive's head jumped off his shoulders. Without ever looking back, the warrior stalked back to his ride, forked it, kicked it to snarling life.

The cavalcade rumbled into motion again, right for the companions. "I don't know about you," J.B. said, "but I got a bad feeling about this."

"Get into the wag," Ryan called down the open hatch. "Get ready to roll."

"Where to?" Mildred called up.

"Away."

The truck with the big Browning stayed where it was to provide a fire base, Ryan noted glumly. Its thumb-thick bullets would punch through the Hummer like handblaster slugs through wet paper. The foot soldiers came trotting down the street and took up positions across from the garage, covering the double doors with their longblasters. A BAR-man was winged out to either side on his belly with his weapon's bipod down.

J.B. whistled. "Them suckers're toting FN FALs and M-1 Garands. And they pack a punch."

"Then there's that wrist laser," Ryan muttered.

The strapping young warrior in the feathered head-dress had been holding back, waiting for his minions to get into position. Then he gunned his V-twin engine with a blat like a submachine gun burst, streaked forward down the street, threw the bike into a dust-raising sidewise skid that brought it to a perfect halt facing the garage doors. He gazed up with a haughty expression on his aquiline features and barked something.

"What's he say?" Ryan asked.

"Beats me," J.B. said. "Sure sounds like he means it, though."

"I say, Ryan," Doc's voice wafted up from below, "but yonder fine young bravo has just called upon us to—"

"Throw out your weapons," the warrior called, "and give up at once!"

"English?" Ryan asked. The Armorer shrugged.

Ryan let his Steyr sling-strap slide off his shoulder, laid the rifle carefully on the rooftop. Then he stood. Two dozen rifle barrels tracked him.

"We're peaceful travelers," he called. "Traders. We're not looking for trouble. We just got caught here by the raiders."

"If you wish no trouble," the warrior said, "then surrender now before I lose patience."

"Who are you?"

"I am Two Arrow of the Eagle Knights. I serve Don Hector, ruler of the valley of the Anáhuac."

"Sec men," J.B. muttered bitterly. "Fancy drag, fancy blasters. Just lousy sec men."

"Why do you wish to make us prisoners?" Ryan called. "All we want to do is trade. Or barring that, be on our way."

"You travel these lands without permission. How do we know you are who you say? Now, throw your weapons out quickly. Or we will come and take them!"

Ryan held up his hand. "I have to talk to my people. Just give me a moment, please."

Before the warrior in the gaudy headdress could refuse, Ryan hunkered out of sight. "What do you say, J.B.?"

The Armorer hoisted his fedora and scratched at his scalp. "I don't trust these bastards far as I can pitch that wag with the M-2."

"That's two of us. But what are our options?"

"Well, way I see it, we're outmanned and definitely outgunned. So our choices would seem to be surrender and take our chances with these sweethearts, fight until they blast us down, or—"

A whistling cut across the cloudless sky. Explosions blossomed white among the deserted huts.

Chapter Nine

"Or, I was gonna say, divine intervention," J. B. said. "'Cept, unbeliever that I am, I didn't expect it to actually happen."

More whistles, more blasts. Ryan peered over the parapet. The street below had emptied miraculously. Apparently not even the haughty Two Arrow was above scooting for cover with rockets dropping at random into the ville.

"Hatch!" Ryan yelled, snatching up his Steyr. "Move!"

"I'm way ahead of you," J.B. called back. And he was, scuttling for the open hatch in a high-speed duck-walk, clamping his fedora onto his head with one hand. He dived down the hole into darkness.

Ryan followed.

The Armorer was perched on the Hummer's rear bumper. Ryan dropped down beside him. There were faces full of almost comical surprise turned back toward them.

"Ryan, what—?"

"Just drive, Millie! Out the doors and cut it left."

Mildred asked no more questions. With the two men

clinging to the rear of the wag like baby opossums, she slammed the accelerator home. Juice from the nuke battery surged into the engine. The big Hummer shot forward as if launched from a crossbow, smashed the doors out of its way with a screeching of splintering wood. Thick wood claws raked Ryan and J.B. but they held on grimly.

No sooner had the wag cleared the garage than Mildred turned hard left. The Hummer heeled over on its suspension. It fishtailed, slamming its right rear bumper against the house opposite. J.B. yelled as his hands were torn from their purchase on the Hummer's rear hatch. Ryan caught him by the back of his leather jacket. Then the wag's cleated tires grabbed the rutted road and it lurched forward.

The Browning machine gunner had abandoned his pintle mount when the first rockets slammed in, not wanting to be caught on top of a firebomb if the truck took a hit. With no more rockets coming in and the quarry escaping, he remembered his duty—or decided he was more scared of the feathered warrior than blazing death. He sprinted back to the truck from the shelter of a house, swarmed up the side of the cobbled-together mount, grabbed the Browning's spade grips and punched the butterfly trigger with his thumb. The big machine gun bucked and roared, pushing the heavy truck back to squat on its rear suspension. The 700-grain .50-caliber bullets sprayed the street at random, knocking lose vast chunks of facades, turning whole adobe bricks into gouts of khaki powder.

Mildred didn't need the splitting-earth roar of the big .50-caliber weapon to remind her of the fix they were in. At the first opening she thought possibly wide enough to pass the Hummer, she cranked left again between blocky houses. The wag fishtailed right, then left, banging off the mud-brick buildings in showers of chips and dust and making J.B.—who now had both hands holding on again—and Ryan wave from side to side with their feet streaming out like pennons in the wag's wake.

A wall in the way was bulldozed into dust and flying chunks. Then the Hummer was clear, jouncing across a field of half-ripened beans as first J.B. and then Ryan scaled the back and clambered monkey fashion across the torn-up roof to drop down the pintle mount hole into the passenger seat. Nobody pursued them from the village.

"WELL, WASN'T THAT an amusing little damned adventure," J.B. declared, doffing his fedora to wipe sweat from his head. With Mildred still at the wheel the Hummer was making its way toward the big lake and the ruined city in its midst, mainly for want of a better destination. "We come into what we think is Happy Valley and the next thing we know we're caught in a war between cannibal muties and sec men with enough firepower to knock over a good-size barony by their lonesomes. Led by a sec man on a big bike wearing a rag and a feather duster. Gee, why don't we settle down right now and start raisin' families."

Mildred, who had been loudest arguing for the peace and prosperity of the valley, shot him a glare. "Look, buster, you just don't get a village like that happening without a long spell of stability allowing people to better themselves and their surroundings. It just doesn't happen."

"She's right," Ryan said from the back seat. His single eye was tracking relentlessly over the landscape, which continued to consist of rocky hills and ridges and lava flows interspersed with patches of green grass. "The people who built that village had the means to do it right and keep it up. That means they weren't stretched across the knife edge of survival and weren't in the middle of any kind of war."

"Before," Jak said from the rear.

"Yeah, yeah, I know," J.B. said, thoughtfully settling his hat back on his head. "Sorry for playing designated killjoy again, Millie. I hate to admit it, but even a crusty, cynical old bastard like me allowed himself a spell of wishful thinking."

"It's a good thing you apologized," Mildred said. "I'd hate to have to cut you off. Especially after such a close brush with death."

"Yeah, that old life-affirming thing."

"It seems apparent the occupants of the village we were so unceremoniously forced to decamp enjoyed a lengthy halcyon time—"

J.B. shook his head in half-feigned admiration. "'Halcyon.' Now there's a hell of a word, Doc, even comin' out of your mouth. What's it mean?"

"Kingfisher," Jak announced.

Everybody turned to look at the slight albino youth.

Wise as he was in all phases of the brutal fight for survival, he was as illiterate as a rock and not widely known for intellectual curiosity.

"And just exactly how do you know something like that?" J.B. demanded.

"Doc tell me," the boy said, dropping his eyes. He didn't particularly enjoy being a center of attention, even among his friends.

"Lot kingfishers on bayou," he added by way of explanation.

"It is good to see the seeds of knowledge may find purchase and bloom even on the most barren and unpromising ground," Doc said before anyone thought to ask what a fish-eating bird might have to do with peace. "Now, as I was saying, the unhappy villagers unquestionably enjoyed a long spell of comparative peace and plenty. But just as manifestly those days have, quite recently, ended in massacre."

"Not massacre," Jak said, half under his breath. "Not enough chills. People ran."

Ryan nodded. "True. But to pack it all into a shell casing, times have been good, back in that ville, but the good times just ended."

"Which means," Mildred said, "our timing sucks. Again."

"So what now, Ryan?" J.B. asked.

The one-eyed man shrugged. "Krysty needs a safe place to shelter until she can fight her infection. Bad trouble's hit the first ville we found, but that doesn't mean it's taken over the whole valley."

"But from the way you told us the sec men acted," Mildred said, "they don't exactly seem like prizes, either. I'm glad you opted to run from them."

"Something about those sec boys," J.B. said. "Just here in my gut it hits me that they acted a whole lot more like some kind of conquerin' army than people coming back to their homes. Even coming to take their homes back by force."

"The people in that ville were never that well armed," Ryan said. "Or they wouldn't've been killed or driven off in the first place. The muties outnumbered the sec men we saw four, mebbe five, to one or more. But they didn't hang around once that patrol hit town."

"And they were smart to hit the road, given how heavy the biker boy and his little pals were packing." The Armorer got that cagey gleam in his eye and rubbed the grizzled stubble beginning to sprout on his chin. "But y'know, Ryan, if those muties—"

"Not just muties," Mildred corrected.

"Right, hon. If those raiders'd been at all comfortable in a ville, they could have still laid the original world of hurt on that sec patrol. Even stones and sticks can do some damage against machine guns and fancy laser blasters. Street fighting's like that."

"Which only goes to support what we have already surmised," Doc said, "that the marauders are functionally nomadic and have but recently arrived in the valley, or at least this part of it. What I find intriguing, John Barrymore, is our deliverance from the dubious mercies of that security patrol, through the agency of a mysterious barrage of missiles. Who loosed those projectiles in so timely a way? 'Twas as dramatic as the lightnings of Zeus, and every bit as unlikely."

"Well, gents," Mildred said, "we may be about to find out."

The wag was slowing. A man had stepped out from a toothy black jut of lava boulders into their path. As most of the humans and muties they'd seen this day, he was short and dark, with a shock of hair as glossy black as volcanic glass. It was held out of his eyes by a green rag tied around his temples for a headband. He wore a short-sleeved shirt mottled in dark brown and green camou, olive-drab pants and sandals. Aside from a knife in a scabbard on his belt, he showed no weapons. His hands were raised in the universal no-threat sign.

J.B. stood up through the gunner's hole in the roof, covering the man with his Uzi. The man's grin never wavered. He was clearly no fool, and wasn't taking them for fools, either. Anybody confronted with a person or persons appearing out of nowhere covered them at once with whatever weapons were to hand as a matter of course, it was clear, here no less than up north.

At the same time Ryan felt his companions' tension, chose not to voice what was, after all, obvious: the man was choosing to expose himself to risk as a sign of willingness to parlay, showing himself unarmed to emphasize that he intended no harm. But that didn't mean he didn't expect any harm done him to be avenged in one hell of a hurry.

They were being watched. Weps were sighted-in on

them right now. Given what they'd seen in the alley so far, that could be pretty serious indeed.

Doc opened his door and stepped out into the hot sun. *"¿Qué tal, amigo?"* he called.

"Fireblast, Doc," Ryan hissed under his breath. "What the hell's he think he's—"

Mildred held a palm up to him. "Ease off the trigger, Ryan. He's nuts but he isn't stupid."

"Doc speaks Mex-talk, remember," J.B. called down softly.

"Yeah," Ryan said. "Keep both eyes open anyway."

"Oh, I already spotted a few beady eyeballs around us already," the Armorer said in a cheerily conversational voice. "Peeping at us over the sights of longblasters, of course. If these people wanted anything but to palaver, they'd already be dragging us out leaking like the legendary Bonnie and Clyde."

"It's all right," Doc called. "This young gentleman's name is Five Ax. It is a very traditional sort of name hereabouts, dating from pre-Columbian times. He is, he tells me, a Jaguar Knight from the City in the Lake. He leads a party of scouts. He claims, and I incline to credit this, that they saved our collective bacon from what he terms Baron Hector's men."

Ryan shrugged, set the Steyr's butt down on the floor with its long barrel pointing toward the Hummer's roof, got out himself.

"And how exactly did they accomplish that?"

Five Ax's grin widened. He held his left palm up, skimmed his right across it and thrust his right hand forward into the air. "Whoosh, whoosh," he said. "Rockets."

Ryan glanced up at J.B. One shoulder of the Armorer's jacket hiked up in an almost-imperceptible shrug.

"Rockets it was," he said. He strode forward and thrust out his hand. "I'm Ryan."

Five Ax took Ryan's hand, looked him in the eye and spoke.

"He says he's pleased and honored to meet such a great warrior chief from the north," Doc said.

"Spun him a real line of it, did you, Doc?"

"I told him no more than the truth," the old man said loftily. "Of course the proper presentation did your repute no harm."

"Well, tell him I'm also honored to meet such a brave warrior. Thank him for saving our asses, while you're at it. Lay it on thick as you like."

"Already done, friend Ryan. Still, a trifle more effusiveness can scarcely go amiss…"

He conversed for several moments with Five Ax. The Jaguar Knight was young, not much more than Jak's age, though considerably thicker through shoulder and chest. He carried himself with the easy assurance of a veteran; for all the fancy-pants title, he seemed much business and little bullshit.

"He's offering to guide us to the City in the Lake and his baron, Don Tenorio," Doc said at length. "He seems altogether confident he can get us both past Don Hector's sec patrols and the marauders, whom he terms Chichimecs."

"Is everybody here named Don?" J.B. demanded.

"It's a title, silly," Mildred said. "Like 'mister.'"

"Thank him for saving us from this Baron Hector's patrol. And try to work out some kind of diplomatic way of asking why. Are his people at war with Hector's?"

Doc spoke to the young warrior. Five Ax responded with laughter. "He says they are not at war with Don Hector, but that relations are not the best between them, either. One derives the distinct impression our new friends are not exactly dismayed that we presented them an opportunity to take one of Hector's patrols down a peg, especially one led by one of his Eagle Knights."

"Eagle Knights, Jaguar Knights," J.B. called. "Seems like a lotta knights."

"It would appear they are roughly equivalent," Doc said. "Comprising the elite of both baron's sec men, and also their personal bodyguards."

"Elite, hmm?" Ryan looked over their self-proclaimed rescuer appraisingly. Two Arrow the Eagle Knight had been maybe as tall as Ryan himself, muscled like an old-time statue of a god, and acted as if he thought he were one to boot, swanking around on his hog-zapping hapless muties with his wrist laser and chopping parts off helpless captives.

Jaguar Knight Five Ax—odd names, oddly similar— was a scrubby little guy who however looked as if he could run up one side of Mount Popocatépetl and down the other without breathing heavy, and also as if he'd crawl through a mile of sewage to jump out of your crapper and slit your throat, should that happen to be his duty.

It might not be so easy to pick one over the other as a pure man chiller.

"What do you think, J.B.? Anybody?" Ryan asked over his shoulder.

"Let me put it to you this way, Ryan," called Mildred, who had her head out the window but was remaining in the driver's seat in case a quick getaway should be called for. "We all know appearances can be deceiving. But this bunch we *don't* know for a fact are murderous assholes."

"And there you have it," J.B. said.

Chapter Ten

"Chichimecs," Five Ax said quietly.

"Chichimecs, huh," Ryan agreed. They were belly-down on the crest of a serpentine cooled-lava flow, watching a party of maybe twenty of the mixed norm and mutie marauders pass by below. Ryan was looking through one side of Five Ax's pair of binoculars.

The raiders displayed the same wide spectrum of weaponry they'd seen among their attackers in the abandoned ville, ranging from a stone club in the warted hand of a mutie, up through bows with crooked arrows and makeshift muskets, to a lever-action carbine or two and at least one AKS. The distribution was sort of a pyramid, with the low-tech weps predominating. Ryan did see one thing that made his blood run chill inside him and made him glad Mildred had decided to duck for cover in that garage: a human carrying an unmistakable RPG-7, a predark Soviet antitank rocket launcher that could pop open the Hummer like a stinkbug on a hot iron stove.

The scout made a gesture like a slow-motion downward patting of the air, which Ryan took to mean they would wait. The two couldn't really talk, although Five

Ax obviously understood at least some spoken English. But they found they understood each other pretty well without speaking; any communicating that needed to be done seemed to be accomplished with a few compact gestures.

Five Ax waited as the afternoon shadows lengthened and the Chichimec band passed. Then he slipped backward down the slope, got cautiously to his feet, picking up his rifle. It was a Lee-Enfield Mk IV in fairly decent condition, the mark with the peep sight back at the rear of the receiver. It wasn't a finely tuned precision weapon like Ryan's SSG, nor yet a bullet sprayer like J.B.'s Uzi. It was just business, a lightweight, robust bolt-gun that went bang when you pulled the trigger and shot pretty much as well as you did out to most conventionally useful ranges. It had a detachable 10-round box magazine; Ryan didn't know whether it still fired the original .303 Brit cartridge it had been designed and built for, or whether it had been rechambered to fire the somewhat more powerful NATO .308. On the whole it was a blaster a lot like the man who carried it.

The Jaguar Knight made no noise Ryan's keen ears could hear above the breeze, nor had he much disturbed the sparse vegetation where he'd lain. He was, like Jak, the sort of man whom Trader might have said barely cast a shadow when he moved. Come to think of it, Ryan reckoned Five Ax would have fit in well with the picked professionals of Trader's caravan, once upon a long-lost time.

They moved back to the Hummer, where Jak

crouched on top of the roof, looking more like some kind of predatory animal than usual in the buttery late-day sun with his white hair blowing around his face, and J.B. was just buttoning his fly from relieving himself among the weeds. Krysty was sitting up in the back of the wag with Mildred helping her drink. She saw Ryan and gave him a wan smile. It was obvious she was hurting. He made himself smile back to encourage her, and she lay down out of sight, assisted by the stocky black woman.

Five Ax spoke to Doc, who was sitting on the Hummer's wide hood with his back against the windshield and his long, lean legs out in front of him. "He says that should be the last of the Chichimecs we encounter. They do not like to get too close to the lake, although they have been growing bolder of late. We should be able to reach the city with time to spare before the sunset. Which even our redoubtable young friend seems to think is a very good thing indeed."

Five Ax nodded, looking serious, just hovering on the edge of uneasy. Ryan wondered what was abroad at night that would put the wind up a seasoned warrior like that. Perhaps the giant rattler wasn't the only monster in these parts.

"Now, THAT'S A PRETTY impressive sight."

They had been catching glimpses of the lake all along. Now they came over a last rise and here it was.

The sun was falling into the jagged mountains, walling the valley to the west. The light was an amber color that seemed to invest everything it touched with richness and with sadness. The shadows seemed to stretch forever.

In the near twilight the water was gunmetal-gray. From the middle of it rose a drowned city. Buildings, skyscrapers, jutted from the placid water. Some, intact, soared high into the pale blue and dove-wing-gray sky. Others were snapped-off stumps, their break points still ragged and fanged with girders. Still others lay toppled, some half submerged, some more than half, like giant quiescent water worms. Lights were becoming visible among the structures, the nearest still perhaps a mile away across the water.

Five Ax guided them around a big hill covered with scrub and woods that rose like a ramp from near the shore into the west, toward the mouth of a narrow causeway stretching out to the half-toppled and half-drowned city. The mouth was guarded by a tangle of razor wire and a miniature adobe fort. As the broad-shouldered Hummer rumbled down the path toward the causeway, sentries in the minifort swiveled the perforated barrel of a tripod-mounted machine gun to bear on them.

"Stop here, my friends," Five Ax said by way of Doc. "I'll talk to them and get us through."

"Do that," Ryan said, glad he had his Steyr stowed for the moment out of sight. He didn't doubt the sentries would pass the scout, nor did they seem reflexively hostile, merely cautious. But he knew how easily accidents could happen where loaded and cocked blasters were concerned. Especially when authentic threats lurked in the vicinity—which these days, granted, was pretty much everywhere and all the time.

Five Ax popped out of the vehicle, waved his arm and shouted. The sentries greeted him with cheerful cries of recognition. To the friends' relief they promptly traversed the gun to aim out into the dusk gathering among the green fields and ridges and snaky black twists of lava flows.

"Our youthful friend is explaining to his comrades-in-arms that we are mighty warriors and traders from the north," Doc translated. He had climbed out to stretch his storklike limbs. "As we already gathered from what Five Ax has said, apparently they have seen our like before, from time to time."

"I hope the earlier visitors didn't pop out of the volcano the way we did," Mildred said. The travelers were always uneasy at the prospect of others stumbling onto their secret mode of travel—not to mention escape.

"Can't be that many people using the mat-trans network," Ryan said. "We'd run into more of them if there were."

A couple of guards in baggy civilian clothes came out of the minifort and dragged the coiling razor-tape tangles out of the way with salvaged swimming pool hooks. "Death Slinkies," Mildred muttered. The others looked at her blankly.

Five Ax seemed eager to get across the water and into the city. Everybody got back in the wag, and Mildred drove it out onto the causeway. The sentries carefully dragged the wire tangles back into place the moment they had passed, then scampered gratefully back inside the thick mud-brick walls of their fortification.

The causeway was of crushed volcanic rock, black

with patches of a deep rust red. The porous pebbles used to metal the surface made squealing, crunching sounds as the tires crushed them. The freshening sunset breeze brought a smell of cool, fresh water through the wag's open windows—although from somewhere, possibly the ville they had been holed up in earlier that day, perhaps another hapless target of the Chichimecs' depredations, drifted the faint but distinctive scent of distant death.

Boats skimmed the green water, some with triangular sails turned yellow by the light's fading, some driven by oars, a few showing no external means of propulsion and hence no doubt driven by some kind of motor. They seemed to all be heading for the City in the Lake, in which lights were beginning to glimmer awake.

J.B. still rode shotgun. Ryan was in the back seat with Doc between him and their guide. Mildred had complained the arrangement meant the nineteenth-century scholar blocked her vision out the rearview mirror; Ryan had countered that traffic from behind was the last of their worries.

Jak was still back in the rear compartment with Krysty, who was moaning sporadically and tossing her head from side to side but seemed thoroughly unconscious. The boy reached chalk-white fingers over the seat back to clutch Ryan's shoulder.

"Light," he said. Ryan turned to look back toward the sentry tower. Sure enough, a light was shining from its top, blinking rapidly. "Signaling."

From somewhere up ahead in the city a flicker responded, this clearly from a mirror reflecting the sun's last light. "You folks have some pretty good communications," Ryan told Five Ax through Doc.

"How else do you think we knew how to intercept you when you cut out of that ville?" the young man said, and grinned his infectious grin. "It was Two Arrow himself who told us you were there in the first place, when he reported back to Hector on his talkie. That's why we like to use the reflecs. Can't listen in unless you know the code."

"This Don Hector's bunch got commo good as yours?" J.B. asked.

"No," the Jaguar Knight said, shaking his head. "At least we don't think so. They haven't shown any sign of having as efficient a system as we do. But they might be holding something back."

Ryan nodded, rubbing his chin, which was raspy with late-day growth. The more he saw of this Five Ax the better impressed he was. The young scout was able to see beyond that which stared him plainly in the face. Not everybody had that gift.

Off to their left his eye caught a flicker of motion, a dull glint of reflected glow no brighter than an ember in a nigh-dead campfire. There came a mighty splash.

"Whoa!" Mildred exclaimed. "What in the wide, wide world of sports was that?"

"*Pesca,*" Five Ax answered matter-of-factly.

"A fish? A *fish?* That was a hell of a big fish, amigo."

"We get a lot of food from the lake. Nothing like a good trout steak. Only thing better is a nice slab of fresh giant axolotl."

"Tell me 'axolotl' means something other than I think it means, Doc."

"An axolotl is still a large, neotonous form of salamander. A giant axolotl is, one infers, well…an extra-large specimen. I take it that was not the response you hoped for from me, dear lady?"

"They eat giant mud-puppies here," Mildred said hollowly.

Jak smacked his lips. "Go some right now."

Ryan's stomach rumbled. It had been many wild hours since it had last felt the fall of food. "I'm with you, Jak. I hope Don Tenorio can spare us some chow."

Five Ax nodded vigorously. "Don Tenorio will honor you with a mighty feast. All the giant *axolotl* you want. And also dragonfly eggs."

"Sounds mighty tasty," J.B. said.

"I'm in hell," Mildred muttered.

Chapter Eleven

Don Tenorio turned back from the giant window that constituted the west wall of his office. Out across the lake the last declining remnants of day showed as a thin band of blood-colored glow behind the western peaks. The light show from Popocatépetl and Iztaccíhuatl easily outshone them. The crimson fire fountains flung into the face of night by the distant mountains was reflected hellishly in the smooth waters of the lake.

He turned, swirling tequila in his glass. "It is rare that we are privileged to receive visitors from your land," he said in heavily accented but clearly comprehensible English. His voice was startling deep and mellifluous, coming from such a slight figure. "Two years, I believe, have passed since the last time."

Ryan stood next to a wall-size shelf of hardcover books, with titles in English, Spanish and some languages he didn't recognize printed on their spines. He was nigh stunned with fatigue. But his spirit was too restless within him to allow him to sit. Even having seen Krysty laid down on clean, crisp sheets in the infirmary of Don Tenorio's headquarters, under the care of staff who had met Mildred's exacting standards, wasn't enough to free him to rest quite yet.

Uncertainty was a fact of life in the world in which he'd grown to manhood. But certain kinds of uncertainty could turn out to be facts of death. He had some questions that were restless to be asked.

Of course, the growling in his stomach might've had something to do with his continued wakefulness, as well. Neither he nor his companions had enjoyed any kind of proper meal since their last feed in the Popocaté-petl redoubt, in what had proved to be the very early hours of that morning.

"You mean somebody else made it down before us?" asked J.B., who sat next to Mildred on a sofa with a ponderous dark-stained wood frame and cushions upholstered in gleaming brown leather. "What with the hot zones and bands of chem storms up north of here, I kinda figured we'd be the first."

"Ah, but no, Señor Dix. There have been others in my lifetime, although I have never ascertained whether accounts of visits before my time were mere legend or not." He smiled. "Most of our visitors have, much like yourselves, been interested in exploring the possibilities of trade."

Ryan glanced at J.B., who was studiously gazing off across the night and the lake. That had been the story they'd agreed upon in advance: that they had come to Mex-land seeking to open up trade routes, traveling down the desolate and sparsely inhabited west coast, but that some unspecified disaster along the way had cost them most of their goods. The story was, as the Armorer said, thin as the seat of a ville rat's drawers. But all agreed it was better than the secret of the mat-trans— not to mention at least marginally more believable.

"Our last set of visitors from *el norte*," Don Tenorio said, "apparently anticipating that we Mexicans had been reduced to the status of primitives by the war, came among us intending to emulate your long-dead countryman, William Walker. Ah, Doctor, I see you know the name."

Doc sat in a leather-covered armchair beside Tenorio's desk. He was playing with a five-inch globe of polished stone somehow painted or printed to represent the Earth, that he'd picked up off its brass and mahogany stand on the desk. "I do, indeed, Don Tenorio. Although he was a bit before my time."

Their host blinked at the tall, skinny man. Out of the baron's sight J.B. rolled his eyes toward the ceiling. Fortunately the nineteenth-century scholar, while mostly maintaining, had already slipped out of phase with reality a few times in Tenorio's presence.

"Fortunately, between us, Don Hector's people and mine, were able to frustrate his plans—ah, María, what is it?"

A dark, pretty woman dressed in a colorfully embroidered linen dress came into the room. She was tiny, no more than four feet tall, though voluptuously built. She spoke softly to the baron in Spanish. He answered in the same language before turning to his guests.

"At last our dinner is prepared," Don Tenorio said.

"My apologies for such delay, for I know you must be famished. Still, it isn't often that I entertain guests so distinguished as yourselves, and so it took my staff, hardworking though they are, extra time to prepare an appropriate repast."

"Didn't really need to bother," J.B. rumbled. "I'm so rad-blasted hungry I could eat the ass end out of a dead—"

"We're delighted and honored that you've gone to such trouble on our behalf, Don Tenorio," Mildred said loudly, rising from the sofa. "I'm sure the meal will be well worth the wait."

PERHAPS BECAUSE SHE WAS every bit as hungry as she had kept J.B. from too graphically describing himself as, Mildred ate the sumptuous meal Don Tenorio had provided as eagerly as everybody else. Of course it didn't hurt that the grilled meat, like everything else, was liberally doused in a thick sauce, sufficiently sharpened with chili that other tastes were muted at best. Nor that the room was lit only by candles, well enough to eat by but not any great aid to identifying what one was eating. Still, it was perhaps just as well for her twentieth-century sensibilities that nothing obviously discernible as dragonfly eggs was laid out on any of the heavy earthenware dishes set on the expanse of white linen tablecloth.

Still, at one point when she had mostly sated her appetite, Ryan heard her mutter as she studied a chunk of baked flesh impaled on her fork, "Mud puppy—the *other* white meat."

Don Tenorio's dining hall was another room in the truncated skyscraper he had appropriated as his headquarters, so situated as to look directly south, providing a splendid view of the volcanoes. Popocatépetl was in especially fine form this night, hurling constant arcs of red molten lava, brilliant as filaments in a light bulb. The travelers all marveled that they had, not twenty-four hours before, found themselves in the midst of that.

They had been describing life in the Deathlands to their host, who was brimming with questions although he did in fact display a fair degree of knowledge as to conditions there. Ryan tore a piece of rolled tortilla away with his teeth, chewed and swallowed, then as he dipped the raw end of the flat bread in the pungent reddish sauce, said, "We've been wondering why it is there's so little background radiation hereabouts."

Don Tenorio was taking a swig of cool water, which seemed to be his drink of choice, from a heavy fired-clay mug. For such a wizened little guy he ate and drank with gusto befitting the fattest sec boss. Maybe his emotional intensity burned it all off.

"Perhaps, my friends, you wonder, and are too polite to openly ask, why our once glorious Mexico City, once the most populous on Earth, is such a shattered ruin, without having been bombed as intensively as your great cities in the north? Indeed, the city was not bombed at all. Which is the answer to the question you did ask."

The companions were way too seasoned to contradict a baron—*alcade,* his people called him—at his own dinner table, even one as mild-seeming as Tenorio. But they all looked up and around at one another. Even ruby-eyed Jak, who normally could be distracted from feeding by nothing short of immediate mortal peril, glanced up from the leg of something Mildred fervently hoped was chicken he was holding in both hands to tear at with his sharp white teeth.

"I see your skepticism. Yet I speak the truth. With your indulgence I will tell you the sad tale of our city's fall."

J. B. waved his own well-gnawed leg of whatever. "Speak your piece, Baron. We're all ears. Well, and gullets."

"We were spared direct thermonuclear bombardment during the great war, as your instruments indicate. But that does not mean we were spared the wrath of the combatants, nor indeed a *matanza,* a slaughter no less comprehensive, in the end, than that suffered by many cities reduced to radioactive glass craters.

"We were not targeted directly because we lacked all significance in the geopolitical sense. To be sure, we had the greatest population of any city in the world. But what of that? We were a neutral country, and while in practical terms we were friendly with *los Estados Unidos,* that fact was of no military consequence. We had no nuclear weapons of our own, nor any force-projection capabilities, as the ability to attack others in different parts of the world was then called. We had barely an army, and that was often strained to keep the peace in our own often unruly states.

"Now I take you for *científicos*—educated folk. I am

sure you know, at least in broad outline, the history of the war itself. Our doom was caused by the earthshaker nukes the Soviets planted along the eastern arc of the Pacific Rim, the so-called Ring of Fire. The fearful vibrations they created, that sank so much of your western seaboard, struck terrible harmonics in the ground beneath our feet."

As if to emphasize his words a tremor shimmied up through the travelers' feet, rattling their bones ever so slightly as it made the dinnerware shift and clink on the table.

"This has always been a region of extraordinary seismic activity. Not for nothing have those who dwelled in the Valley of Mexico long called themselves the Sons of Shaking Earth. Destructive, deadly earthquakes were nothing new. Indeed, many of our newer and most imposing structures were built specifically to withstand great earthquakes."

He gestured around with his fork. His headquarters lay near the southern edge of the city, affording a nearly unobstructed view of the lake. Lights shone from the windows of a few buildings looming nearby, candles and torches and lanterns, dim ghosts of the electric starlight that had once illuminated the city's heart. The other skyscrapers were present merely as monolithic shadows, perceptible principally where they blotted out the real stars.

"Which is the only reason as many survived as did. Most did not, even of the mightiest structures. There are limits to how strongly we can make a thing, and no matter how powerful our creativity, it seems our ability to destroy is always stronger."

"Ain't that the truth," J.B. said.

"The people, it is said, were dancing in the streets to the sound of cathedral bells, rung to celebrate our deliverance from the bombing, when the first great tremor hit. Tens of thousands died in the space of a few minutes as giant buildings were thrown down on their very heads."

"And let me guess," Mildred said with a fork half raised to her full lips. "They turned out to be the lucky ones."

"You are very wise. For while they died screaming, they died almost upon the instant. Not so the ones slain next, when the great volcanoes exploded. Just as no quake in our recorded history compared to those that struck, wave after horrible wave, on that terrible day, neither did any volcanic eruption compare to what happened then. Popocatépetl and Iztaccíhuatl each lost over a thousand feet of height in one huge belch. Huge clouds of superheated gas and incandescent ash rolled out in tides of death across the valley. They didn't reach so far as the heart of the capital itself, although the suburbs were stricken, like Pompeii of legendary times. But the great city was not spared a blizzard of gray ash, falling to a depth to cover cars parked or wrecked in the streets, higher than the tallest man's head. Those who had been outside or had been driven forth by the collapse of the buildings they had occupied drowned in a sea of choking, stinging ash.

"The shocks, the eruptions, the rains of ash continued—not for days or weeks but for years, all through-out the skydark and beyond. Yet in the end they proved not the worst of our tribulations. Oh, no." He shook his head in sorrow.

"If I might venture a guess," Doc said, gesticulating with his fork, "a couple of the Four Horsemen had yet to visit you."

"Precisely so, Doctor. Although in truth our people, such as survived the shaking and the suffocating clouds, were mostly spared the lingering death of Famine."

He drank from his goblet. "Only because Pestilence struck them down before they could starve. Undoubt-edly you know, from your own history if not your own experiences, how tenacious human life is. Even the greatest and most comprehensive disaster will generally leave survivors in its wake. And however wretched or reduced they are, they proceed with their lives, create a daily routine that is tolerable to them. Such, literally, is life. But the plagues that followed the tremors and erup-tions were so vicious and swift that they literally cleansed the rubble of survivors. Most of our current scholars believe that within two months no humans re-mained alive in what had been the largest collection of humanity in our history. In fact, they now debate whether the plagues were altogether natural, or whether they were some kind of biological-warfare organisms, unleashed upon us incidentally, as what was called in those days 'collateral damage,' or whether some force hostile to us, perhaps domestic terrorists, struck at us in our time of greatest vulnerability. However it happened, our mighty city was destroyed and purged of life. And so it remained for most of a century."

He seemed an unlikely sort for a baron, their host, this Don Tenorio. He was a small, dark man, clearly on the downward slope of middle age, spare, graying, in fact perhaps a bit gray overall. His features were spare, his mouth a slit, his nose a great beak, in general betraying more than slight relationship to the human Chichimecs the companions had encountered. He seemed not just to lack but to be the antithesis to the sort of flamboyance, the larger-than-life swagger that characterized the Deathlands barons they had encountered, the good, at least comparatively, as well as the bad. He seemed more suited to be a clerk, a shopkeeper, a bureaucratic mouse not big or imposing enough even to be a rat.

But as they sat at his table and ate his food and drank his wine, both copious and fine, Ryan began to perceive him in a different light. Nor was it simply the light of candles Don Tenorio used to light his dining hall, a trick, Ryan gathered, like the heavy wooden furniture and blankets patterned in muted but multiple colors hung from the walls, to transform the sterile chamber in a reclaimed skyscraper, smelling inescapably of moisture and mildew and in the occupants' subconscious if not actual fact, of ancient death, into something approximating a hall in some fine adobe villa built on dry and solid ground.

As he spoke, the *alcade*'s skin seemed to take on an almost transparent quality, and his eyes to burn, as though they were thin membrane and dark lenses showing forth the light of the spirit and vision that burned inside.

Jak was frowning. He nodded out the window. "Why much water?"

"An excellent question. Mexico City was built upon a lake. Its predecessor, Tenochtitlán of the fierce and terrible Aztecs, itself lay in the midst of Lake Texcoco. In time Texcoco was virtually covered over, paved over, by Mexico City, as were several other substantial lakes nearby.

"With the continuing powerful quakes, the waters rose, or the land sank, or perhaps both. Indeed, so it happened throughout this great catchment basin that we by tradition miscall a valley, which in fact has no outlets for water, so that no rivers flow out of it. Heights were cast down, others thrust up. The normal work of millions of years of geological formation occurred in short years, in some cases weeks. We believe it was the single most violent seismic upheaval, not in written history, but in the whole year history of the human species. The whole land was transformed, so that when the people emerged from caves and shelters after the skies cleared and the nuclear winter ended, it was as if we had been transported to another realm.

"As I have indicated, not all the consequences of the disaster were bad. The valley, which had long been blessed with greater rainfall than the desert lands to the north, began to receive even more than before. And for the most part our rains were pure, not the acid rains and chem storms that have so ravaged your own homeland and indeed much of the northern reaches of our country. This weather pattern has persisted. We receive abundant water for irrigation. In the days of the Aztec, the waters of Lake Texcoco were brackish with salts carried down from the mountains. Nowadays the waters of the lake, which we also call Texcoco, are fresh, fit for irrigation or, suitably sterilized, for human consumption.

"Even the volcanic ashfalls are a blessing as well as a curse. They create rich growing soils, causing the very lands they smother to spring back more fruitful than before. So our valley has been a relative haven in our tormented world. While the tremors and eruptions continue to take a toll, they have also helped to isolate us from a hostile outside world."

"Yet you seem to be seeking contact with that world," Ryan said. "Welcoming us for instance, not to put too fine an edge on it."

"I believe the benefits inherent in peaceful trade outweigh the risks from such contact," Don Tenorio said. "As you have observed, and as I have hinted at, we are not without means of defending ourselves."

"And cooperation with Don Hector has been part of those means of self-defense?" Ryan asked.

Tenorio raised a thin gray eyebrow. "Most perceptive, Señor Cawdor. We reentered the long-dead City in the Lake a generation ago. At the time that was all the safety we required. Most residents of the valley believed the ruins were cursed, that it was death so much as to set foot among them, which was why the wealth present here remained totally untouched for the better part of a century. For years it was true enough, what with the plagues. But eventually the spores or whatever carried the contagion died out and lost their potency. Or perhaps the only humans to survive to our time were genetically immune to the plagues."

"If I might be so bold as to make an inquiry, Don Tenorio," Doc said, "how does it happen that you and certain other folk we have encountered speak English, much less so fluent and excellent a form as you yourself display?"

"Ah, but you flatter me, Doctor. As you may be aware, for a long time we Mexicans had a love-hate relationship with our neighbors to the north. Yet by your day, right before the war, English had indisputably become the international language. So learning that language had become institutionalized here. It continued to be taught even through the Great Skydark. Its knowledge has come to be associated with greater education, and hence with greater status—with class, if you like. Which is why Don Hector, who is in many ways a virulent traditionalist, encourages his elite, his priests and Eagle Knights, to learn it—to differentiate them from the commoners."

He patted his lips with his napkin. "Ah, but it grows late, and doubtless you are fatigued from your ordeal. I will not torment you with further questions. I hope you rest well, though, for there remains a world of things I wish to ask you of."

"I SHALL SEE YOU gentlemen in the morning," Doc said. "In the meantime, I am off to the chambers our host has graciously provided, there to renew my long-standing acquaintance with Mr. Jack Daniel's." The tall, gaunt man hoisted his salvaged bottle to his companions.

"'Night, Doc," J.B. said. "Sweet dreams."

Doc showed him a rare, sad smile. "Ah, John Barrymore, but for one such as myself, the sweetest dreams are no dreams at all." He went into the building, leaving his companions leaning on the terrace rail and shaking their heads.

"Where's Jak?" Ryan asked.

His friend grinned at him. "Some sweet little *señorita* snagged him, is my guess. They seem to think he's what they call *muy bonito*. Red eyes and all."

He took a swig from his own bottle. "Ah, youth. It's wasted on the young. Me, I gotta admit I'm glad Millie's even more tired than I am. It's about all I'm gonna be able to do to totter all the way to my bed before I pass out. I'm beat."

The terrace they stood on had once been a restaurant overlooking the street from several stories up. The slowly heaving night-black water now came almost to their feet. It was a peaceful night, quiet but for the sporadic cries of some unknown night bird— or night something—and the distant grumble of the volcanoes, punctuated by explosions that sounded like a giant's knuckles knocking on wood far away. The Armorer held up his bottle and admired the way the dark liquid within caught the starlight as he swirled on.

"Laphroaig single malt, as I live and breathe," he said. "I tell you, Ryan, I'll eat and drink damn near anything that I can get my hands on. But that doesn't mean I don't appreciate the best when I run across it."

"Cow steak's better than wolf steak, any day," Ryan agreed, leaning on crossed arms. He had stopped his own drinking of anything but purified lake water early in the meal. He wanted to keep his head clear.

"You said a true thing there."

"So what do you think of our host?"

"Don Tenorio? Seems a nice enough old codger. Mebbe too nice to be a baron."

"Not too nice to ply us with alcohol on empty stomachs, I noticed."

"Yeah. But that's just boilerplate. Trader would have done it, too, just to feel out somebody he didn't know and was none too sure of. What's that line Doc's always quoting? 'In weenie warthog' or something?"

"In vino veritas."

"There you go." He took a pull at his bottle. "I do wonder how Don Tenorio's going to want to be paid for all this lavish hospitality."

"We have novelty value, right now," Ryan said. "He seems to have a curiosity. And since he's had visitors from up north before, not all of them friendly, it's of real value to him to get what news he can."

"Yeah, right now. But pretty soon we'll be old news. I got a feeling this baron has something more in mind."

Ryan shook his head. It wasn't a gesture of denial; it indicated he flat didn't know. "Mebbe. All I can say is, he seems legitimately friendly enough right now. And we can all use the rest, not just Krysty."

The moon was rising like a giant self-luminous bubble squeezing up from the lake. J.B. saluted it with his bottle. "And speaking of which, I believe I'll take me to my room and let you get along to her."

He started away, stopped, turned back. "Oh. Just remembered. I want to ask the Doc what all that business was about that Walker fella."

"I already did," Ryan said. "Back in Doc's time, little before actually, he led a party down to a place in Central Merica, ways south of here. They aimed to take over."

"How'd that turn out?"

"He went to the wall, eventually."

"Figures." The Armorer nodded sagely. "Another dude just had to be baron, and all it got him was the chop."

THE WINDOW WAS OPEN in the dark infirmary. That surprised Ryan; in most of the big buildings in these old dead cities, you couldn't open the windows. The breeze was fresh and cool and smelled of the water, and only a tiny tang of sulfur from the endless eruptions.

The moonlight came gushing in the window and splashed over Krysty where she lay asleep in the bed, among white sheets for one of the few times in her life. They did all right for themselves here, the baron and his colony of scavvies. Krysty looked pale even for her, her skin almost greenish in the moonlight. Still, her breathing was regular—her mouth was open and she snored gently—and her cheek, when he touched it with the back of his hand, gently, so as not to rouse her, seemed cooler to him.

Taking off his long coat, he shook it out and spread it on the linoleum floor beside her bed. He pulled his SIG-Sauer, pulled back the slide far enough to confirm it was loaded by the dull gleam of brass in the moonlight. Then he eased the slide shut again.

They were in the proverbial position in which, should the baron have wished them harm, he could have done it to them at any time. But it went against Ryan's grain, and long years of hard lessons in the company of Trader, tough and survival-wise as an old gray rat, to take security for granted. A baron's son himself—and exiled through the treachery of his own kin—he knew how fickle a baron's mercy and hospitality might be. And while this baron seemed almost unnaturally easygoing, even benign, that didn't exactly lull Ryan into complacency; was this Don Tenorio really hard-assed enough to take the measures necessary to protect himself, far less his current honored guests, from hostile outsiders, who didn't seem in short supply in the valley? Or insiders for that matter—as yet the travelers had no real skinny on the internal politics of Don Tenorio's sunken ville.

He would sleep well. But he'd keep his blaster near to hand. He used the decocker to ease the hammer down on the chambered round, ready to be cocked again at the squeeze of the trigger, slipped on the safety. He set the weapon on the floor beside Krysty's bed.

He bent over her and kissed her forehead. Then he laid himself down on his coat and fell instantly asleep.

Chapter Twelve

"What do you use for fuel in this beast, Don Tenorio?" J. B. asked, shouting to make himself heard over the roar of the big boat's motor. The gleaming white craft was raising a big bow wave of pale foam as it thrust itself across the surface of the lake.

"Alcohol," the baron called back from where he stood on the flying deck atop the cabin behind and above them. "We have developed techniques to distill it from the algae and weeds that grow in the lake."

J.B. nodded appreciatively. To his friends, gathered near him on the foredeck up toward the bow, he said, "Sometimes even whitecoats do some good, I guess. But if you catch me about to take a sip of any of their home-brew, do me a favor and shoot me right there."

"Indeed," Doc said. He had his coat off, his sleeves rolled up, his lank hair streaming in the breeze of their passage. His cheeks showed an unusual amount of color.

"Nautical life seems to agree with you, Doc," the Armorer remarked. "Too bad Millie's feeling a bit off. I reckon she'd enjoy this little junket."

"With full respect, John Barrymore," Doc said, "I suspect her plea of illness was but a ruse, and that her true desire was to spend the day abed reading volumes from our host's extensive library."

"Mebbe so. Couldn't exactly blame her if she needed a break from sight of the rest of us."

They were circling the semisubmerged remnants of what had been Mexico City's downtown area. When that was done Don Tenorio planned to take them on a tour of such of the sunken streets as were safe for navigation. Even from out here on the open water they were getting some idea of how the baron's people lived. Small boats, most of them fishing by the looks of things, dotted the calm green surface. Close in by the buildings were moored houseboats, some salvaged whole, like Tenorio's cabin cruiser *Paloma Blanca*, others seeming to have been cobbled together from scavenged materials. Among them floated large platforms, wide flat rafts with enough gunwale to hold in a layer of soil, dotted with growing green shots of various crops. It was a trick, Don Tenorio proudly explained, that they had borrowed from the ancient Indian inhabitants of Tenochtitlán.

J.B. glanced sidelong at their host, standing above them at the rail. Over one shoulder protruded the long slender barrel of a Browning M-2 set in another improvised mount. In a way the cabin cruiser might still be what it started life as, a rich man's toy. But it was one with teeth. Nor was the baron himself unarmed. He wore a white shirt with loose sleeves, dungarees, a belt with a big wide turquoise-inlaid silver buckle, and strapped onto it a black combat holster. In the holster rode, cocked and locked, a blaster the Armorer had blissfully identified as a .40-caliber Witness, a lightly modified version of the classic CZ-75 license-built by Tanfoglio in Italy. It was an altogether businesslike fighting blaster, and seemed startlingly out of character for their spare, small, almost bureaucratic host.

"Look at him up there," the Armorer muttered. "He's enjoying this way too much. He ought have a bandanna around his head, an eyepatch and a cutlass in his teeth, like a pirate in an old-time pic book."

"Where'd you ever see pic books with pirates in them?" asked Ryan, who had grown up reading a tattered copy of *Treasure Island* from Front Royal's baronial library.

J.B. shrugged. "My mama told me about them," he said. "She actually had herself a few books, growing up."

"We don't hear you talk about your childhood very often, J.B.," Krysty said with a radiant, if slightly wan, smile.

IT WAS THE MORNING of their third day in the City in the Lake. The first, the morning after their arrival, the companions had mostly slept—even Mildred, after she was finally convinced the baron's med people were competent to look after Krysty. The next day had been spent lounging, eating, talking with Don Tenorio and some of his lieutenants who spoke English, such as young Ernesto, his bespectacled chief aide—who was along for this cruise, although constantly fussing on the talkie—and his rather glum and cadaverous-looking sec boss, Colonel Solano. Krysty had already begun to regain consciousness for protracted periods, and her fever had greatly receded. Mildred had been busiest of any of the companions, shooing the others away from Krysty's bedside after brief visits to keep them from tiring her out, insisting that Krysty herself sleep and drink as much fluid and soup made from the chickens the scavvies kept in profusion as she could.

Just as Mildred had predicted, given rest, comparative security, and maybe a bit of a boost from Gaia, what with all the seismic energy being released in the area, Krysty's immune system had driven back the nasty infection caused by the shit-smeared crossbow quarrel, and gone a long way toward healing the actual wound. Had any other patient suffering similar insult tried to climb out of bed inside a week to ten days, Mildred maintained, she'd have stunned them with a bat. But physician that she was, she had learned to trust Krysty's instincts about the redhead's own healing processes. If Krysty thought what she needed today was fresh air, sunshine and a little light exercise, then fine; Mildred was happy to kiss her and the rest goodbye and to spend the day propped up in a real bed drinking chocolate sweetened with honey, another venerable local tradition that had been revived in the modern-day valley.

J.B. SHRUGGED IN RESPONSE to Krysty's remark and looked away to the green rolling country stretching north. Its serene beauty was deceptive. One of the things making Ernesto twitter even more than usual were reports that the Chichimec horde, under their mad prophet

Nezahualcoyótl, was on the move, devouring crops—
and villagers—like mutie locusts within twenty miles
of the Lake. They were moving slowly but ominously
closer each day.

"Not much to tell," J.B. said.

Completing the expedition was the young albino Jak
Lauren, his white hair whipping his scarred lean face,
sunlight twinkling on the jagged bits of metal worked
into his jacket. His arms were folded on the railing at
the boat's prow. He walked a small leaf-blade throwing
knife along the backs of the fingers of his right fist like
a stage conjurer with a coin.

The boat had nearly circumnavigated the ruined city.
Now it swung to port to avoid a fallen skyscraper, faced
with shiny dark-red stone, that stretched like a finger
into the lake. A pelican perched on a corner of its roof,
which stood perhaps two feet out of the water. As the
boat growled past, it spread its great white wings and
flapped majestically away.

The small, spare *alcade* had vanished from the flying deck above them. Now he strolled out onto the foredeck. "You've seen what it looks like from the outside,
my friends," he said in that rich voice, which seemed it
by rights should emerge from a much grander, more imposing personage. "Now would you care to tour the
streets of our city?"

"Sure," Ryan said. "I'm interested in seeing your
operation."

"Then see it you shall."

Don Tenorio held up a spare brown finger. The helmsman in the glass-enclosed cabin put the wheel over. The boat heeled to starboard, curved toward a watery avenue that led between two looming buildings, one of which had broken off a hundred feet or so above, another that soared, apparently intact, a good twenty stories.

The boat slowed to a putting creep. "With the constant earth tremors, things are constantly falling into the water," Don Tenorio explained. "Also existing snags shift unpredictably, or structural steel members can be thrust without warning into channels that yesterday were clear. Besides, we don't wish to swamp anybody's home or garden with our wake."

He had a point. Off their port bow floated a growing plat perhaps a hundred feet square, its furrows of dark soil sprouting knee-high corn plants. To their starboard rode a houseboat of sorts, or perhaps a floating shanty, rising two stories above its gunwales and seeming to have been cobbled together of colorful panels of plastic. Or to be in the process; two men and a woman were engaged in fixing a new sheet to the upper story, the woman on the roof, one man on a ladder that the second man steadied from the deck. The woman and the man on the ladder waved cheerfully to the boat as it prowled past.

Don Tenorio raised a hand in reply and beamed. "For a century people shunned this city, thinking it accursed—believing horrific spirits stalked its streets and canals. We had to sneak to the ruins in our boats like thieves in the night, lest we be attacked for running the risk of disturbing the evil ghosts and bringing their wrath upon the surrounding villages. Danger we found here in abundance, even death. But no curse.

"For our daring we have won great riches. And now that we have, through our sweat and ingenuity, regained a foothold in this once-great city, we can dare to hope to envision the day—maybe not in our lifetimes, maybe not for many lifetimes of our descendants—when it is one day great again."

"A most inspirational dream," Doc murmured. "May you and your followers realize it."

But Ryan felt a chill scurry like a small scaly mutie down his spine as they passed between the giant structures and into the ruin itself. Only the shade, he told himself. But then Krysty caught his eye and gave him a slight smile that was almost a grimace, and he wondered if her scant, sporadic doomie powers were showing her some foreboding glimpses into the future of the baron and his pioneering people.

Not ours, he told himself, or she'd say something. He moved to her side, the right, laid a hand on her unwounded shoulder. She reached up to cover it with her own.

In some places the remaining structures crowded to either side of them like glass and stone and steel cliffs. In others they fell away to leave the *Paloma* crossing broad swatches of open water covering what had been plazas to begin with, or places where nothing taller than the lake was deep had survived the quakes. From one such the companions all pointed and made wondering noises at the spectacle of three skyscrapers, twenty stories high and more, that had been felled by one falling against the other so that they lay tilted like dominos; the last was propped on the semicrushed remnants of a building that had either been built shorter or had itself snapped off.

"Impressive devastation," Doc observed.

Just how many followers Don Tenorio had trying to wrestle the city back from that devastation, chaos and the elements, neither the *alcade* nor Five Ax had specified. Although they seemed well-meaning and open-spirited, perhaps too much so for the age, Ryan had to admit they were far from foolish. Their habit of talking freely, even expansively, of their efforts seemed always somehow to skate around giving information that might be of great use to ill-wishers—such as their numbers. Still, from circumstance, Ryan knew they had to number in the hundreds, perhaps as many as a thousand.

"Haven't made much of a mark on the place, however many of them there may be," J.B. said, sidling up to Ryan. They had been together so many years it was often as if one could read the other's mind, a communion Ryan also shared with Krysty and, to a lesser extent, the other companions. The Armorer had been his comrade almost his entire adult life, since the early days in Trader's caravan.

Ryan's old friend was also right, as usual. As they cruised cautiously along the waterways between the half-destroyed structures, they saw pockets of concerted activity—here, people clearing rubble from a floor two stories above the green water that had been completely exposed by the devastation; there, people loading cardboard boxes into a flat-bottomed boat. All of them greeted their passage with a cheerful wave. Most of them seemed to be armed, carrying handblasters holstered or standing watch with ready longblasters.

The timbre of the water wag's engine changed. Tenorio glanced up from his chart as the big boat began to slow still further.

"I've arranged for you to view one of our explorations," the *alcade* said, approaching Ryan and the rest in the prow. "It will give you a chance to meet some of us doing the actual work, see how we live our lives."

Ryan nodded. He was a little dubious himself. The wag was approaching the flank of a building faced in glazed stone of a rusty red color that leaned crazily against the black tower next to it. A bumper of tires had been hung between two glassless windows with a blue nylon rope so that they hung level just above the water. A houseboat was anchored a few yards down the street. Evidently it had been moved to allow the *Paloma* room to pull in. As the boat slowed, a crewman tossed a line up to an open window. Hands grabbed it, made it fast within, then a rope ladder was tossed down.

"My friends?" Tenorio indicated the ladder. "I regret the inconvenience of having to scramble to get inside."

"We done worse," J.B. said, rubbing the back of his neck, "mebbe a time or two."

By unspoken consensus Jak, with his predator's instinct for danger, swarmed up first. Krysty went next. She negotiating the swaying ladder with neither hesitation nor visible difficulty. Ryan still wondered if she wasn't being ballsier than was good for her. Still, he trusted her judgment implicitly in all things, and who would know better what she could handle?

As he followed her up into the cool depths of the building, the unmistakable sound of a muffled shot came echoing from within.

Chapter Thirteen

Ryan rolled over the top, came up with his SIG-Sauer in hand. Or tried to. What he actually did was half roll, half skid down the canted concrete floor until he fetched up into what proved to be a waist-level web of bungee cords. After only a moderate amount of flailing with his left hand, he was able to get his feet under him and recover. He was glad he'd had the blaster on safe.

Laughing silently, Jak helped him disentangle with his left hand. His right held his shiny Python. Krysty stood down along the angle where floor met wall with two bearded male scavvies, her own blaster in hand. The younger and trimmer of the pair was just holding his hands up to her in a back-off-the-trigger gesture.

"Our scout," he announced in accented English. "She's fine. No threat."

The others joined them with a minimum of comedy. Doc slid down on the seat of his pants, maintaining great dignity. The carpet had been devoured long since by some sort of ugly crud, so that now all that remained of the floor covering were patches of powdery yellow fungus. Ryan didn't have the heart to tell the older man the seat of his trousers was now bright yellow.

The scavvies on station were introduced. The one who spoke English, a middle-size guy with thick chest and shoulders, very sleek black hair and carefully trimmed beard framing his broad oblong face, was Ricardo. The other, a big, unkempt guy with frizzy wiry hair standing out in gray clumps to either side of his bald head like scrubbing pads, a scarred face with an unhealthy-looking potato of a nose, and an imposing paunch pushing out his blue-gray mechanic's-style coveralls, was Teo. He wore a .45 1911 auto. Ricardo had a Beretta.

Ricardo explained to them that they were surveying. Their team, the three of them and their scout who had fired the shot from somewhere off in the ventilation system, were basically mapping out what parts of the buildings on this block were accessible, what they had been and how likely they were to reward further work, either exploration or hauling out goodies.

"This was just an office building," Ricardo explained. "Not likely much useful. Still—" He smiled and shrugged. "Who knows what we find?"

"How are you doing?" Ryan asked Krysty, making his way next to her where she sat on the sloping floor with her knees up. She had made sure not to plant herself in a patch of the chrome-yellow mold.

"Fine, lover," she said. "Really. The energy I'm getting from all around is fantastic."

"If you say so," he said.

A cry floated out the hole in what had been the ceiling that gave into the HVAC ducts. A moment later a figure came crawling out hand over hand on a rope that had been tied to a heavy, rusted hunk of desk and let into the hole. Ricardo scrambled up the wall to lend a hand.

The scout allowed himself to be helped out and down, although the way he moved indicated he didn't really need it. Or *she*, Ryan realized. The face was so smudged with grime and overhung by a hard hat topped with a battery-powered lamp that it was hard to tell at first.

"Allow me to introduce Claudia," Ricardo told the visitors with pride. "She is my *novia*. What do you say? My fiancée."

Her face split in a bright smile. She came scooting down the angled wall. She wore a backpack. On the outside of it was lashed, of all things, a huge dead mutie rat.

The foreigners were quickly introduced. Claudia expressed pleasure at meeting them in Spanish, duly translated by Doc. She seemed a pretty, vivacious little woman underneath the gunk.

She had been creepy-crawling the other rooms and offices accessible through the ductwork. This, apparently, was her job: the nasty, claustrophobic and dangerous work of crawling through the bowels of a steel-and-concrete stiff, looking to strike prime salvage. She had not found anything very worthwhile on this jaunt. Until the rat had lunged for her face from a side vent, at which point she had popped it neatly between the eyes with her handblaster.

Now she unslung the rat and held it excitedly up for inspection. It was a suitably nasty-looking specimen, body a good two feet long, its orange incisors as long as Ryan's little finger. It looked to have a ruff or mane of quills like a porcupine, but that might have simply been extra-long guard hairs matted by immersion in none-too-clean water.

Jak eyed it with keen red interest. "Good eats?" he inquired hopefully.

Claudia grinned even wider and bobbed her head.

THEY HAD LUNCH on the houseboat, which served the trio as mobile workshop and base of operations. Mutie rat wasn't on the menu; the scavvies told their guests that to be digestible it had to be slow-cooked many hours in a covered pot, then marinated in red chili sauce, at which point it became an excellent tamale filler. Instead there were chicken enchiladas and beans.

J.B. talked shop with Teo; the large, lumpy, cover-all-clad man was the general fix-it guy and machine doctor, who both kept the mechanisms the team used, such as pumps and generators, alive and kicking, and examined scavenged equipment to determine its function and whether it was ever likely to be able to be coaxed into performing that function again. He wasn't particularly knowledgeable about blasters, which of course were J.B.'s abiding passion, but the pair had managed to lose themselves in a discussion of small engines. Doc, whose knowledge of Spanish, while both wide and deep was decidedly nontechnical, did his best to keep up the translation. Fortunately much of the jargon was similar in Spanish and English.

Tenorio was discussing the progress of the team's

survey of the block with Ricardo and Claudia. His two bodyguards were squatting up on the roof, smoking hand-rolled cigarettes and batting the breeze, apparently out of preference. Ernesto was back on the water wag, worrying on the radio.

Cleaned up, Claudia, the intrepid dead-skyscraper spelunker, proved to be a strikingly pretty woman, almost certainly not as young as she looked, with fine features, big dancing dark eyes and a restless manner. As she talked, she kept playing with her prize find of the day: a squat, three-inch-tall, wind-up toy in the shape of a green lizard with a row of yellow spines down its back. It still worked; Claudia would wind the plastic key and it would waddle across the table, growling.

"What do you reckon that thing is, anyway?" he asked Krysty.

She looked at him as if the question were double stupe, at the very least. "It's Godzilla."

Claudia looked at them. *"Sí, sí. Es God-zee-ya."*

"I'll be switched," he said as the little monster fetched up against a big bowl with faded fruits painted along the rim. It continued to try to advance, little wind-up motor grumbling and stumpy feet churning. "I remember when I was a kid, how disappointed I was when I found out he wasn't real."

"Then you grew up and found out there were plenty of real monsters to go around," Krysty said, smiling.

"Ain't it the truth."

She was obviously not all the way back to normal, because she didn't correct his grammar. She hadn't done that often lately. Instead she looked again at a framed print hanging on the wall beyond the head of the table, over Don Tenorio's shoulder. It reproduced a stylized kind of painting of a woman in a hooded robe surrounded by golden radiance, standing on a crescent shape like a moon, only black. This time Claudia noted her interest and spoke, seriously for once.

"She says that is the Lady of the Valley," Doc translated.

"I've seen a lot of those pictures around since we arrived," J.B. remarked between bites. "People still hold to all that religious stuff down here?"

"Oh, yes," Tenorio said. "Veneration of the Lady had deep roots. After the conquest by the Spanish she appeared in that manner you see pictured to an Indian as the Virgin of Guadalupe. But before that she had been worshiped for centuries by the Indians of the Valley as Tonantzin. In both guises she is among other things a spirit of the Earth."

"Gaia," Krysty said.

He smiled. "Given the seismic activity you've experienced here, no doubt you can understand how a goddess of the Earth might play a major role in the lives of our people through time."

"Yes," Krysty said with a smile. "I can."

"DIDN'T YOU ALWAYS TELL ME Gaia wasn't a person?" Ryan asked when they were back aboard the *Paloma*, putting for home.

"Yes," Krysty said, seated once more in the deck chair in the prow.

"Then what's with all this 'Lady of the Valley' stuff? You acted like you knew what the Mexes were talking about."

"The people themselves personalize the forces of the Earth. They envision those forces as a lady, a mother-goddess. Because the forces are so very strong here, their belief is likewise."

"So she's just a luci of some kind? A vision that ain't real."

"The forces are real, so she is real, here in the valley. She's the way the people perceive the reality—they put a human face on it."

He shook his head. "This is all miles beyond me."

She reached up to touch his cheek. He felt the slight stubble that sprouted by afternoon no matter how raw he scraped his face each morning rasp beneath her fingertips. "Don't worry, lover. The important thing is Gaia's power is great here, greater than I've ever felt before, and it's helping me heal from what Mildred tells me was a very nasty injury."

"Guess you're right."

He was relieved to hear the slightly unsteady footfall of Doc on the deck behind him. He turned.

"It would appear the *alcade* is more relaxed about allowing his subjects to carry weapons than most barons of our experience, friend Ryan," Doc remarked. Tenorio himself was back by the cabin discussing an unrolled chart with Ernesto.

"He sure hasn't uttered peep one about our packing," J.B. remarked, rolling up to join the little group.

"Where's Jak?" Krysty asked him.

"Back aft, watchin' the wake as if he expects to see naked women splashing in it."

The Armorer was carrying his Uzi on its long Israeli-style sling that allowed it to ride horizontal at just above belt level, ready for instant use. For his part Ryan had left his Steyr sniper rifle back in their quarters. His SIG-Sauer P-226 seemed sufficient, especially given how well-armed their host's escorts were. Aside from the team manning the big Browning in the pintle atop the control cabin, he had two bodyguards, no doubt Jaguar Knights, one armed with a Heckler & Koch MP-5 K, a compact 9 mm submachine gun with a foregrip shaped rather like a miniature table leg as well as a pistol rear grip, the other with a long FN FAL .308 battle rifle. The longblaster man was wiry. The boy with the machine pistol, blocky. Both were short; both cheerful as virtually every one of Tenorio's scavvies the companions had encountered to date seemed to be, but both also seemed tough as the flows of black chilled lava that seamed the valley. The escorts weren't smoking and joking just now; like the heavy machine gunners, they were intently scanning the water and the rubble rising to each side.

"Boys don't look like they're watching just for practice, do they?" J.B. asked Ryan.

Having finished his discussion, Don Tenorio stepped forward to join his guests. "Your people are pretty sharp-looking, Don Tenorio," Ryan said. "So much it makes me wonder what they're looking out for."

The small, spare man shrugged. "The city is full of dangers. The most prevalent, obviously, are environmental—falling debris, the sudden collapse of a building, snags beneath the water. But there are living dangers, as well, some human, some animal, some…" He shrugged expressively.

"You keep patrol boats out on the water, I notice."

"Oh, yes. The more so since the Chichimecs invaded the valley in force. Sometimes they try to send raiding parties into the city. And sometimes they succeed, because the ruins are too huge for us to throw a completely effective cordon around, even if we stripped everyone from our work of reclamation, which would defeat our very purpose. So we stay armed and alert. Also there are…things…in the water and in the city itself, and some of them are a great deal more sinister than the rat Claudia killed. The giant *axolotl* and bass are edible and provide an excellent source of food. Others seem to regard us the same way. Those folk who held that death still stalked the drowned streets and buildings were not altogether wrong, even though the plagues had long since lost their virulence."

Krysty shook her head. "I don't understand why you have muties in and around the city, since it was never nuked and there's so little background radiation."

"We have wondered the same thing, Señorita Wroth. Many mutant beings, such as the giant rattler you encountered coming over the mountains, no doubt wandered down from the radiation belts to the north in search of prey." The companions had given their hosts a carefully edited account of their journey, especially the escape from the eruption, that made no reference to the mat-trans. So far they seemed to accept that the companions had driven down from *el norte,* skirting the rad wastes by keeping to the coastal region west of the valley's sheltering ring of mountains.

"How then might one account for such aquatic denizens as the great *axolotls* and fish, Don Tenorio?" Doc asked.

"That has provoked much debate among us, Doctor. Some suggest the young may have swum down from the north in the rivers that flow into the lake. Others object, pointing out that the zones of heavy radiation lie on the other side of the watershed, in the lands we call the Great Chichimeca, the realm of the Chichimecs. They suggest that there may have been agents at work in producing mutation other than simple radiation. Some exotic form of biological warfare, perhaps. Those who favor the migration theory point out that in all the extensive scientific literature we have recovered and cataloged there is not the slightest hint of such research. The biowar proponents answer back that such research would be classified the most secure secret, the files encrypted…and so the debate rages."

"Just like whitecoats," J.B. sniffed. "Always wrangling about stuff that doesn't actually add up to diddly-squat."

"Ah, but I would beg humbly to disagree, Señor Dix. Whether we are seeking new knowledge or trying to reclaim what our species has lost, we cannot know in advance what bit or piece might help to lift us—lift the world—from the misery and devastation the war left in its wake."

"You also don't know when you might resurrect some of the knowledge that brought all the destruction about," Krysty said.

"*Usted tiene razón*. You speak truth, fair lady. Yet we persist, recognizing the risk. What have you encountered in this life that does not entail risk, even of deadly peril?"

Krysty smiled and inclined her head, acknowledging his point. Her distrust for science and technology didn't outweigh her own regard for truth. She maintained her integrity no matter the cost, which was often not small in the world they inhabited.

The Armorer barked a brisk laugh. "Life's fatal, that's for nuke-blasted sure."

They were crossing another open area. This one, however, wasn't entirely devoid of buildings. A pyramid of stone steps rose from the midst, its base submerged in the lake.

A shadow crossed Don Tenorio's spare features when his guests pointed it out. "The great sacrificial pyramid of Tenochtitlán," he said. "Many thousands of lives were offered to the old gods there, oceans of blood streamed down those steps. It was discovered, excavated and partially restored before the war."

He shook his head in bleak amusement. "An irony that it survived untouched, of all things."

The skinny bodyguard said something in Spanish. "Or perhaps not. As Ésteban reminds me, Don Hector asserts it's proof of the power of the ancient gods, whose worship he seeks to resurrect in the valley."

A gap-toothed grin split the longblaster man's dark face. He spat over the rail in the general direction of the sacrificial pyramid.

As they passed it, Doc pointed with his cane toward a party of three scavvies, roped together and scaling the apparently stone facade of a building just to port of the boat's course, which tilted perilously to the northeast. "What system do you use to assign tasks to your subjects, Don Tenorio?"

"Assign?" Their host blinked. "Sometimes I offer suggestions, even bonuses and awards for particular tasks. But seldom do I 'assign.' I do not hold so much control as you appear to believe, my friend. Mostly my people do as they see best, for their own profit and the advantage of us all."

"You keep a mighty loose rein on your subjects for a baron," J.B. said.

"I fear you have been laboring under a misapprehension. I am no baron. I'm not even a mayor, although it amuses my associates to call me *alcade*. The people of the city are not my subjects. They are free companions—stockholders, if you like, in what centuries ago would have been called a company of adventurers."

"Don Tenorio. *¡Mira!*" came a cry from overhead. The assistant machine gunner was pointing ahead.

A cloud of dust roiled from a cavity that might once have been a shop display window. A young woman stood amid the dust, holding a rag to her face and frantically waving for attention.

The woman screamed something. "Cave in!" Don Tenorio exclaimed. "We must go to their assistance."

The pilot had already increased the throttle. The boat reared back slightly on a mobile mound of green scummy water and roared ahead, not fast—it couldn't brake like a land wag, of course—but faster than its walking-pace before. They crossed an intersection, coming perilously near the top of a submerged traffic light. Then the pilot was backing the engine and slewing the big gleaming water wag slightly sideways to kill its forward momentum.

Using long metal poles, the baron's two bodyguards halted the boat's lingering drift toward the building. It bumped up against the sunken wall of the structure, using its own bumper of old tires lashed to the outside of the hull to cushion and protect it. The skinny bodyguard with the FN longblaster jumped into the opening where the woman stood covering her face with a handkerchief and coughing, caught a line tossed him by his burlier comrade, fastened it to a jutting chunk of metal.

Don Tenorio was next over into the building, a structure with mostly intact bluish-black windows that rose three further stories and then broke off. The wide guard with the stubby machine pistol helped hand him across. The *alcade* seemed impatient with the man's solicitude. Shrugging him off, he plunged into the building with his guards, seemingly oblivious as to whether his guests followed or not.

The scavvie woman's face was obscured by the rag she was using as an impromptu air filter. Her hair was as startlingly red as Krysty's; but unlike the crimson of Krysty's sentient locks it was a deep red that glinted with metallic highlights in the morning sunlight like fine copper wire. She was taller than average for the people they had encountered in the valley, although shorter than Krysty. Ryan caught an impression of lithe but well-padded athletic grace, of jade-green eyes flashing him a somehow appraising glance above the rag. Then she whirled and was gone into the shadowed interior.

J.B. looked inquiringly to Ryan. His Uzi was up and ready, which meant he was, too. Ryan nodded. "Let's follow. Eyes wide."

Krysty was on her feet. "You sure?" Ryan asked her.

"Sure am, lover. If there're people who need help, I'll do what I can." She smiled. "A little exercise will do me good."

Ryan helped hand her across to Doc, who had jumped over ahead of them. Then came Ryan, and lastly Jak, still turning a leaf-bladed throwing knife in his chalk-white fingers.

They raced through a room empty but for decayed and colorless carpet lying in fungoid patches on the floor. Whatever furnishings or decoration had once occupied the room had since been shaken loose or otherwise stripped. Into the guts of the building, the woman led the way, followed by Don Tenorio and his pair of guards, the companions trooping after. The interior was dank and rank with the smells of mildew and stagnant water, dead marine life and again, a lingering sweetish stink that all knew well as a hallmark of human death.

There was no way the smell could have persisted for a century. Ryan wondered if it was the result of some kind of psychic emanation or, more likely, simple illusion created by expectation. He mentioned the thoughts to J.B. in a quick, low murmur.

The Armorer chuckled quietly. "There's not a reason in the world somebody might not have cashed in here in the not too distant past, too," he said. As had Ryan, he kept his voice hushed, though neither could have said why. "Leastwise the dust thrown up by the cave-in seems to have mostly settled already."

They pounded up two flights of diamond-panel metal stairs with big blotches of some kind of actual fungus growing on the peeling enamel of the walls. Their footsteps echoed like the beats of great barbaric drums in the enclosed well, reverberating back up at them weirdly distorted by the water that flooded the lower levels. In his mind's eye Ryan saw a vision of just such drums atop the resurrected pyramid they had passed, voices booming to drown out the screams of the victims....

He shook his head. Not too healthy, mooning over fantasies when a chem storm might be rolling in.

They broke out into an echoing space lit poorly by lanterns; the water threw back the dim yellow light in ripple patterns against the walls and the faces of the party. Ryan realized they were on a gallery toward the top of what had been a several-story atrium. On the level above, the walls fell back farther away into a wider open space. Below them, a busted-off stair protruded from stinking water whose black surface glistened with

just a hint of poisonously pearlescent taint, as if just a
bit of oil had been spilled on it. A curved metal pipe
serving as a handrail had peeled away from the steps to
nowhere and jutted into the air, its end corroded and raw.

As they all followed the redheaded scavvie woman
around two sides of the gallery, Krysty's steps faltered.
Ryan caught her quickly by the biceps, fearing she
might topple over the safety rail into the murky water.

"You all right?"

"Not me," she said, shaking her head. "*Us.* Something here, something bad…"

A few yards ahead of them their guide stood waving
them through a door. Don Tenorio started to go through
first. His bulkier bodyguard, the slab-faced man with the
shorty machine pistol, shouldered the baron aside almost brusquely and stepped through first, his blaster
held ready in both scarred hands.

A boom and a flash of blue-white fire filled the
atrium.

Chapter Fourteen

Screaming horribly, the bodyguard reeled back onto the catwalk. As he turned, Ryan saw that his face and the now-smoldering front of his khaki shirt were torn with dozens of tiny holes, some round, some ragged, some bizarrely shaped like the letter T. Ryan had seen such wounds before. They happened when somebody poured a handful of carpet tacks down the barrel of a blaster, usually a muzzle-loading black powder makeshift, and fired them off into a human target. The tiny wildly gyrating projectiles went every which way and bled velocity like a severed artery. They were entirely ineffectual beyond the range of a good healthy spit. Fired from close enough for the muzzle-flare to set the target's clothes alight, though, they could ruin your whole day.

The bodyguard lurched into the rail and cartwheeled over it. The clench reflex tightened his finger on the trigger as he went over. The little bullet-sprayer was still flaming and yammering when his body disappeared into the dark water with a splash.

Ryan caught a glimpse of the red-haired scavvie woman standing by the door, gloating light gleaming in those strange green eyes. He was already drawing his

SIG-Sauer. He sensed a weight descending toward his back, started to turn. Something slammed the back of his head. His skull filled with spark-shot darkness.

HE CAME BACK to consciousness on his knees in the gloom of the atrium. He had been elsewhere for just a few seconds, apparently, briefly stunned rather than unconscious. He felt a quick spasm of relief. A head blow that actually put you out generally left you with a bleeder in your skull that would chill you sure.

Of course, chilling seemed a likely item on the agenda in the not too distant future. He could feel the absence of his handblaster. Rough hands yanked him to his feet. One started to tug on the hilt of his broad-bladed panga.

A dozen dark, wild-haired men dressed in loincloths surrounded them: Chichimecs. They were armed with the usual chronological grab bag of weaponry from clubs and spears to at least a couple of smokeless powderblasters. Two of the ambushers held a furious Don Tenorio by the arms as the copper-headed woman spoke tauntingly to him. Ryan blinked to clear the vision in his one eye, which still swam with big green-and-purple afterimage blobs. It seemed as if there were more marauders across the well of the half-drowned atrium.

With a gesture like an irate egret shaking out his wings, Doc broke away from the captor who held his arms. He jabbed another in the chest with the tip of his cane. "You have no cause to lay your foul hands upon my person, sirrah!"

The Chichimec stared at him more in shocked surprise than anything else. Then his dark face twisted in a rage-filled snarl. He grabbed the end of the cane and raised his own weapon, one of those flat clubs edged with jagged shards of volcanic glass, to strike Doc down.

Doc yanked back on the handle of his cane. The slim steel blade hissed free. The raider's face sagged into a look of even greater surprise.

Like a striking serpent, the sword darted forward to bury itself in one of those dark staring eyes.

The Chichimec shrieked once and then fell bonelessly, dead on the instant. The marauder who had held Doc earlier wrapped his arms around him, trying to pinion them to his sides. It was too late; Doc had already managed to claw the bulk of his LeMat free. He turned sideways, thrust the blaster up under his captor's chin and lit off the shotgun underbarrel.

The blast tore off the man's face.

Ryan was already in motion. He rammed his elbow back into the gut of the man who held him on the left. Then he pivoted his hips to drive a forward elbow smash into the hinge of the jaw of the man clutching him from the right. The man uttered a strangled scream as his jaw broke and slid, horribly, a handsbreadth to the side. He was bastard tough. Even as he clutched his shattered face with one hand, the other raised an obsidian sword club to strike back.

As quick as thought, Ryan's panga whispered free. He chopped it right down into the fury-and-pain-distorted face, splitting the skull to the bridge of the nose.

Ryan sensed motion behind him, launched a savage back kick without looking. The man who'd been to his left went backward over the rail. He screamed horribly as he landed on the busted-off handrail. The gore-smeared raw end punched clean out his bare chest.

By that point there was a whole lot of screaming going on. Ryan had quick impressions. Jak's right hand, ghost-pale in the gloom, darted like a snake repeatedly striking as he threw his sharp little knives into eyes, throats, bodies, not caring that most of them wouldn't do lethal damage. All that was needed was distraction, to spoil aim or to allow an ally to land a kill shot. Krysty's hand whipped out, pressing the barrel of her Smith & Wesson blaster into the gut of a Chichimec, and fired twice. J.B. felled two captors with an overhand right and a hand-edge smash to the throat, then spun and sprayed Chichimecs on the opposite side of the well with an ear-shattering burst from his Uzi.

The wiry bodyguard had twisted himself free of the raiders who held him and hurled himself at his baron's two captors. The four were down in a thrashing tangle in the doorway. The copper-headed woman, a tiny black blaster in her hand, was dancing around the tangle spitting like a cat in fury at not finding a clear target.

Ryan followed down the man whose skull he'd split to yank his silenced SIG-Sauer from the waist string of the dead man's loincloth. He fell onto his side and rolled, momentarily unsure whether to chill the woman who had lured them into the trap or to try to find the Chichimec who had wound up in possession of the body-guard's longblaster. His brains had been rattled by the rap to the head. He wasn't quite as razor-edge decisive as usual in combat.

The Chichimec who had appropriated the long-barreled FN FAL stepped up and slammed the steel-shod butt of its wooden stock against the back of the bodyguard's neck with a sound like an adz splitting a log. That settled that. Ryan fired two sighing shots into the middle of his back. He went to his knees, then fell onto the still form of the scavvie he'd butt-stroked.

Copper hair flying, the woman spun to point her tiny black blaster at Ryan. He rolled to shift his aim point to right between her breasts, which even under the circumstances he noted pushed out the front of her olive drab blouse impressively. Not that Ryan had ever scrupled to chill a woman, however attractive, when circumstances called for it. But the real issue would be who was in position to get a shot home first…

For just a moment, two wild green eyes and Ryan's single cold blue one locked each other above their gunsights. Then the woman went flying up and back into the air.

Ryan stared. There were very few occasions in his life when he'd been so taken by surprise by a twist of events that all he could do was gape. This was one.

A tentacle, dark-striated and slimy, held the woman around her rib cage, aloft above the water. Others waved in the air around her.

She screamed, not in terror but in evident fury. She fired the handblaster downward. It made little popping sounds that were almost comical and didn't bother whatever monstrous mutie held her in the slightest.

One of the ambushers had grabbed up the fallen FN FAL. He rushed to the rail, aimed downward at the churning water from which half a dozen tentacles sprouted like sentient plant stalks, fired a burst. As usual, it was a bad idea to fire a .308-caliber rifle full-auto. The recoil walked the barrel straight up in the air and put him flat on his skinny ass.

The woman had thrown her useless handblaster away. *"Macahuitl!"* she screamed. *"Macahuitl!"*

Ryan wondered if it was a prayer or a curse. It was neither. One of the handful of Chichimecs still on their feet tossed her one of the obsidian-edged clubs. Then his face erupted in a gush of black blood and dough-colored brains as Krysty, far too much a woman of the Deathlands to fight fair, fired a shot into the base of his skull from touch range. He went down with his hair burning in reeking blue flames.

The marauder woman fielded the sword club deftly. She hacked it savagely down into the tentacle that gripped her below the arms. The volcanic glass, sharper than a surgeon's scalpel, half severed the leg-thick member. Greenish ichor spouted, covering her face and chest. The tentacle spasmed, hurling her through the air onto the catwalk on the far side of the atrium.

Holding his SIG-Sauer in both hands, and none too steadily for all of that, Ryan backed cautiously away from the rail. Another pair of tentacles plucked another howling Chichimec from the far side.

Ryan looked around quickly, trying to take stock of the tactical situation. It was, basically, battle over—at least, on this side of the well. Krysty stood with her back to the wall. Her sling was gone. Her left hand was splayed on the plaster as if for support, the right held her .38 warily ready. J.B. stood near her, prudently far back from the rail, Uzi ready and aimed out across the well in case either the monster or the raiders decided to take any further interest in the companions. Fortunately they seemed to be amusing one another more than sufficiently.

Doc and Jak were helping to disentangle Don Tenorio, drenched in blood from crown to knees but apparently unharmed, out from what remained of his two captors. Their bare backs looked like hamburger. He still clutched his green-steel Witness, whose slide was locked back on an empty mag. Ryan nodded approvingly. The baron or *alcade* or whatever he was might have been a scholar instead of a fighter, but when the caps were popping he'd given a game account of himself.

Ryan moved to Krysty's side, slid an arm around her trim waist. She looked up at him. Her face was greenish pale.

"I guess Mildred was right after all, lover," she said. "This was a bit too much exercise for me."

She slumped against him.

"YOU AND YOUR COMPANIONS saved my life today," Don Tenorio said. He held a goblet of salvaged brandy in his hand as he stood on the terrace of his headquarters gazing south across the lake to where the smokies bled glowing molten stone. The sun had set. The sky behind the volcanoes was ashy-mauve. Overhead, the deep purple was pierced with stars.

Ryan sipped at his own goblet. It wasn't the first time he had tasted such high-quality predark liquor. He was a baron's son, after all. Still, he had to admit these scavvies did well for themselves.

The red tiles of the floor shifted beneath his feet. The corners of his mouth tightened. He wasn't exactly unfamiliar with earth tremors, either, but these were so frequent it began to gnaw at a man's nerves. He started to wonder if each little shake was all, or whether it was just the tune-up for a mighty blow.

"You did a pretty fair job saving yourself," Ryan said.

Tenorio turned back, favoring his guest with a smile's ghost. "Let us agree that you and your companions helped to keep me alive."

Ryan shrugged.

After they had dined together, the *alcade* had asked if he might speak to Ryan privately on the terrace. Ryan had agreed, but reluctantly. By mutual consent, he led the group. If he gave orders, the others followed them. But they were a team, a family. He wouldn't, except under emergency conditions, take any decision affecting the group without consulting them. And he disliked anything that even smacked of dealing behind the others' backs, of cutting them out of the loop.

But, provisionally at least, he trusted Tenorio. And just listening to their host speak his piece wouldn't chill anyone.

"It was already my pleasure, that you should be my guests so long as you pleased. It was and is my hope we might be able to establish some kind of trade relations with the north, although it will be a good many years before such becomes practicable. If ever. But now I owe you a mighty debt of gratitude."

He sighed and set the goblet down on a table next to the half-full decanter of salvaged cut-crystal. "Despite these things, there is a favor I am compelled to beg of you."

Ryan set his own goblet down. "Within reason, you got it."

"You may or may not find my request reasonable. I want to ask you to act as my emissary to Don Hector."

Ryan regarded the smaller man a moment. Immaculately turned out in a collarless cotton shirt and light blazer, Don Tenorio bore no resemblance to the bloodstained apparition that had helped him support an unsteady Krysty on their rapid retreat from the ambush site in the derelict building.

"I'm not sure what kind of a reception we could expect from your neighbors, Don Tenorio," Ryan said. "They weren't too friendly to us the first time our paths crossed. And today I don't think we helped their cause much, spoiling their attempt to snatch you and laying waste to a squad of their commandos."

The raiding party had been dressed and armed as Chichimecs. But they had all been human, and while none was fat, they had all been visibly better fed than the half-starved marauders who had besieged Ryan and his friends in the mechanic's garage in the abandoned ville. The final proof had been the scavvie woman who had first lured them into the trap and then fought the unknown mutie monster's tentacles not with panic but with tigerish ferocity. Tenorio knew her as Felicidad Mendoza, daughter of Don Hector's sec boss.

"I still can't quite understand that play of theirs," Ryan said. "Mebbe they could have passed as a group of Chichimec raiders who had slipped in. And then they send in somebody as distinctive-looking as that woman—somebody known to you and your sec people. Pretty much seems to undo the whole purpose of a ruse."

Don Tenorio shrugged. "There may have been aspects to their plan that remain hidden from us."

A score of Tenorio's own sec people, led by Five Ax, had gone into the building after Tenorio and Ryan's party had escaped. They had taken no prisoners; they'd found no one alive inside. They had recovered the body of the wiry bodyguard, neck broken by the buttstroke from his own rifle, and ten fake Chichimec bodies. None was that of Felicidad Mendoza. They had dumped a few pounds of dynamite wired up with underwater fuses into the atrium in hopes of dealing with whatever was living down there. How successful that had been nobody knew; no mutant chunks had floated to the surface after the depth-bombing and none of them had felt like diving in for a closer look.

Ryan didn't blame them.

They hadn't, however, left in a hurry. The Jaguar Knights even recovered six or seven of Jak's throwing knives from dead raiders. It was mostly a matter of convenience, since Jak could file the things from suitable bits of scrap metal in a surprisingly short time. But he had been pleased, since you really couldn't have too many of the weps. Ryan had been surprised they had bothered. But the scavvies seemed to have it as a point of pride—*pundonor,* they called it in Mex-talk—that once they were inside a building nothing would drive them out short of imminent collapse.

"Also," Don Tenorio said, "Señorita Mendoza, while a fierce fighter and utterly without fear—as we ourselves witnessed today—has also a reputation for being... How do you say? Somewhat precipitous. 'Rash' perhaps is the word."

"It'll do."

"Under Don Hector the only honor and status to be gained by women is won by bearing children. Despite that, and despite the iron discipline Hector clamps upon his people, there seems to be no controlling Felicidad. Some even say she, even more than the gross beast who is her father, is the author of the terror by which Don Hector increasingly rules his folk."

"You make the prospect of a visit seem mighty attractive, Don Tenorio."

"I am sorry. I must speak candidly, my friend. Please believe me when I tell you that I believe the risk to you in serving as my representatives would be slight. Don Hector does live by a code of honor. And he has always respected flags of truce in the past, even after relations between us began...to grow difficult."

"Why send us, then, instead of some of your own people?"

Don Tenorio frowned thoughtfully, fingered his chin, went to gaze again at the volcanoes. The sky was black now, but for a blue band behind the mountains to the west.

"To make a fresh start, I suppose. To try to reopen meaningful communications. We have never been truly friendly, his people and mine, since he began to consolidate the villages of the valley. With the coming of the Chichimecs down from the north, he has grown insistent that all the valley should be united under his rule. He has subjugated independent villages. He has even suggested that he might consider himself compelled to subjugate us, as well. This we would resist.

"We do not emphasize warrior skills as he does. Despite the fact that my personal guards are highly trained, and enjoy styling themselves Jaguar Knights in response to Hector's corps of Eagle Knights, my security forces under the good Colonel Solano are small indeed. But most of my people, as you are aware, go armed. And the city would be a hard place to take from us by force. In truth, I don't think Hector could do it, for all his peasant conscripts and sec men and even his Eagle Knight elite."

As he spoke, he seemed to wander, his voice growing quiet. He shook himself and turned back to Ryan.

"Any conflict between us can only strengthen the hand of the destroyers from the north. My people will never accept Hector's methods, much less his rule. Why does he have to reign over us? We would cooperate in any way. We could to fight off the invaders. It makes no sense—"

He shook himself again, as if to break the spasm of a futile debate Ryan sensed he had held with himself many times before. "I do not expect you to plead our case to Don Hector. What I want is for you to see if you can get him to talk with us—with me, again."

The volcanoes rumbled like far-off thunder. Out onto the terrace came Colonel Solano himself, Don Tenorio's own sec chief. He was a tall, lean man with a neat mustache and sharply creased khaki clothes that, while not actually a uniform, looked quite a bit like one. With a brisk, professionally neutral nod to Ryan, he went to the *alcade* and bent to speak quietly in his ear.

"It seems a new element has arisen," the baron said as the colonel quickly left. "Don Hector has sent his own emissary across the causeway, an Eagle Knight under a flag of truce. He has brought an invitation, with a guarantee of safe passage, for you and your companions to visit Hector in his current headquarters on Chapúltepec."

Chapter Fifteen

"Don Tenorio and his people have served an invaluable function," the tall, strapping man said in a rich baritone voice. "Yet they cannot be permitted to continue obstructing amid growing crisis."

"And how exactly are they obstructing, if you don't mind my asking, Don Hector?" Mildred asked.

It was a warm morning, not really hot, as was frequently the case in the valley. Though the sun was halfway up the sky, the earth and air still smelled of the rain that had fallen the latter half of the night. Fresh. Clean rain, Ryan thought. No chem taint.

He looked to Krysty, who stood near him, arms folded, face shaded by her hat. She smiled.

A man could get used to that. Clean earth, clean air, clean water. A man—and his mate—might be able to settle here. Get some kind of life going.

He almost laughed out loud at his own fanciful nature. Allowing himself to wander into such spun-sugar wishfulness—here in the midst of what might or might not be an enemy camp, with a horde of enemies, human and mutie, just over the northern horizon and bearing down. Mildred was right. The strain of constant road, constant danger, was grinding on them. The bearings in his mind were getting worn.

Out on the beat-down field in front of and below them, thirty nearly naked young men performed calisthenics, practiced combat, unarmed or with old-time weapons, or unarmed defense against melee weapons. They all looked, near as may be, like the companions' host: tall, even for men from the north where the travelers hailed from, copper-skinned, muscular, with long coarse hair the color of spun anthracite. Not clones, but almost might as well have been.

A trio of young men in the fanciful headdresses and the funny-looking partial armor the companions had seen before stalked among them. They were apparently officers or cadre. One of them, Ryan was pretty sure, was Two Arrow, who had led the patrol that had tried to capture them in the sacked ville. He kept flicking glances up at the top of the hill where his *cacique* and the visitors watched from. The glances didn't seem overly friendly.

"Our valley has been invaded, as you are all too well aware, Señorita Wyeth." Don Hector wore a simple, short white robe with gold trim and sandals. His midnight hair was cut square front and back and swung freely just above his impressively broad shoulders. His face was wide, cheekbones pronounced, his jaw a shelf of bone. He was a handsome man, exuding an animal vitality; such was his energy that he seemed barely able to keep still, but was constantly pacing back and forth within the shade cast by the awning. His accent when

he spoke English was more marked than Don Tenorio's. "Nothing less than complete unity of purpose will
permit us to survive this crisis. Don Tenorio's attempts
to stick to what he calls 'autonomy' smacks of selfish-
ness. What's called for is selflessness. Sacrifice."

A hill rose like a ramp practically from the western
shore of the lake, rising gradually to a height of a few
hundred feet above the surrounding farmland and lava
badlands that veined it. At the far end, perched at the
verge of a cliff, lay the jumbled ruins of an old palace.
The ruin was called Chapúltepec Castle, after the hill
itself; *chapúltepec*, they were told, meant "place of the
grasshopper." Don Hector had his current headquarters
in a much more modest but still sizable villa built of
wood or adobe in some woods east of the castle, which
had either better weathered the earthquakes caused by
the Soviet nuke charges or been rebuilt or even con-
structed entirely since the war.

The practice ground lay east of that, at the foot of a
small rise. The companions, their host and his small ret-
inue stood or sat in the shade of a stand on the top of
the low hill, basically uprights of PVC pipe stuck in the
ground and holding up a roof of corrugated fiberglass
of an unusually unpleasant shade of green. Two servants, a young man and young woman in white robes,
stood by, serving them from pitchers of lemonade and
plates of fruit, some of them exotic kinds Ryan had
never encountered before.

The *cacique* had no guards, leaving aside the thirty
or so fanatic man-chillers drilling on the grounds below

them. His sec boss, Mendoza, had accompanied them, however, and now sat at a salvaged tubular-steel-and-plastic picnic table downing lemonade in great gulps and dabbing his broad sweaty forehead with a succession of handkerchiefs.

Ryan had heard Tenorio, who didn't usually seem to go in for uncharitable assessments, describe his rival's sec boss as a "gross beast." The description was adequate, if a trifle underdone. There was a good four hundred pounds of him stuffed into his khaki uniform and spilling off both sides of the camp stool that tremulously supported him. There were huge, dark half-moons of sweat stained into the fabric beneath his arms. His face was immensely wide, a blurred square, that looked as if it had started out strong and maybe even handsome and subsequently bloated up like a corpse's. The contrast to his own boss and the sec men nominally under his command, all of whom looked as if they'd stepped off posters for some predark health spa, couldn't have been more comically extreme.

The hair matted to his head and in his profuse mustache was a deep, rich red with metallic undertones. His dark olive face was spattered with darker freckles, concentrated on a nose that looked as if it had been broken often enough that it had just given over any pretense of having some kind of shape, like the rest of him. Only in the hues of his hair and skin did he bear any noticeable resemblance to his human panther of a daughter.

Don Hector ignored his obese sec chief, seeming to enjoy strutting and holding forth for his outland visitors. He gestured down at the warriors struggling and shining and sweating in the sun.

"My Eagle Knights," he declared. "My personal bodyguard and commandos, all devoted to me. Not that all my people aren't, of course. But these in particular have demonstrated their total commitment and zeal."

"Interesting you train them so extensively with knives and clubs and whatnot, when some of them carry lasers," J.B. remarked, polishing his steel-rimmed spectacles with his handkerchief.

"They practice the traditional martial arts of their forebears. It strengthens their cultural identity as well as their bodies and minds. And also, of course, training in the use of simple weapons or no weapons at all serves the most practical of purposes. More technologically advanced weapons may break or run out of ammunition or energy. And then a warrior must fall back on his fists and feet and cunning. And his warrior spirit."

"That's surely true," the Armorer said, "but a good many people don't know it."

He put his glasses back on. "Where did your boys get those fancy laser bracelets we saw in that abandoned ville, anyways, if you don't mind my asking? They're about the most advanced I've seen or cut sign of."

"We discovered them in a hidden laboratory, one that was apparently buried underground even before the war. Our scientists are working on duplicating them, of course."

The companions looked at one another, trying not to be obvious about it. Was there another redoubt hidden hereabouts? Had Don Hector and his people been the ones to clear out the base on Popocatépetl's flank?

"It's a very impressive show, Don Hector," Ryan said. "But I have to wonder why you're going to the trouble of showing it to us. After all, we're pretty much just visiting."

The baron laughed. A big, echoing sound. "That in itself makes you special! We have had so few visitors the last hundred years or so."

He gestured for the maidservant to refill his goblet, which was massive, carved from milky quartz. "You displayed great courage and resourcefulness in making your way here, my friends. That causes you to be of interest to me, a man much in need of those very traits to meet the current emergency. And my good friend Don Tenorio seems to regard you highly—and while I admit to questioning his military and political acumen, he does have a very keen judgment where value is concerned. And indeed, why may I not, as I gather he has, indulge my curiosity for tidings of the world north of the radiation belts and lethal chemical storms?"

"Your people didn't seem to have in mind inviting us here as honored guests when we first ran across them, Don Hector," Mildred said.

The *cacique* drank. "Surely a woman as perceptive as yourself can understand our need for caution. We are at war. And as you may have heard, rare as they are, we have received visitors from *el norte* before—and not all of them so well-intentioned as yourselves. Apparently they thought to reenact the great myth of Cortés, in which a handful of white men conquers a whole land full of red men."

"Then again, we're not exactly all white men," Mildred said.

Hector laughed again. "Indeed, indeed."

He set his stone goblet down a bit forcefully. "Mistakes have been made. That much is certain."

"What can you tell us about these muties who're invading your valley, Don Hector?" Ryan asked.

Hector raised an eyebrow in showy surprise. "Don Tenorio has told you little? But I see it must be so. How typical of the man. A great man, a visionary and genius beyond doubt. But otherworldly. Totally unprepared to face the often brutal challenges of the real world in which we live. Thus he prefers to hide from facts, to avoid dealing with or speaking of the threat we all face. Here is an example of why the people and the valley must be united under my rule—I do not shrink from the truth!"

He was pacing back and forth in front of them, emphasizing his words with thrusts of a thick forefinger. Ryan reflected that Tenorio had to have a little more taste for confronting harsh reality than his rival baron had let on. He had chosen to grind his face right into it when he had led the first scavvies into the haunted, mutant-riddled artificial canyons and canals of the City in the Lake. Ryan and the others had seen him in action the day before, plunging into danger without hesitation when he thought his people needed aid. Nor had the *alcade* frozen or played the coward when they were ambushed; the fact that he had fired his handblaster to slidelock showed he possessed all the courage and presence of mind any man could use, whether or not he was a particularly efficacious fighter.

The problem, though, was that Ryan was inclined to agree with Don Hector's larger thesis. For all his strengths, Tenorio didn't strike him as the man to face down the Chichimec horde. There it was, the bare fact, as ugly as a stickie and smelling twice as bad. It was also true that in their time as Don Tenorio's guests, though they had spent many hours in conversation concerning both life in the Deathlands and in the valley and city, scarcely a word had been uttered concerning the invaders.

There was a difference, Trader had taught him long ago when he was an untried pup, between physical courage and moral courage. Despite the fact he was no man of action, was it possible Don Tenorio possessed more of the former than the latter?

The tall, handsome baron said something to his sweltering sec boss in Spanish. Mendoza replied in the same language, sounding despondent. Doc sidled up next to Ryan.

"I trust, my dear Ryan, that just because yon hulk does not *appear* to understand English," he said from the side of his mouth, "that we do not take it on faith he truly does not comprehend everything we might say."

Ryan grinned. "Thanks, Doc, but I'm there already. A baron's gratitude, the honesty of a sec boss…"

"*Alike chimerical.* You are a wise young man, Ryan. Still, I did not wish to take aught for granted—"

Ryan slapped him lightly on the shoulder. "Anytime you think you see something I miss, speak right up, Doc."

The old man nodded gravely.

Hector finished his conversation with Mendoza, who now began to eat green grapes from a silver bowl on the table. He stepped up in front of his guests as though mounting a stage.

"For years we have had dealings with the Indian tribes to the north, the people we call Chichimecs. Sometimes we traded with them. Sometimes they raided us for our crops and wealth. Sometimes we sent military expeditions north to discourage them from such acts. But for the most part they stayed in the deserts on their side of the mountains, and we on ours.

"The Great Chichimeca is a savage place. As you may know, the north of our once-great country received more direct damage from the war than did our capital— the price it paid for proximity to *America del norte* and the military bases in Texas especially. The radiation belts and chemical storms that so afflict your homeland extend to the northern reaches of Chichimec territory. Enough that mutants are frequently born into their tribes, especially the more northern ones. These traditionally have been considered witches—evil, but unlucky to kill. So mutant babies are taken out into the scrub and left. Other mutants would come and collect them—or not. Thus the surviving mutants formed bands of their own, living in uneasy coexistence with their fully human kin, sometimes clashing, more often trying to ignore one another. Would you care for food?"

Ryan looked around. "I wouldn't mind some fruit," J.B. said. He went to the table and rooted in a bowl. "What's this one?"

"It's a papaya," Don Hector said.

J.B. took a bite. "Mite sour, but not too bad."

The earth shifted beneath their feet. Out on the training ground, the combat practice continued without notice. Ryan reflexively took a step toward Krysty. She smiled and made a tiny gesture with her hand to indicate she was fine. More than that: it appeared spots of color had come to her cheeks and she was standing a trifle straighter than before. Her hair was stirring around her shoulders in a way that made the servants stare while trying to conceal the fact. Ryan realized the temblors were acting on her like mini doses of jolt. The wound in her shoulder had almost completely healed, although Mildred still had her in bandages and her left arm in its sling.

He turned to see Don Hector eyeing Krysty with keen interest. It wasn't unusual or unexpected; barons taking a fancy to the exotic and stunningly beautiful redhead had caused them more than a few close moments in the past and doubtless would again, if they survived long enough. Still, Ryan had a strange sense there was something beyond simple desire in the sharpness with which those obsidian-flake eyes fixed on Krysty. He went to her side and put an arm around her as if in a casual gesture of affection. She leaned against him.

"Several years ago," the *cacique* continued, taking another drink from his quartz goblet, "a child was born into one of the northernmost Chichimec tribes. It was clearly a mutant, white-skinned, outsize, mute from birth. And yet the people could not bear to expose it as they always had mutant children in the past. No one who came into its presence could think of harming it. The child could influence the emotions of the people. As it grew, it demonstrated the ability to control the feelings of animals and mutant humanoids, as well. The Chichimecs came to call it the Holy Child and to worship it as a gift of the gods.

"Then, a year or so ago, a wandering self-proclaimed priest—a madman, more like—came among the Chichimecs. Nezahualcoyótl, he called himself, meaning 'Howling Wolf' in the old tongue. He claimed to be able to read the thoughts of the Holy Child and to read the future, as well."

"Doomie," Jak said. He had been watching the fighting practice with what appeared total absorption. But perfect feral hunter that he was, he was always keenly aware of his surroundings and what went on among them.

"Or just plain old-fashioned charlatan," J.B. said, doffing his fedora to scratch at his bald spot.

"Or both," Ryan added.

Don Hector nodded judiciously. "Whatever his true abilities, Howling Wolf persuaded the Chichimecs—and it appeared, their Holy Child, as well. It was their destiny to join together with the witches—the ones you would call 'muties'—and conquer the valley. And then, who knows? Perhaps the whole wide world."

He smiled grimly. "This self-proclaimed prophet

may or may not have the slightest notion of how big the world is. But he has assembled a force large enough to conquer the valley, unless we act decisively—and together. Even monstrous mutant creatures, such as the viborón, the giant rattlesnake you said you encountered on your journey into the valley, have come to join the horde. All serve the Holy Child with fanatical devotion."

He took a flower from a basketful on the table and held it daintily to his nose. "Which means they serve Howling Wolf."

"So that's what you're up against, Don Hector," J.B. said, helping himself to another piece of fruit. "What're your chances?"

"We will win," the *cacique* said. "We must. They have numbers on their side, and mindless courage. We have, as you are aware, a decent if not inexhaustible supply of modern small arms. Most importantly we have training, will and discipline—even our common troops, although they are not honed to such a flawless edge as these my Eagle Knights you see in front of you. But—"

He held up a blunt strong finger. "We must have unity. Of action and purpose, which means, unity of command. And that, my friends, is why Don Tenorio and his people must submit. As surely you must see, being wise in the ways of the world yourselves."

"Unity of command's an important principle, Don Hector," Ryan said, "right enough."

An uncomfortable silence descended. Ryan hadn't yet agreed to serve as actual emissary for Don Tenorio, although he had consented to see if he could talk the *ca-*

cique into reopening communications with his rival the *alcade*. The companions' very survival dictated maintaining neutrality for the moment, especially here in the very shadow of Don Hector's palace in the presence of a couple dozen of his bodyguards. Although he personally saw the force in Hector's arguments, Ryan was unwilling to say anything at this point that might seem to commit Don Tenorio to any course of action.

"What do you call those obsidian-edged clubs?" J.B. asked. "I noticed some of the Chichimecs were carrying them, too."

"Ah, yes," Don Hector said. "The *macahuitl*."

The companions looked at one another. The baron pronounced the word "makaweetle," rhyming with "beetle." It was what Felicidad had called for yesterday when her tiny handblaster proved useless against the tentacled unknown that had held her.

Don Hector called out something in a guttural language Ryan knew wasn't Spanish. One of the three sergeants or cademen turned and came trotting up the slope. Sure enough, it was their old friend Two Arrow.

At Don Hector's command, the big Eagle Knight pulled the weapon slung at his belt and handed it over. At close range Ryan realized the odd yoke and arm and shin-guards that made up the Eagle Knight armor were molded out of plastic. The baron examined the weapon a moment, then proffered it to Ryan by laying it across his own left forearm hilt-first.

Ryan picked up the weapon gingerly. It was about the weight and dimension of a conventional metal machete, maybe two feet long and two to three pounds in weight. The thin flakes of obsidian had been cunningly fitted so as to form an almost continuous edge down both sides of the flat hardwood club. The weapon was square-tipped and while handy was blade-heavy, as only made sense for a dedicated hacking-and-slashing weapon.

Ryan handed it off to J.B. Mildred came close to study it over his shoulder. Firearms were her first love when it came to weaponry, but no graduate of med school who had studied and practiced surgery could remain neutral about cutting implements.

"Nice heft," J.B. said. "Do some damage with this, no mistake." He took a couple of passes in the air with the weapon.

He handed the weapon to Mildred. "But stone for a cutting edge?"

"It's a form of glass," Mildred said. "Glass will take a sharper edge than any metal alloy. I've known some docs, mostly Latinos who knew their history, who insisted on the surgeons using obsidian blades when they had to go under the knife themselves. Cuts were finer, cleaner, healed quicker."

She turned the *macahuitl* in her hand and grinned. "Not that I suppose that's a big issue for this baby, huh?"

"As you perceive. The vulnerable point of such weapons is not their ability to hold an edge, but a regrettable tendency to break. Still, my elite warriors—and the Chichimecs—are devoted to them, and not solely because of their traditional resonance with our people."

Mildred handed the weapon back to J.B., who passed

it hilt-foremost to Hector. The *cacique* pivoted and said something in the guttural tongue to Two Arrow, who had been standing staring at the outsiders with a hint of unpleasant smirk and more than a hint of savage gleam in his eyes. The warrior knelt and accepted the weapon back, then stood quiveringly straight.

"Your behavior inconvenienced our guests," the *cacique* said in English. "However, you have served me bravely and faithfully. I have decided to accept your flowery sacrifice.

"Cut your throat."

Two Arrow's brown hand snapped up. The obsidian blade bit into his neck. Ryan clearly heard the stone grate against bone.

The warrior's head lolled to the side. A geyser of blood erupted from his neck as he folded to the ground. Mildred shrieked and leaped back. But the brunt of the bloodflood sprayed Don Hector, who received it unblinking.

Then he turned to his visitors. His eyes seemed to stare out of a horror mask of gore. "Return to Don Tenorio and do me the favor of telling him I will meet with him two days hence at a place of his choosing. Tell him also the truth you have witnessed with your own eyes— that I and I alone possess the will and the means to save our valley from the Chichimecs."

Chapter Sixteen

"He's crazy," Mildred said. "He's flat-out, florid, schizophrenic."

"Jumped back fast, back there," Jak said with a wolf's grin from the rear compartment of the Hummer. "Blood scared?"

"No. I mean, yes! Yeah, I've seen blood before—even been sprayed with it a few times. You people know that. But back in the twentieth century that was something we took seriously, what with AIDS and everything. And besides, it took me all by surprise, dammit. I never imagined he'd *do* something that barking damn crazy."

"Which made it all the more effective a demonstration of the loyalty he commands from his household troops, dusky princess," Doc said.

"Which only goes to show they're as screwy as he is. And while you're at it, you can seal that 'dusky princess' crap in lead and dump it in the Marianas trench, you goofy old coot!"

"Millie, our man Don Tenorio doesn't seem to really want to be a baron," J.B. said. "In this bad old world, what I've seen of it anyway, only those who want it re-

The Gold Eagle Reader Service™ — Here's how it works:

NO POSTAGE
NECESSARY
IF MAILED
IN THE
UNITED STATES

BUSINESS REPLY MAIL
FIRST-CLASS MAIL   PERMIT NO. 717-003   BUFFALO, NY

POSTAGE WILL BE PAID BY ADDRESSEE

GOLD EAGLE READER SERVICE
3010 WALDEN AVE
PO BOX 1867
BUFFALO NY 14240-9952

GET FREE BOOKS and a FREE GIFT WHEN YOU PLAY THE...

Lucky 7

SLOT MACHINE GAME!

Just scratch off the silver box with a coin. Then check below to see the gifts you get!

YES! I have scratched off the silver box. Please send me the 2 free Gold Eagle® books and gift for which I qualify. I understand I am under no obligation to purchase any books, as explained on the back of this card.

366 ADL D34F   **166 ADL D34E**

FIRST NAME	LAST NAME

ADDRESS

APT.#	CITY

STATE/PROV.	ZIP/POSTAL CODE

7	7	7	**Worth TWO FREE BOOKS plus a BONUS Mystery Gift!**
🍒	🍒	🍒	**Worth TWO FREE BOOKS!**
♣	♣	♣	**Worth ONE FREE BOOK!**
🔔	🔔	🍒	**TRY AGAIN!**

(MB-04-R)

DETACH AND MAIL CARD TODAY!

ally bad can hold on to it. He seems a nice enough old guy, for somebody who pays too much attention to whitecoats. But if I was a bettin' man, and of course I am, my jack would have to be on this dude Don Hector. Even if he is crazy as a shaken-up jar full of hornets."

"Barons always crazy," Jak said. "Where big deal?"

"I don't *believe* you people. He's tried to have us killed, not once but twice."

"Neither time on purpose," J.B. pointed out.

"So *he* says. But even, just for the sake of laughs, stipulating that he didn't mean it—correct me if I'm wrong, John, but are you not just as dead if you get chilled accidentally as on purpose? Either way, dirt hits you in the eyes."

"People," Ryan said softly, "this isn't really our fight." He was sitting in the back seat with Krysty beside him, gazing morosely out the window, letting the warm moist air, smelling of clean water and fertile soil and only ever so slightly of the omnipresent sulfur tousle his shaggy black curls.

He had been a little uneasy, approaching the checkpoint at the landward end of the causeway. Tenorio had allowed them to go to Hector without trying to send along any kind of chaperones—or spies. But it would be right within parameters for baronial paranoia for him to decide that, having broken bread and spoken with the enemy, they were never to be trusted back into the city. Or perhaps, not except under armed guard, as prisoners virtual or outright.

But no. The sentries had grinned and waved the way

the scavvies always did to the visitors, hooked back the razor-tape tangles and moved the blocks and gestured them right on through. Did that lack of apparent suspicion in itself indicate pusillanimity on the part of Tenorio on his people? Mebbe.

Mildred sat back and crossed her arms. "It is if we have intention of staying here, Ryan. Making some kind of lives for ourselves other than running from danger to danger, living off the linings of our stomachs until we can scrounge a few self-heats or MREs. But if you-all *like* that kind of life, we can always shine it on. Maybe find our way back through all that lava to the redoubt, jump somewhere else and hope we finally lit in Paradise."

"Now, Millie—"

"Don't you 'now Millie' me, John Barrymore. Don't even."

"I fear our esteemed physician—is that cognomen acceptable to you, *mademoiselle*?—our esteemed physician has a point," Doc said. "I do not believe any bonds unbreakable yet bind us to this place, nor to the parties involved. But if not here, where? And should we chose to light here, at least for the time being, we may find ourselves perforce choosing sides."

"One thing's for sure," Krysty said. "We won't be joining up with the Chichimecs."

The others laughed, but briefly. "There's a point to what you say, like always," J.B. said. "That being, if we stay, we fight. Or we're food. Since I'm not up for getting eaten, that makes our problem figuring out the best way to help fight."

"Tenorio's a friend," Ryan said, "if a baron can be anybody's friend."

"Tenorio's a good man. I believe that, I do. I also believe he's a weak leader. Hector's crazy and he's probably a sadist. Like J.B. says—"

"As," Krysty corrected automatically.

"As J.B. says, what else is new? That seems to be another part of being a baron—you got to be ready to force people and to hurt people to get them to do things your way, so why is it surprising most of them seem to like it so much? It's the job. One thing taken with another, he seems to have the force, both in personality and manpower, to swing the weight. Can we honestly say that about Tenorio?"

"Tenorio and his people would be hard to beat in the city, Ryan," Krysty said. "Mebbe we should think about that. The scavvies have achieved self-sufficiency or near to it in food and water. And we know enough about guerrilla fighting, not to mention city fighting, to realize how hard it would be to dislodge them. For either the Chichimecs or Hector."

Ryan nodded slowly, not quite seeing where she was heading.

"They can't keep people out, though, Krysty," the Armorer pointed out. "We know that pretty damn well, too."

"No, they can't. But getting raiders *inside* the city and getting the scavengers *out* are two different matters. Tenorio's people know the place. It's their home. We have to figure they'll fight for it, and fight hard and well. I have to think that means they could hold out pretty near indefinitely, if they had to."

"So what you're saying is, we could throw in with Tenorio and his mob, and just let the landward part of the valley go hang?" J.B. rubbed his chin. "Mebbe. But I'm not so sure how well that idea sits with me, to tell truth."

"Nor I, J.B.," the redhead admitted. "It's just something I think we need to take into consideration."

"Now, it don't gripe at me because my heart's started to bleed cherry syrup for all those poor sufferin' people out in the valley I don't even know. But, dark night, forting up in the city waiting for the Chichimecs to wear us down, living every day just waiting to die...well, losin' slow is still losin'."

"But have you not just described life itself, John Barrymore?" Doc asked.

J.B. grimaced. "Mebbe. But I guess I like the illusion that I got a chance."

"What do you think, Jak?" Ryan asked.

The albino shrugged disinterestedly. "Cities no good. Moving on better."

"Doc?"

They were approaching the city and the flat island parking lot where they would of necessity have to leave their big wag. Doc began to slow the Hummer.

"It seems we find ourselves faced with a choice between Scylla and Charybdis—or, as may be, between the Devil and the deep blue sea. I believe I am just as glad to abide by your wisdom in this matter, Ryan, for I can see no easy resolution to our dilemma."

"People," Mildred said, "I don't like to be the voice of doom, here. But I think there's something else we need to look at."

"Speak up," Ryan said. "Your thoughts won't do us no—*any* good if you don't let them out."

"Can we live under Hector, any more than the Chichimecs? What if he decides to tell us to cut our throats—or just asks his fat boy Mendoza or this firehaired daughter of his you folks got crosswise of, back in the city—to do it for him? Maybe you have to be a bastard to be a real baron. Maybe you have to be a little crazy. But not this big a bastard, and not this crazy."

Ryan scratched under the lower edge of his eyepatch, where sweat was making it chafe his cheek. "You got your sights lined up right on that," he said after a moment. He sat back in his seat and gazed at the ruined towers of the city, thrusting up right in front of them now.

"Trader always used to say, 'a leader who shows doubt really isn't a leader after all.' Mebbe that's so. Most times it is, I reckon. But we're bound up together by trust, or we aren't bound by anything at all, so I can't lie to you. The plain fact is, right now I don't know whether to pull the trigger or to snap on the safety."

Krysty touched his cheek. "Don't worry, you're not perfect, lover. You're human, and you aren't made of vanadium steel. We noticed that. When the time comes, you'll make the right call."

"Look on the bright side, my dear Ryan," Doc said. "We do not have to make up our minds right upon this instant. Don Hector's agreed to talk to our esteemed host, after all. Who knows what might happen?"

"Something generally does," J.B. said, getting out and stretching. "And that there's the whole rad-blasted problem, in a cartridge case."

THE SMOKIES WERE triple angry this night. The terrace vibrated constantly beneath the soles of Ryan's boots, not, so far as he could tell, from earthquakes, but from the shattering unceasing violence of the eruptions. Their rumble was like the sound of big engines revving nearby, and the occasional blast sounded like a gren going off right down the block. A sort of fiery haze enveloped both peaks, sometimes shot through with flashes of light, terribly intense. A fine ash, sulfur-reeking, floated on the breeze, brushing Ryan's face like clouds of gnats, sticking to hair and skin.

"Don Tenorio," Ryan said, "you've been a good host. But by that token I reckon I owe it to you to give it to you straight and not walk all around the muzzle before going for the trigger. Don Hector's right."

Don Tenorio turned from the railing. His rather sharp features now looked to have been chiseled from stone by a rude, hasty hand. As if he were an idol of an unfriendly god.

"It'll take all you've got to beat back these Chichimecs. It'll take unity of action, of command. If that means giving in to what Hector wants, well, that's the price that's asked for holding on to what you have. Mebbe even your lives."

The *alcade*'s dark eyes flashed. Here's where we see how thin a baron's gratitude really stretches, Ryan thought. He knew he was risking all their lives, but his companions had all agreed he owed Tenorio the truth. He didn't like the idea of trying to lie to the man, that much was sure.

"So this is what it comes to?" Don Tenorio rapped. "The wise white men from the north, come to tell the simple brown men how things will be."

All Ryan could think to do was to paraphrase what Mildred had said to Hector at the training grounds that afternoon. "Well, Don Tenorio, we're not all men, and we're not all white."

Don Tenorio glared a moment longer, then laughed. A silent, openmouthed laugh, the way a wolf laughs. Ryan was reminded for a moment of Jak, of all people, and it came to him to wonder what depths this little undistinguished-looking man might have that he, Ryan, hadn't come close to plumbing yet.

"Forgive me, my friend. I always beg my people to speak only the truth to me, without... How do you say? Sugar-coating. Of course they promise to do so. Of course that is not the way it happens. I am unaccustomed to such directness. You are a brave man, Don Ryan."

"That or triple stupe."

"And that is one thing you are not. Still, no more am I. And I still believe that you are wrong."

Ryan spread his hands.

"First, we would prove very difficult to dislodge from the city, by the Chichimecs or, should it come to that, by Don Hector's forces."

"I realize that. But like J.B. says, making them dig you out building by building, room by room, is just a form of dying slow."

"Perhaps. But the Chichimecs are raiders, customarily so, classically so. Theirs is not the persisting strategy. It is their way to strike, seize what they can carry and leave. On that basis we alone could simply wait them out, if we must."

"I hear what you're saying, Baron. But these Chichimecs don't act like they're here for just a smash-and-grab job. They act like they're fixing to stay. Looks to me a lot more like a migration than a raid."

The small man turned back and gripped the railing hard. Ryan could see the muscles of his shoulders hunch through the thin linen of his shirt.

"I fear you are correct. They are driven by hunger, by greed, and by religious fanaticism, and those are harsh, relentless masters. And they are many, far more than I would have thought possible. The lands to the north must be depopulated save for the women and children and those too old to travel."

He stood staring into the night. After a moment Ryan walked soft-footed to the table where various refreshments had been laid out by María. They were alone on the terrace. Don Tenorio didn't prepare or serve his own food, nor sweep his own floors, but he didn't like to be waited on hand and foot; he couldn't bear to have servants hovering around, although when he worked he tended to keep a stream of eager young aides hopping to various tasks and taking down notes. The ash made the white tablecloth look as if it had been sprinkled with pepper. Ryan refilled his ceramic mug with a punch blended from several juices, not all of them familiar. No alcohol for him this night; he needed as clear a head as possible.

"When we came out here," Tenorio said, speaking out across the lake, "I made quite sure that everyone understood that, while our mission was one of peace and hope and life, we must be prepared to fight, to kill or die, for what we made here. Otherwise, we would have nothing at all. And we have had to defend what is ours. There have been raids, attacks, treacheries—not, I must say, from Don Hector. Not until recently. For a time, indeed, he was a stabilizing influence on the valley, and most welcome. Banditry declined as he rose—I must say that much for his methods.

"So we, and I still believe it is true of most of us, we understand the paradox, that to keep anything, we must be prepared to risk all without hesitation. We will fight if we must. For all that we prosper, we have not yet grown soft, because every day is a fight for survival, against the dangers of the city.

"But…let me explain it to you in this way. I have no children of my own body. I cannot, and I suspect you cannot know how devastating such a fact, such an admission is for a man of this land. It means that in a true and real sense I am something less than a man. But that is how it is."

He turned to face Ryan. "I will not say that the people of the city are my children. That would be obscenely patronizing. I will say that what I would leave behind as my legacy is a better life for *our* children, the children of the city. Unending war is no such legacy, even if we someday win.

"What I would gladly do is welcome everyone, the people of the valley, the Chichimecs, even the poor so-called witches. You've seen the size of the city, the magnitude of the task involved in reclaiming it, rebuilding it. Not all the people of the valley, humans and mutants alike, could finish the task in my lifetime. But I know that will not happen. We must fight the Chichimecs. We must rout them."

"Which brings us full circle," Ryan said, "back to Hector."

"Back to Hector. He is a far better war leader than I. I respect and honor him for it. I am willing to do what I can to help, and most of my people are, as well."

"Then why not give him what he wants?"

"Because he will not be content with our assistance, with mere alliance. He insists on having power over us. I cannot for the life of me comprehend why. But I do know this—my people will not accept the burdens he would lay upon us. You saw today, I believe, what I am speaking of."

Ryan had nothing to say.

Don Tenorio sighed. "And so you can now perhaps see why I was sharp with you before, unforgivable a breach of hospitality though it be. I can neither deny Don Hector nor give him what he wants. I—"

A screaming came across the sky. Ryan tensed, unsure of how to respond. His instincts cried out for him to seek cover, but reason told him whatever was making the racket, it was too late to hide from it already. Nor did Don Tenorio show any sign of bolting. The small, gray man didn't even flinch, and Ryan was rad-blasted if he would show less stone than a bookworm of a merchant.

There was a crack like the loudest thunder Ryan had ever heard. He looked wildly up at the sky. What seemed to be huge but not very bright shooting stars were passing overhead, trailing smoke. One of them struck the building right behind Don Tenorio's headquarters with a flash and breaking of glass, passed through like a bullet.

"Fireblast! What's going on?"

"Tonantzin's tears, we call them, the tears of our ancient earth goddess. More prosaically, they are bombs thrown out by the volcanoes."

Ryan stared at him with his lone eye. "They throw them this far?"

"Rarely. But yes. As you can see."

Light spilled onto the terrace as the door was flung open. Ryan's companions spilled out, blasters in hand, staring around with wild eyes.

"What in the name of everything nuke-blasted is going on?" J.B. demanded, brandishing his Smith & Wesson M-4000 shotgun. "Are we being shelled?"

Ryan had to moisten his lips before he could speak. "Lava bombs," he said. "From the smokies."

"Dear God," Mildred said. She stared off toward the south. "It looks like somebody pried the lid off Hell."

She turned to Ryan. "If they'd been going off like that

when we were leaving, when we came across the mountains, we'd never have made it!"

J.B. put his arm around her shoulders. She pressed her face into the hollow of his.

Krysty was at Ryan's side. She alone held no weapon. Her eyes were calm, but her hair stirred around her shoulders as if agitated.

"You knew it wasn't an attack," he said softly.

She nodded. "I could feel it." Her cheeks were flushed again.

Don Tenorio was eyeing them intently. "You are most finely attuned to the forces of the Earth, are you not, Señorita Wroth? If you will forgive my asking."

Arm around Ryan's waist, she turned to face him. "I am…you might say, bound to Gaia. To the forces of the Earth. I draw strength from them."

He smiled. "My people already are saying you are touched by the Lady of the Valley."

"I'm only tuned to the forces of the Earth, Don Tenorio. Nothing more."

He shrugged. "As may be. You are clearly a woman of remarkable power. Even I, who have small feel for such matters, can sense that. Now, if you will excuse me, friends, we can all hope the worst fury of the eruption is spent so we can rest."

He started to the door. When he reached it he stopped and turned back. "One thing, *señorita*. This land is not altogether like your Deathlands to the north, where I understand people have largely turned their backs upon religion. Many of the old beliefs remain strong within the valley—stronger in some places than in others. In future you might be wise to be as discreet as possible about the strength of your connection to the earth spirit, however you call it. There are those who might fear such power, those who might envy it—and those who might try to use it. Now, I bid you all good-night."

He was gone.

"Now what in thunder do you suppose he meant by that," the Armorer asked, "that somebody might try to 'use' Krysty's power?"

Doc ran his hand through hair already tousled by sleep. "I hope, somehow, we never find that out, John Barrymore."

NAKED, HER CINNAMON-SATIN skin shining in the torch light, Felicidad Mendoza knelt in front of Don Hector on the cool stone of the temple. Naked, he sat upon a polished stone throne. She was rendering him obeisance with her very skillful lips and tongue.

He moaned and writhed and sweated. Then he seized handfuls of her spun-copper hair, thrust his hips violently. He uttered great guttural cries as he spent himself.

She took it all in and never batted a jade-green eye.

When it was done, she rose, eyes kept carefully downcast. "I hope that my lord will accept my sacrifice," she said. Her breasts were large and rode high. The nipples were small chocolate caps upon them. Beneath her flat dome of belly and between her panther-muscled thighs, her pubic bush gleamed like filaments of burnished metal in the flicker of the torches. She crossed her wrists behind her and stood nude in front of her lord.

The throne had been carved from a single piece of onyx and polished to mirror gloss. It was uncomfortable as hell. Don Hector had purchased from the scavvies down-filled cushions to ease his baronial backside, and upon these he now lolled, sated.

"Given what a botch you made of the attempt to take Tenorio, I should accept a full flowery sacrifice of you," he said musingly. "Perhaps grilled alive in a steel brazier on a bed of glowing coals?"

"I shall accept what gifts my emperor chooses in his wisdom and mercy to bestow on me." Actually the term she used meant literally, first speaker. In the valley of Mexico that had long been synonymous with *emperor*, and that was how he heard it.

"Tush, tush, my child," he said, wagging a finger, all indulgence now. "You mustn't use that term…yet."

"If I have given further offense—"

"All right, all right. No need to lay it on so thick. Look at me now, and explain to me why you screwed up so badly."

She did as he bade. "I anticipated, thanks to the intelligence reports gathered by my father, that Don Tenorio would at some point go on an inspection tour on that armed cabin cruiser of his, as he does every few days. When our contact in his palace passed word that he had set forth, we executed the trap we had already prepared. By that point, thanks again to our own intelligence assets within the city, we knew that the strangers from the north would be accompanying him. We judged that they would sweeten the prize we would bring back to Your Resplendence."

She shrugged. "They proved more formidable prey than we reckoned. I of course accept full responsibility for the miscalculation and our failure."

He nodded his jutting chin on his fist, as if scratching it. "What in the gods' names were you doing there, Feli? After myself, you are perhaps the most recognizable dweller in all my domain."

"The object in disguising our raiding party as Chichimecs, if I may presume to remind Your Celestial Refulgence, was in the event we were discovered before springing the trap. Once we had captured Don Tenorio, and his *gringo* guests, and conveyed them here to await your soon-to-be-divine pleasure, there would be bloody little point to trying to pretend we were a pack of muties and savages out of the northern wastes, now would there?"

"Perhaps. But had you not permitted yourself to be seen during what turned to be the abortive attempt, our rivals might still possibly believe the attack was carried out by the savages. Or at least they couldn't prove otherwise."

"As I said, I misjudged. My life, it need not be said, lies upon your palm."

"Enough, enough. We've settled that. You are far too valuable, not to mention beautiful, for me to discard…lightly. You are a brilliant schemer, Felicidad. Your skills at intrigue are nonpareil. But you are rash. Sometimes rash enough to spoil your own cunning efforts."

The nude woman shrugged again, causing her breasts to ride impressively up and down her rib cage. "It matters little. Tenorio is a maguey worm. A strong man would be plotting his revenge. Tenorio pleads with us to reopen negotiations, he all but apologizes for successfully defending himself."

Hector frowned thoughtfully. "You do him discredit, my lovely little feather. He realizes well enough that only I have the means, the manpower and the generalship to defeat the Chichimec hordes. He still thinks to use me, manipulate me to do his dirty work for him, while he and his pack of merchants are free to grub like rats in the ruins of the city, and gain treasures they had no share in creating!"

He was almost shouting now. She flowed to his side like honey down a plank, caressed his cheek. She fell to her knees; her fingers trailed down his well-muscled chest and his belly, the ribbed muscles of which were only beginning to be softened by a hint of paunch. Then they trailed farther down.

"We shall give him the talk he wants, all the talk he can stomach, won't we, great chief?"

He trailed his strong brown fingers though glinting strands of her hair that had worked free of the knot she had gathered it into atop her head, and smiled. "That we shall. And remember, the foreigners are not to be harmed. Especially the woman."

She frowned. "Why not?"

"Because I say so," he said, allowing a touch of whip-crack into his voice. Then he stroked her cheek with the backs of his fingertips. "I sense great power in them. Especially in the woman."

"So you will replace me with another woman with red hair—provided her hair is naturally that unpleasant shade, of course?"

He laughed. "No. I may take my pleasure of her yet—that remains for me to decide."

She stiffened and looked down. "Of course."

"No, no. Look at me." He put a curled finger beneath her chin and raised her face. "You know what use I can put her to, and the others. You know what it means to me. To you, too, if you continue to serve me well—without question nor further mishap."

"I shall give of my all each day to thee, O Lord."

"That's my girl. And now to more personal pleasurable matters…"

Chapter Seventeen

Though sadly faded, the stripes on the big tent were many-colored, retaining a hint of their earlier gaudiness. "I cannot help but believe," Doc said as the companions marched with Colonel Solano, Five Ax and the rest of the small party accompanying Don Tenorio up to the meeting place, "that the fanciful shadings of yon pavilion lend an unwonted note of frivolity to these proceedings."

"It's what the tent-rental place they salvaged it from had in the appropriate size, Doc," Mildred said. "Scavvies can't be choosers."

J.B. winked. "Mebbe it's a little commentary on this whole fandango by that sly old coyote Tenorio."

Doc frowned loftily. "He seems to regard these talks as of the gravest moment, John Barrymore. Still, there may be aught in what you say."

"Gotta admit I'm not too comfortable having you here," Ryan said sidelong to Krysty, walking up the slope next to him. He carried his Steyr SSG-70 slung, muzzle down. As had the crest of the hill on the lake's northern shore where the striped tent had been erected, the path to the tent had been cleared of scrub and rocks for the convenience and comfort of the dignitaries. Just offshore, Don Tenorio's cabin cruiser *Paloma Blanca* rested at anchor.

"I'm fine." She was. What had been an angry pus-weeping hole in her shoulder was now a red blotch that had seemed to shrink almost visibly when Krysty had stripped down to show Ryan the night before—not that he had spent long watching before getting involved in other activities. The colossal outpourings of seismic energy, it seemed, supercharged more than just her immune system. His knees were still wobbling.

"Don Hector was paying a little more attention to you than seems good for us on our last little jaunt," he told her.

"He's not exactly the first baron we've run across to admire me." She smiled to take any perceived edge off the words.

"It's what those other barons did as a result of admiring you that worries me."

She laughed. "I'm afraid I'm with Mildred. Maybe it's just my vanity, but I think any hypothetical crush the *cacique* might harbor for me is about the last of his character flaws we ought to be worried about."

"That's a point," Ryan conceded grudgingly.

Five Ax was walking along beside them, wearing desert-camou shirt, khaki shorts, rubber-tire sandals and an MP-5 SDK, Heckler & Koch's full-size brother to the stubby little 5K model, complete with a built-in noise suppressor fattening the barrel. The Mexican army or national police or whoever's arsenals the scavvies had turned up sure hadn't stinted themselves in firepower, by the evidence both of Tenorio's group and Hector's party trudging up the other side of the hill. The wiry little Jaguar Knight commando was listening in on their conversation, not eavesdropping, since nobody was making any attempt to be private. Now he laughed and spoke rapidly to Doc.

"He suggests you entertain no worries on that score, friend Ryan," the old man translated. "Don Hector, so the barracks rumor has it, has little use for women as women. If you will forgive me the implied indecency, my dear Krysty."

"No, Doc, I'm shocked and appalled."

The old man's long face slumped. She laughed and fisted him in the ribs. "Gaia, I'm joking you! There's very little you can say to me that I didn't hear before I was weaned. Or see."

Five Ax spoke again. Doc was blushing and too obviously flustered yet to speak. Mildred, whose Spanish had improved greatly with fairly intensive use over the last few days, caught up the slack. "He says the exception is the Red Haired Serpent," she said.

"Red Haired—"

"Felicidad Mendoza," Krysty said.

"Dead on target," Mildred said. "I hear she's a real piece of work."

"DON'T LIKE THIS," J.B. murmured from the side of his mouth.

Ryan cocked the brow of his one good eye at his friend.

"Hector's sec boss Mendoza made zero fuss about us packing," the Armorer amplified

The outlanders were at the back of the tent, standing in a clump or sitting in folding chairs the scavvies had provided. The real dignitaries, the barons, their sec chiefs, and a single bodyguard each—Five Ax for Tenorio, a gorgeously plumed and laser-braceleted Eagle Knight for Hector—were up at the front talking over a heavy oak table. Hector wore a robe fringed in gold, Tenorio a simple white shirt with open collar, khaki trousers and hiking boots. The two sec bosses looked almost identically glum.

"Tenorio and Solano didn't kick up a fuss about Hector's people coming heeled, either," Ryan said. "Not Mendoza's .45 nor that laser-blaster thing."

"Don't that strike you as a bad sign all of its lonesome?"

Ryan shrugged. "Same rules apply as always—keep both eyes open."

"Wonder where Little Miss Copperhead is," Mildred said.

"Up to no good," the Armorer guessed.

"Don't reckon Hector wants to remind Don Tenorio of her existence right this moment," Ryan said. "Plus we hear Hector hasn't got much use for women at the council table, remember?"

"I'm disappointed. I've been sort of looking forward to seeing her in action."

"No, you're not," Ryan, Krysty and J.B. said simultaneously.

The meeting seemed to be going well. The two barons were pitching their voices too low for Ryan to make out what they were saying, even if they'd been speaking a lingo he understood, which of course they weren't. But their tones seemed amicable.

Krysty's eyes suddenly widened. "Ryan—" She clutched his hand in a drowner's grip.

"Krysty, what—"

"Something…bad," she whispered. "About to happen."

Tenorio and Hector rose as one, stepped around the table, embraced each other.

The roof fell in.

RYAN FLOUNDERED as the faded but colorful cloth swaddled him. It was surprisingly heavy. He shouted, *"Krysty!"* The cloth muffled his voice.

He fell over.

The cloth seemed to have got itself twined around his legs and the butt of his sniper rifle. He struggled to draw his panga, but the folds of cloth were fouling his arm; the blade was too long to get free of its sheath. Heavy fabric pressed close in on his face, filling his nostrils with dust and the omnipresent ash, making it difficult to breathe even as his lungs burned from the exertion of struggling to get loose.

He heard a tumult of cries, shots. "Krysty!" he cried again. It was like a bad dream, one of those terrible dreams, where danger threatens and nothing you do works, where your impotence is total.

The cloth split across right in front of his face, allowing sunlight and blessedly cool, fresh air to flood inside. He grabbed the first thing he saw, a pale arm. Then he saw that at one end was a strong but very feminine hand grasping a folding knife, and at the other end was Krysty.

"Give me your hand," she shouted to him, reaching down with her free hand. They clasped each other's wrists and she hauled him to his feet—even without using her Gaia linkage to enhance her strength, which drained her so brutally she saved it for the direst emergencies, she was strikingly strong for a woman.

By the time he was upright his SIG-Sauer was in his hand. He looked around. A dozen or more of what he took for Hector's sec men—not Eagle Knights, but more generic goons in khaki uniforms—were milling over the collapsed tent. As he took stock, he saw Colonel Solano, looking dazed, trying to struggle free of the swathes of cloth.

A dazzle of ruby brilliance. The city sec boss's head exploded in a cloud of pink steam.

An Eagle Knight, possibly the one who had accompanied Hector, was standing several feet from the toppling, blood-geysering corpse, a *macahuitl* in one hand, the other upraised to aim his armlet-mounted blaster. Ryan snapped his SIG-Sauer out in front of him into a two-handed combat grip. The Eagle Knight saw the motion, started to swing his arm around to bring his laser to bear.

Ryan didn't know whether the fancy partial armor the Eagle Knights wore was some kind of bullet-resistant synthetic, although he guessed it was. To be safe he lined the long barrel of the silenced P-226 up so that the Eagle Knight's head seemed to be right on the front sight like a pumpkin on a post. He squeezed the trigger once, again. The weapon made its explosive cough. Because he was loaded for defense, not stealth, and because he was running low on subsonic rounds, he was firing full-power Parabellum ammo. Had the bullets flown past any objects they would have made cracking sounds almost as loud as an unsuppressed muzzle report. Neither copper-jacketed bullet happened to pass near anything on its flight into the Eagle Knight's face. His head jerked back and he crumpled.

Another Eagle Knight in full drag was running at Ryan with obsidian-blade sword upraised. Apparently he didn't rate one of the prized wrist-lasers. He was high-stepping to navigate across the fabric, which seethed like a stormy sea with the angry, frantic efforts of those still trapped under it to get free. Ryan turned to face his charge, drawing his panga with his left hand; the big and powerfully muscled swordsman was already too close to be taken down by any handblaster before he split Ryan's skull to his teeth, much less by the jacketed 9 mm ball rounds from his SIG, which carried more penetration than punch. At his side Krysty also spun, but even if she could fire in time, the 158-grain lead slugs from her .38 weren't going to be enough, either.

Above the commotion Ryan heard a ripping sound. Right in the sec man's path a shine of steel in the sunlight appeared through a fresh rip in the faded but colorful cloth. The Eagle Knight ran on heedless, eyes rolling with whites showing on all sides, as if he could smell his victim's blood already.

At his feet the cloth erupted with a chattering roar. Strips were blasted upward. The Eagle Knight screamed as bullets lanced up through his thighs, his scrotum, his balls, to smash his pelvis, jelly his bowels, rip his lungs to hissing shreds. He did a wild death dance and fell backward.

Like a mutant monster from some drowned basement in the City in the Lake, J.B. surged free into the afternoon air, his Uzi smoking in one hand, the little razor-edged Tekna knife he'd used to win his way free in the other.

He sprayed bullets at Mendoza's uniformed sec goons. A couple fell, others fled.

Ryan's friends were popping through the fabric like mushrooms through bizarrely striated soil after a rain. Jak hauled Doc to his feet with surprising strength and wheeled, his right arm whipping forward. A khaki-uniformed sec goon screamed, dropped a leveled 1911 .45, clutched as if to hold back the blood diluted by clear aqueous fluid that jetted from the ruin of his eye, around the bare-steel shank of a throwing knife. Even as Doc brushed at his coat with the hand holding his swordstick, his right hand came up and his big ungainly LeMat boomed. A sec man aiming a lever-action carbine at him dropped, clutching the hole smashed through his belly by a .44-caliber lead slug, as if the pressure could squeeze out the intolerable pain.

Mildred had cut her way free with a scalpel, Ryan wasn't sure where she'd carried it to get it into action so quickly. She took her side-on target shooter's stance, blasted two quick shots from her Czech-made ZKR 551. Two more of Don Hector's sec men went down, each with an identical, perfectly circular hole in his forehead, punched by her flat-tipped, wad-cutter bullets.

Five Ax was free, too, hauling Don Tenorio out of the rip he'd slashed in the cloth with his own knife. The *alcade* looked stunned but showed no injury. Five Ax shoved his baron downslope toward the beach, away from Hector's camp on the far side of the hill. He snugged the butt of his machine pistol to his shoulder and fired three sputtering suppressed bursts into the place where the fallen tent was mounded over the big oak conference table. Ryan guessed he reckoned Don Hector was underneath.

"Here comes everybody!" J.B. shouted, slamming a fresh mag into his Uzi and firing a blast down the hill's far side at the valley sec forces starting to swarm up it. "Time to cut stick and go!"

Mildred grabbed the back of his jacket and hauled on him. "Take your own damn advice, you crazy sawed-off fool!"

Stuttering thunder split the afternoon air that reeked with burned propellant, blood and spilled guts. Everybody without exception fell down flat on their faces, including the sec forces surging up the landward slope of the hill.

"By the Three Kennedys!" Doc exclaimed with his cheek to a red stripe faded pink. "Are new volcanoes being spawned about us?"

The Armorer looked back toward the lake and uttered a ringing rebel yell. "No, that's Ma Deuce her own bad self, singing the sweetest song this child ever heard!"

He reached down and snatched up his battered fedora.

"Five Ax!" Ryan yelled. "Take Tenorio and go!" He jammed his SIG-Sauer into his waistband and unslung his rifle as the Browning on the boat fired another burst. The rate of fire wasn't slow, but the noise was unbelievable. It wasn't just noise; Ryan could feel the muzzle-blast pounding the skin of his cheeks like a brisk wind from at least an eighth of a mile away. The thumb-thick bullets threw up tan-earth geysers higher than his head where they raked the hilltop. The Jaguar Knight gunner was smart enough to fire well away from the tent, where he might chill his baron or one of his friends. It didn't matter; Hector's sec boys were still hugging the planet, except for those still on their feet on the same side of the hill as the terrible bullet-sprayer. They in turn were rabbiting over the hill and into the scrub as fast as said feet could beat.

The companions coalesced into a clot around Five Ax and his baron as they retreated downslope. Ryan brought up the rear, the Steyr raised almost to his shoulder. As they reached the foot of the hill, a dark face peeked up over the crest. Ryan yanked the butt to his shoulder and pulled off a snapshot. To his amazement the .308 bullet caught the sec man right at the top of his forehead and flipped the cranial cap right out of his skull. It wobbled in a crazy arc through the air and out of sight, hair and scalp still in place.

"Splendid shot, Ryan, my boy," Doc said, reaching a hand to help the one-eyed man clamber over the railing of the *Paloma* as he came slogging through shin-deep water.

"Pure triple-stupe luck," Ryan said. But he was grinning fit to split his head as he said it.

THE BIG, WHITE WATER WAG growled away from the shore at moderate speed, so as not to tumble the somewhat dazed survivors around the deck. Nobody expected any of Don Hector's people to get in the line of fire of the Browning heavy machine gun.

Not any of Hector's people did. A lone figure came pelting down the slope, dark hair flying wild and free, torn and soiled white robe hanging off one shoulder.

"Come back!" Don Hector shouted after them in Spanish. "It was not my doing! My underlings betrayed me, they acted against orders—please, please, Don Tenorio, believe me!"

He tore off the robe, threw it aside. Wearing only a loincloth, he fell to his knees in the dirt and began to weep and tear his hair, imploring forgiveness so loudly they could hear him plainly over distance and the engine noise.

"That's enough out of you," Ryan said as Doc translated to the group standing raptly by the aft rail. He cinched the shooting sling of his Steyr around his left forearm, raised the cool steel buttplate to its home in the hollow of his shoulder, bent his eye to the scope, brought the crosshairs together on the middle of that muscular, hairless chest. He sucked in a deep breath and let it halfway out, mentally calculating the motion of the boat—not too hard, since it was mainly up and down; the cruiser was driving directly away from shore. His finger squeezed.

The SSG barrel was yanked skyward as the shot cracked off.

Ryan looked around, his lone eye the color and temperature of an Arctic winter sky and no more friendly. Don Tenorio's small soft hand was still clamped on the barrel.

"No, my friend," the *alcade* said. "That's not the way."

"He was ready to chill you in cold blood, the coldest," Ryan snapped, not caring he was speaking to a het-up baron in the midst of a knot of that baron's sec men with their own blood running high. "Don't you have the sand to let me do what's crying to be done?"

Don Tenorio put both hands on the younger man's broad shoulders. He had to reach way up to do it. At the contact, Jak growled low in his throat and started forward. Krysty lifted a hand. The albino boy stepped back, but his ruby eyes still smoldered. Five Ax had reflexively brought up his MP-5. Now he let the fat barrel fall offline and turned away, looking shamefaced.

"Ryan, *mi hijo,* listen to me," Tenorio said. "I don't care about Hector. If his life was mine to take now I'd snuff him out, be he awake or asleep, in blood hot or cold. He's earned far more deaths than you or I could ever give him. But my people aren't strong enough to rout the Chichimecs by ourselves, and Hector's people won't follow me any more than mine will follow him. We need him."

Ryan glared at him a moment longer.

"Mebbe you do have what it takes to be a baron, after all," he said. "But you sure picked a fine nuke-blasted time to show it!" He turned and stalked forward.

Chapter Eighteen

The armory was lit by electric lights, away up near the ceiling of the vault. Not bright but steady. The companions looked around in surprise as Don Tenorio ushered them in.

"We have scavenged generators, which we have modified to burn the alcohol we distill," the *alcade* explained.

"You don't use them at your residence," J.B. pointed out.

Tenorio shrugged. "Except for the radio room, it's not necessary. Here, we find it useful to be able to see to work. The ventilation system is helpful, as well."

They were in the basement level of a building fronting on the plaza of the step-pyramid. The structure hadn't been submerged at the base, although its upper two-thirds had been sheared off and fallen into the next street over, obstructing it. The armory level had been sealed and waterproofed, so that no dampness had seeped in.

Jak gazed around at the racks of rifles, mostly Garands and FN FALs, with a few racks of BARs thrown in. "Sweet," he said.

"This building was a headquarters of a special operational branch of the federal judicial police," their host explained. "Apparently they were created to cooperate with the American government in prosecuting the war on drugs."

"I was wondering where all the weaponry your people and Hector's tote was coming from," Mildred said. "When I visited here I was told in no uncertain terms that private firearms ownership was major illegal."

The *alcade* smiled. "And such proscriptions worked about as well here as elsewhere, as well as the war on drugs, for that matter. You'd be surprised what we've found in private dwellings. Nevertheless, as you surmise, our heavier armament comes from military and paramilitary police arsenals such as this one. They tended to be very well built and sealed. We've successfully salvaged several that were altogether submerged."

"Nasty work," J.B. said.

"Dangerous and difficult. But highly profitable. Don Hector pays handsomely for the weapons and munitions we provide him." His voice took on a tint of irony at the mention of his rival baron.

Ryan, who had been admiring the collection of blasters as raptly as the others, suddenly swiveled his head to stare at Tenorio. "You sold him those wrist-mounted lasers. His people never found them."

"Yes, we did. And I have often wished we had not. Did he tell you otherwise?" The older man chuckled dryly. "I suppose that shouldn't surprise me."

"Why'd you sell blasters like that to a crazy man the likes of Hector?" Mildred asked.

"We didn't realize fully what they were."

"How's that possible?" Ryan asked.

"Come with me," the baron said. "I shall explain."

He led them to a stairway down, where he once again switched on the heavy flashlight he carried, powered by a scavenged D-cell battery. Through muted echoes and weirdly shifting shadows they descended.

"While the computer equipment in this facility was functional when we found it, the disks contained no data. We surmise that this joint facility was used in part to conduct off-budget research on behalf of some agency of the United States government, possibly the famous Defense Advanced Research Projects Agency, possibly the DEA, possibly someone altogether different."

Ryan glanced back at Doc, whose eyebrows were raised in comical surprise. The nineteenth-century professor had intimate experience with a supersecret and off-budget U.S. government research project: the Totality Concept and its Operation Chronos, which had snatched him from his own time and hurled him a hundred years forward to the end of the twentieth century.

They descended into another cool, musty chamber. Tenorio switched on the overhead lights at the entry and clicked off his flashlight.

"Dark night," J.B. breathed. "This is a real treasure trove."

The *alcade* smiled at him. "I see you appreciate the equipment here."

The Armorer all but stumbled forward, half dazed, like a latter-day wine fancier who had stumbled into one of the fabled lost cellars of Cali. "Bridgeport…Clausen lathe…looky here—an old Monarch toolmaker's lathe, I mean it was old when they laid this place down. A real jewel. And this—"

He paused by a box-shaped object the size of a small wag, ran his hands over its red and white exterior. "This here's some kind of multiple axis CNC machine—a living steel mill." He sighed and removed his hands from it as reluctantly as he might have from a lover's skin.

"I'd have no clue how to work this baby, even if it still runs. This is stuff outta legend."

Mildred moved to his side, put her arm around his waist. He took off his spectacles and polished them reverently.

"You are knowledgeable indeed, Señor Dix. Even though the machines are functional—" he walked to the Monarch, a relatively small machine, gray-enameled and with smooth, almost melted-looking contours, switched it on, engaged the clutch; the head spun, motor purring with cat-smooth power "—none of us possesses any but the most rudimentary skills at machining."

He gestured. "There are devices here more advanced even than the tabletop CNC mill that has so impressed your armorer, machines whose functions we can but dimly guess, if at all. It was down here that we found stored a dozen peculiar objects, like bulky plastic armlets."

He switched off the lathe. "In those days we were quite naive, more enthusiastic than wise. This structure was among the first we explored extensively, since it was one of the very few not flooded. We were excited by the rich trove of weapons stored above. Those at least we understood—perhaps I need not tell you that by disposition and education, we were traders and explorers, not fighters. We have some skill with weapons now, and knowledge of them. It was gained, as you might imagine, by sheer brutal experience. In the end, we happened to mention our find to Don Hector, then a young village *alcade* himself, a man obviously on the rise, with intellect and vision. He made us an offer for the mysterious objects. Because we needed resources to expand our toehold in the city, we accepted."

"And he figured out what they were?" Ryan asked.

"One of the cases had a manual in it. Can you believe how naive we were?"

"'Every weapon has a manual,'" Mildred said.

"How's that?" J.B. asked.

"Nothing. Just a quote from an old movie."

"We also discovered a number of energy cells subsequently," Tenorio said. "We sold them to Hector." He shrugged. "What could we do? They only fit the laser weapons. And Hector was our friend then, already helping to protect us from raiders. It was a mutually beneficial relationship. One which we thought would endure."

"What happened, Don Tenorio?" Krysty asked.

Jak snorted. "Power."

"Of course your young friend is right, *señorita*. From what began as a defensive alliance of independent settlements in the valley, he saw he could begin to weld himself an empire of sorts. And also…"

The *alcade*'s words trailed away, as if his spring had wound down. He looked older than they had seen him look before.

"And also what, Don Tenorio?" Doc asked.

Tenorio shrugged. "Perhaps it's nothing. But he also began to be first interested, then obsessed, with the traditions of the valley."

He looked at them. "The *ancient* traditions, from the days before the Spanish arrived—of human sacrifices to monster gods. It has always seemed to me that the change in his character dated from the time he began to delve into them."

Ryan and Krysty shared a glance. "I can believe it," she said. "There's much dark power in that one."

"There is power and there is darkness, surely. More than that, I cannot say. But come."

He led them through the large chamber, which was crowded by mechanisms mostly unfamiliar to Ryan. From the rapt but puzzled expression on J.B.'s face, the one-eyed chiller could tell his friend didn't recognize them, either.

"We're gonna have to hog-tie him to keep him from spending all his time down here," Mildred said with a twinkle in her eye. "This is pure toyland to him."

"Won't work," the Armorer chortled, rubbing his square work-hardened hands. "I'm an escape artist."

"Have to get our host's permission first," Ryan reminded him.

Don Tenorio glanced back. "You are all my honored guests for as long as you might choose to stay. This was so before you saved my poor life not once, but twice. But I hope you will forgive me if I consider ways I might make use of your extraordinary skills and ingenuity, to our mutual benefit. I would be happy to provide Señor Dix total access to this workshop, for instance, and such assistance as he might prefer, if he would be willing to share whatever knowledge he can glean about the purpose and workings of these mechanisms with us."

J.B. looked at Ryan, his eyes seeming to swim behind the round lenses of his glasses. He reminded Ryan of a kid who'd had a spotted puppy trail him home and was now beseeching his daddy, "Can I keep it?"

"You are going to have to keep him sedated to keep him away now," Mildred said.

"See no reason to say no," Ryan said, "for as long as we stay."

"And I hope that is a good long time," Tenorio said. "In particular, I wish to speak to Don Ryan concerning such matters this very evening. But now I have something else I would like you to see—our pet mystery."

At the far end of the high-tech wonderland of a workshop was a plain metal door, enameled olive drab. Aside from the relative absence of nicks and weather-fading it was absolutely as generic as a door could be. So why was Ryan suddenly licking his lips to moisten them and feeling a slight acceleration in his pulse?

Tenorio threw open the door. This time a light came on by itself. Inside the door was a small vestibule, then a much larger, more imposing door.

Also a very familiar sort of door.

There was a big sign beside the second door. Peligro, it said in big red letters, and also Danger. And below, in English and Spanish, was a warning: Tezcatlipoca Redoubt. Secured Facility. Authorized Personnel Only. Intruders Will Be Killed Without Warning.

Below it was a simple keypad. Also very familiar.

"We have not yet mastered the sequence to allow us entry," Don Tenorio said through the pulse thunder in Ryan's ears. "Someday, perhaps even with your assistance, we shall learn what lies beyond this door."

WHEN THEY RETURNED to the cabin cruiser, which was moored in a drowned street next to the plaza, there was a message waiting that had come in by radiophone. The scavvies' talkies wouldn't function deep in the bowels of a building, with all that structural steel around. Once aboard, the *alcade* listened to what his bespectacled and ever-serious chief aide, young Ernesto, rapidly told him. Then he approached his guests.

"I hope you will not find it inconvenient if we make a detour rather than return directly to my quarters."

Ryan looked around. "We don't exactly have plans for the rest of the evening," Krysty said, summing up the group's sentiment.

Tenorio nodded, uncharacteristically brisk and silent.

"What's going on?" Ryan asked.

"I prefer to show you, if you will bear with me."

The big, white water wag worked its way to the north edge of the drowned downtown, detouring only around blocked avenues or known hidden snags. The pilot was giving it as much throttle as he dared, relying on his knowledge of the dangers and the blue-white glare of a spotlight mounted alongside the .50-caliber. As always the blaster was manned by a Jaguar Knight.

Fallen buildings obscured their view until they entered the final block that led to the city's northern edge. Then they could see columns of smoke rising pale against the star-shot black sky, lit from their bases with flickering glares of yellow and orange, for all the world like miniature volcanoes.

"Smokies?" Jak asked.

"Villes," Krysty answered grimly. "Those are houses burning."

Tenorio nodded.

"A display of petulance by our friend Don Hector?" Doc wondered.

"Chichimecs," the *alcade* said. "Their whole army is on the march south. Advance patrols are setting light to villages before them."

"I thought they didn't burn the villes they captured," Ryan said, "since they're looking to move in and stay."

"It seems they now choose to announce their presence in a very graphic way. I believe it is a challenge."

Ernesto emerged from the red-lit cabin to murmur to his boss. Tenorio listened, frowning slightly.

"And now it seems we have received an emissary from Don Hector bearing a profuse apology," Tenorio told the companions. "Also a parcel."

"A parcel?" Ryan asked.

The baron nodded.

IT SEEMED the smokies had decided to yield stage to the burning villes. Their eruptions had died back to sullen furnace glow on the overcast above Popocatépetl and Iztaccíhuatl, and the occasional deep-throat grumble echoing across the oil-dark water.

Ryan again stood alone with Don Tenorio on the terrace of his headquarters. This time instead of refreshments there were two containers on the table. Ryan avoided looking at them.

"Here is the favor I would beg of you, Ryan Cawdor," Don Tenorio said. "I would ask you to aid me as my war chief, commander of my forces."

Ryan looked at him, his gaze bleak. It took him a moment to register what the small, slight baron had said, and not simply because it had come right out of the blue. Krysty had taken sick immediately after dinner; she'd eaten with her customary appetite, then promptly thrown it up. Mildred suspected she hadn't recovered fully from her infection, even though the wound itself was healed, or possibly that her immune system had directed its efforts so totally to healing the injury and fighting off the infection from the dung-smeared crossbow bolt that a secondary infection might have gotten a foothold in her stomach. Mildred was tending her now in the spare but comfortable quarters Tenorio had provided Ryan and Krysty. The physician had urged him not to worry about Krysty.

"Come again, Baron?" he said. He couldn't believe the message his ears belatedly got through to his brain.

"I asked if you would take command of the city's defense forces."

Ryan rubbed his jaw. It had grown stubbly, though he had shaved his chin clean that morning, as he did when he had luxury of time and water.

"With due respect, Don Tenorio, I walked away from being a baron, so I'm not likely to agree to be sec boss for any man. I'm sorry."

Tenorio shook his head. "You misunderstand, my friend. I was planning to ask this of you before poor Colonel Solano was murdered this afternoon. I can find another sec chief. He had a few able lieutenants. What we lack is war leadership. From your tales of past deeds I perceive you have ample experience in war. You are clearly a leader of great ability, to hold your group together on such a long and perilous journey—of which I gather this is only your latest. And the resourcefulness and resolution and ability to *command*—not just men but situations—which you have displayed impressed me deeply."

"But you have warriors, too. What about Five Ax and your other Jaguar Knights?"

"They are brave and skillful, indeed. But they are also young and…how would you say? Limited by their lack of experience. Five Ax is a superb commando and small unit leader. Perhaps some day he will mature into a strategist, as well. But that time remains in the future. In the meantime we must go to war against the Chichimecs—now, tomorrow. And we must march alongside the forces of Don Hector, while always looking over our shoulders at them. I despair at that necessity, but necessity it is. The Chichimecs have forced our hand. For all his courage and even his intelligence, young Five Ax is not the equal to that task."

"I'm not sure any man is," Ryan said.

"As it happens, Five Ax himself believes you are. He nominated you for war leader, although the notion had occurred to me before he spoke."

"It's a pretty huge responsibility you're asking me to take on, Don Tenorio. Your people don't know me."

"You are far too modest. Everyone in the valley knows of the intrepid band of traders from *el norte*. Including, I have no doubt, the Chichimecs. Nezahualcoyótl has astonishingly good intelligence sources among Hector's people and even here in the city."

Ryan suspected that was a good indication Tenorio needed a sharper, more active sec boss than the unfortunate colonel had been. Since he was dead set in not considering that position, whatever else went down, he kept his peace on the subject.

"You can't expect too much from us. You can't expect wonders. We'll help you against the Chichimecs. I've spoken with the others and we're agreed on that. But for anything beyond that…we're just people."

"All heroes are 'just people.' All villains, too."

"Mebbe you're right. Reckon you are. But I don't know enough about your forces. Don't even know how many fighters you got."

"We can certainly provide for you all the information you need."

"Not hardly. Not overnight. I can't just waltz in here and have any idea what I'm trying to do."

The *alcade*'s shoulders slumped. "Yet we must go to battle soon. And I can't leave my fighters at the mercy of Don Hector."

"I sure was wrong about that one," Ryan admitted. "He can't be trusted, no matter what he does to try to convince you."

At that both men turned and looked at the objects resting on the table. The emissary who had crossed the causeway under a white truce flag had been insistent on the *cacique*'s behalf that the attack that afternoon had been carried out against Don Hector's wishes and against his express orders. His sec boss, Mendoza, had performed the treachery on his own initiative.

To demonstrate his good faith, and sincere contrition for the treacherous assault, Don Hector had sent Mendoza's head in a clear glass jug. His eyes and mouth were wide open in a look of agony and horror. Next to the jug rested a largish earthenware pot with a lid. This contained what was purported to be the sec boss's heart. Tenorio had told the companions he presumed it had been carved from Mendoza's chest while he was still living, in the traditional manner.

"Poor Mendoza," Don Tenorio said. "He really wasn't a bad sort. Not truly cut out for secret police work. Which is no doubt why it's his head in the jar."

"I tell you what. I'll go out with your people, do

what I can to help in the upcoming battle. It'll give me a chance to learn about them. Then if there has to be a continuing campaign—and sure enough there's going to be—these Chichimecs'll just pull back to come at you later if they start getting the worst of things, and I doubt you and Hector together have enough people to bag them all, keep them from getting away—if the war goes on, we'll see what I can do for you."

"But who will command my forces? I can't just turn them over to Hector."

"No. You can't. You've got to lead them."

"But what am I to do? I have no idea how to command troops in battle."

"You read a lot of history, don't you?" Ryan didn't bother to specify predark history; that went without saying. Here, as up north in the Deathlands, what was known of the years since the Big Nuke wasn't written down. It was passed along in oral traditions, spotty and more than half mythologized when there was any truth to the tales at all. Or when people even bothered. What a lot of people felt, even if most couldn't articulate it, was, Ryan knew, *The past? Look what it's done for us. Fuck it.*

"I have, yes." Tenorio said.

"Military history?"

The *alcade* smiled. "I remember an impressive list of names—of battles and who won them. I know when they happened and where. As to what actually happened and why—"

He spread his hands. "I might say I know enough to

be dangerous. This would not be true. I don't even know enough to delude myself I know anything of use."

Ryan nodded decisively. "Tell you what, then. Let me leave Doc back with you while the rest of us go out with your troops. He's a big student of history. Might even say he was part of history himself. He knows his way around a fight from firsthand experience as well as reading about it. He can advise you, at least keep Don Hector from leading you down any slaughterhouse chutes. Beyond that, you got good judgment and sense. You'll just have to rely on them."

"So it must be, I suppose."

Ryan looked back to the grisly trophies on the table. "I gotta admit I'd feel better about this," he said, "if it was a red-haired woman's head in that fireblasted jar."

Chapter Nineteen

"Now this," J.B. said, affectionately patting the dark-blue steel receiver of the Browning automatic rifle cradled across his lap, "is what going to war is all about."

It was a high, wide day, bright blue above with just a few fluffy clouds rolling along, mostly green around them, although the southern sky was smudged with a nasty pall of smoke. They didn't look that way much, being as they were headed north toward the invading human-mutant horde. They had a dirt road to drive, and it had been several days since rain, which meant the valley's mostly foot-slogging defenders were at least spared the infantryman's ancient nemesis, mud.

Three of the companions shared the big wag with the nuke battery. Ryan drove. Jak rode shotgun in the machine-gun mount—which now mounted an actual machine gun, an M-60 7.62 mm blaster lent them by Don Tenorio out of the FJP armory—and J.B. was sprawled in the back seat chortling over his own loaner auto-blaster. Krysty was sick with her relapse, delirious with fever. Ryan had left her back in the city in Mildred's capable, and at least confident-seeming, hands and tried to shut a door on all thought of her and lock it down tight for the duration of the fight; a man who headed into a major blood-spilling with a divided mind was asking to wind up at air temperature. Doc, per Ryan's suggestions, remained back at the joint command post with Don Tenorio, advising him on tactics and generally keeping an eye on him, with the help of half a dozen Jaguar Knights, who while upset about missing out on the fight understood the need to discourage any further lapses of judgment on the part of Hector's underlings.

Upset at missing out on a fight. Ryan shook his head. What a concept.

Ryan had the wag crawling along beside a marching column of two-hundred-odd city troops. Well, armed scavvies, at any rate; aside from the handful of so-called Jaguar Knights, who had chosen to train themselves into pretty good facsimiles of old-time commandos, they didn't seem to have much notion of a military way of doing things. Still, their spirits were high and they seemed ready to fight. Most of them *had* fought, against the various deadly dangers lurking in the city if nothing else.

Ryan knew that was the biggest factor in determining how people did in combat. If you'd been shot at before, or even had to struggle for your life against some kind of immediate danger, you were that much less likely to break, to lose your head and get yourself or your buddies chilled. Seeing the elephant, Doc called it.

Also, at least all the scavvies had weapons, even if half of them carried no more than handblasters. That was an edge they had over Don Hector's motley bunch.

Ryan had been surprised and even a little disappointed on first getting a look at the vaunted valley army. There were about thirty Eagle Knights, including five or six of the laser-armed officers mounted on motorcycles. There were maybe fifty generic sec men in scavenged khaki uniforms, not always complete and not all identical—apparently it was the thought that counted. They were fairly well armed, with at least longblasters. The Eagle Knights carried submachine guns, FN FALs, a couple of BARs. The sec men's pieces ranged from FNs and Garands down through bolt guns—some ancient military Springfields and Enfields, some sporting rifles—to shotguns and lever-action rifles. A very heavily armed force, by postdark standards, mounting pretty serious firepower.

Not so the three or four hundred hapless valley peons who made up the bulk of Hector's army. These had apparently been conscripted right out of the villes and fields. A fair number of these had seen the elephant themselves, in Don Hector's various little wars and police actions as he'd sought to bring the valley under control, or in patrols and skirmishes against the Chichimecs. They'd fight.

But most were green as budding apples. They'd been trained to march, and been taught discipline—or at least been trained to fear their commanders, which Ryan knew some thought was the same thing. But they were visibly terrified, rolling their eyes in anticipation of contact with the enemy.

No more than half of them armed with blasters. Such

blasters as they had did tend to be higher tech and quality than what the Chichimecs carried. The lucky ones
got bolt-action rifles or even one of a few Garands. The
others who actually carried guns had to make do with
weapons all the way down the firepower food chain to
single-shot shotguns and even a couple of little skinny
break-action rifles that J.B. swore had to fire .22 Long
Rifle—a round that would kill you just as dead as any
other, and indeed could cause insidious internal bleed-
ing that was hard to detect or treat, but that wouldn't be
anybody sane's first choice as a battle rifle. Of the other
half of the troops, some carried machetes or cane cut-
ters, which were essentially machetes with long handles,
some long enough to qualify as pole weapons. Others
just had clubs, and some…well, maybe they had pocket
knives tucked away somewhere.

"The real stickie in the swimming hole in all of this,"
J.B. said, "is ammunition." He was examining his own
stock that had come with the Browning, .30-06 rounds
loaded into 20-round magazines, plus a couple cases of
cartridges in boxes, in the optimistic hope that he might
have a chance to recharge his mags.

With a whine of a 250 cc engine, Five Ax came rock-
eting up to them on a Honda dirt bike, back along the
column from scouting up ahead. That was the bitch
about being separated from Doc and Mildred: they were
the ones who spoke, and more importantly understood,
Spanish. Fortunately, a decent minority of the scavvies
could communicate passably in English. So for that
matter could most of Hector's officers—caste distinc-

tions being the sort of thing he liked to encourage. But where Five Ax was concerned, he and Ryan had never from the outset had much trouble talking to each other even though Ryan knew no Spanish whatever and the Jaguar Knight spoke no English. They just naturally seemed to share a commo channel.

"Chokepoint ahead looks clear," the Jaguar Knight got across, "but I don't like it."

"I hear you." Ryan already knew what he was talking about. Starting just a couple hundred yards ahead of them now the road ran along a hogsback ridge on the left-hand side for perhaps a quarter mile, while on the right, paralleling it no more than a hundred yards away, ran a lower but still elevated spline of weed-grown lava flow. Ambush heaven.

"Aw, now," J.B. said, tongue firmly in cheek, "what are we getting all spooky about? Don Hector promised us there's no Chichimecs nearer than two, three miles from where we are now."

"Yeah, right," Ryan said mirthlessly. They were working to a timetable, which meant that they couldn't do a halfway decent job scouting the heights; *real* recon meant going on foot, quiet and methodical, not roaring around in a wag or on a bike, which Five Ax well knew. The necessity of joining up with Hector's forces in time to deploy properly also meant they couldn't jump off the road and drive cross-country around one or another jaw of the potential trap.

He stopped the wag, got out. Taking his lead, the column came to a halt, fell out for a smoke and a swallow of water from their bottles. To keep up appearances, there was a city man named Obiedo in charge of the force, but Tenorio had passed the word that any suggestions Ryan might see fit to make were to be treated as commands.

Jak stayed snuggled up to the receiver of his machine gun. It wasn't just that he enjoyed the potential power riding around in the thing. He was staring at the pass up ahead as if invisible laser beams from his ruby eyes might spring out and melt away concealment from around any ambushers. He knew they were headed straight into potential death ground as well as anybody.

There were two other wags with the column, carrying extra water and ammo, each mounting a .308-caliber MG, one an M-60 like the one mounted on the Hummer, the other an FN MAG-58. They stopped, one halfway back the column, the other pulling rear guard. Their gunners were likewise alert behind their mounted blasters.

Ryan made use of a gift from Don Tenorio, a little low-power Simmons monocular—a baby eight-power telescope that would ride in a pocket, which they'd scavenged out of the drowned city. Not the finest precision optics, but very handy, and just the ticket for a one-eyed man.

"Nothing," he said, lowering the scope. "Which don't mean there's nothing there. Five Ax, make sure everybody's eyes are open. If we get jumped, our best chance of survival is cut left and go balls-out right up that ridge."

Five Ax nodded. He understood that the best thing to do in an ambush was to charge straight into the teeth of your ambushers. Ryan wondered if the essentially civilian scavvies understood, as well. He voiced the concern to J.B. as he got back in the wag.

"Might," was J.B.'s response. "Raids and ambushes are probably just what they're used to."

"If not,'" Jak growled from behind his blaster, "too late now."

And then it was too late.

Another bike scout had gone riding down to the far end of the pass: Claudia, the fearless spelunker, one of the few women with the city force. She slowed, turned to ride back to the column.

Suddenly, Chichimecs swarmed over her, seeming to boil up out of the ground like wasps out of holes.

Chapter Twenty

Claudia was carrying a Ruger Mini-14 with a folding stock as well as her old M&P handblaster. She managed to get the carbine into action one-handed. Ryan heard shots crack as her engine whined to sudden acceleration.

Neither did any good. The raiders were all over her at once, pulling her off the bike and wresting the blaster from her hands.

The marching scavvies heard her scream. The mutie and human mob was seething in a mound over and around her like pack predators.

"Eating," Jak said tersely.

With a shriek of his engine and a squeal of rubber spinning on hard-rutted earth, her lover Ricardo started to peel away to her rescue. "Stop that man or he's dead!" Ryan shouted.

A burly bearded scavvie with a scar down one side of his face and a slung M-16 stuck an arm out and clotheslined Ricardo right off his ride just as he launched himself. He felt onto his back and lay stunned.

Others were stung into action. They began to run along the road, drawing or unslinging blasters.

"Five Ax, stop them," Ryan yelled. "It's a trap! They're trying to lure us in to rescue her."

Five Ax began hollering commands. He rode his own bike forward in front of the men running up the road, cutting in front of them like a sheepdog. They stopped, staring at him in angry consternation.

"Jak," Ryan said quietly.

The M-60 blasted off with an ear-tearing snarl, rocking the Hummer back on its suspension. The scavvies who had run down the road ducked as the rounds cracked over their heads. A couple flung themselves facedown on the road. The rest scattered into the scrub, right where Ryan wanted them.

Jak was no ace blasterman, but did know enough about machine guns to fire bursts, booming clusters of four or five or six rounds. He dropped his first one into the road fifty yards short of the feeding frenzy. Then, using the dust thrown up by the bullets striking ground, he walked his fire right into the tangle of limbs and bodies. Ryan thought he saw a mutie brandish an arm torn off the beautiful female scout. Then the bullet storm was upon them.

The M-60 was nowhere so lordly as mighty Ma Deuce; it fired rifle rounds, the same as Ryan's SSG, in fact. But it fired a lot of them. And while the .308s didn't have the power to turn a body inside out the way the .50s did, there was nothing weak about them, either.

At this range Jak's bursts took the Chichimecs and their human prey like a scythe. Blood and parts splashed. Claudia's screams were drowned by those of her assailants, and then all went quiet.

Several ambushers broke away with red mouths and tried to bolt back to cover. Nice try; they died.

In a scatter of seconds nothing lived on the road. Jak came off the trigger. The last ejected empties and metal links from the ammunition belt tinkled down into the hardpan. There was a lot of silence. The valley was a bowlful of it.

After a moment Ryan became aware of the wind sighing through the grass and down the pass. A meadowlark sang; somewhere a mourning dove called out his territory with soft hoots. Birds didn't have a care for humans and their spats; never had. Except for vultures and crows. Glancing up, Ryan saw there were already two of the former on hand, black crucifixes wheeling against the sky.

Ryan came out of his briefly suspended state. Things were about to start happening in bunches. He leaned into the wag, grabbed out his Steyr and a pack with rats, extra mags and some grens stuffed into it.

"J.B., take the wheel," he said. "Take the wag up along that hogsback on the left. Bastards'll be all along it. You'll take them in enfilade. Burn them out, then pour in to the flanks of the rest when they come down the road at us. I'll send Five Ax and the other scooter scouts along."

J.B. laid aside his BAR and scrambled into the front seat. "You?"

"I'll run the reception committee down here."

J.B. nodded and the Hummer roared away. Ryan quickly explained what he wanted to Five Ax with words and gestures.

Ricardo had caught his breath enough to commence weeping and wailing. He abruptly broke away and went running right at Ryan, arms pinwheeling, shrieking like a man on fire. Fortunately he'd left his 12-gauge Winchester Defender scattergun slung. Ryan, holding his Steyr in both hands, waited him out, timed him. When the burly berserk man got in range, Ryan wheeled the butt of his Steyr up and around and laid it against the side of his head. He did it as gently as possible under the circumstances, which wasn't very, more pushing with the wooden stock like a paddle than swinging free. It was done as much to preserve the alignment of the optics as to save the bearded scavvie's life. Ricardo went sprawling, clutching at the dust and moaning.

Ryan looked around, caught the eye of a scavvie he knew spoke English. "Get him squared away. If he tries for me again, I'll chill him now. The rest of you, get off the road, spread out in a line facing up the road, find yourself some decent cover and get ready to rumble."

They stared at him for a moment. He was acutely aware of being a stranger among them. He had been reluctant to make use of his supposed authority. Now he saw no choice.

The man he'd told to see to Ricardo looked up from where he knelt beside him. Miguel, Ryan thought his name to be. "This isn't where we're supposed to fight," the scavvie said. "We're supposed to meet Hector first."

"This is war, friend. You fight where it finds you, not where you planned."

Time was getting short. The Chichimecs were probably

on the move already under cover, knowing their ambush was spoiled. "Time's blood," Ryan said. "Your move."

Miguel shouted in Spanish to his comrades. They broke up, disappearing into the scrub on both sides of the road. Miguel dragged the dazed Ricardo out of sight.

In a moment Ryan was alone except for the two wags. He gestured them to come up, then pull off to either side of the road to lay down a serious fire base. It would be better tactics, he knew, to wing them out to either end of the firing line, lay down interlocked fields of fire, but he knew what was coming. He was afraid of the Chichimecs creepy-crawling up through the brush and dead ground and taking them out with grens or pipe bombs or a plain old body-swarm. Better to let the groundpounders buffer the wags; they couldn't afford to lose the heavy weps, especially this early in the game.

And now from the pass ahead came the first evidence that an attack was coming. A spatter of shots was thrown at the scavvies as they dispersed and went to ground. Big puffs of white smoke thrown out by blackpowder blasters rolled up into the sky.

Without rushing it, Ryan moved to a grassy mound crowned by some kind of bush. He took up position behind the low mound, got the Steyr's bipod steel buttplate into his shoulder, his cheek welded to the stock, his eye up to the telescope.

He had expected a certain amount of anger when the *gringos* took it upon themselves to chop pretty, popular Claudia to worm bait along with her attackers. But though ville dwellers, and for the most part no warriors, the scavvies were anything but sheltered. They well understood that sometimes the best gift one friend could give another was a quick death.

Ryan laid his crosshairs on the road. A party of Chichimecs had appeared halfway along the pass, trotting in the open with a tireless coyote gait, carrying the usual random assortment of bloodletting implements. Laziness and bloodlust were getting the better of judgment. He grinned and aimed at the chest of a big guy with impressive steerlike horns and a military-style, bolt longblaster, a Springfield or a Mauser.

Before Ryan could drop the hammer, the two machine guns from the scavvie supply wags spoke. The Chichimecs on the road were bowled over. Ryan saw his target's right arm ripped off. The horned man fell kicking.

Ryan shifted his aim to a norm-looking guy with an M-16 shagging his mostly bare ass into the brush, led him, fired. The Steyr's barrel rose irresistibly as he threw the bolt by long-engrained reflex. When it came back down, there was nothing but weeds in the glass. Deep down in his belly he felt a flash of self-disgust. He'd never know for sure, but he had a marksman's sense he'd missed the bastard cold.

Shots were cracking now from both sides and to the front. More black powder blaster smoke suddenly blossomed from the ridgeline to their left. Ryan heard somebody off to his left start to scream. Then he heard the unmistakable snarl of a machine gun.

His blood froze. What if they had an MG of their own up there? They'd smoke his wags, sure as nuke shit. Unable to elevate the rifle properly from a prone position, he rolled into a seated posture, cinching his left arm up in the shooting sling, aimed the rifle at the crest in hopes he could spot the raiders' bullet-sprayer if they had one.

HE NEEDN'T HAVE worried. The Hummer and the half dozen motorcycle scouts trailing prudently behind its comforting mass and still more comforting M-60 had reached the heights of the crestline. As Ryan had foreseen, they found several dozen Chichimecs armed with longblasters strung out along the ridgetop in a line away from them. Since the ambushers had set up to sweep the column down on the road with fire, they had made no effort to conceal themselves from the sides.

J.B. stopped the wag and bailed out with his BAR as Jak poured blazing death right along the Chichimec rifle line. More concerned himself with letting potential targets escape than his own safety, the Armorer just stood flatfooted by the open door, shouldered the heavy automatic rifle and began splashing muties and human raiders with well-placed sprays of .30-06.

To either side of him Five Ax and the other riders just stopped their bikes, shouldered longblasters and fired from the saddle. The raiders went over like bottles being shot off a bawdy-house bar.

The Chichimecs were hard-core bastards, J.B. had to give them that. Some of them actually turned and shot back. One of the scooter scouts slumped abruptly, drilled clean through the heart by a .30-30. As he and his light bike toppled into the grass, his comrades chopped down the human who had chilled him and everybody else in sight.

J.B. tossed his Browning into the back seat of the Hummer with blue smoke still trailing from its muzzle, jumped back behind the wheel and put the hammer down. The wag's nuke-powered electric engine was surprisingly quiet as it shifted its mass into motion, or maybe it was the ringing in his ears from all those shots going off. He took the wag bucketing along back of the ridgeline with Jak hosing down anything that moved or looked as if it might as they passed.

To the left, a wide brown guy popped out of a bush, raising a blaster made of pipe wired and taped to a rude wooden stock. "Here, catch," J.B. said, tossing him a pineapple-style M-26 gren from which he'd thoughtfully pulled the pin. The spoon went spinning away with a musical little twang. Reflex took over and, amazingly enough, the mutie *did,* catch it that is, dropping his improvised blaster to field the gren two-handed. He was staring down at the fizzing bomb cradled in both hands when J.B. swept by. The Armorer heard the blast but didn't get to see it shred the mutie's upper torso and blow off his face and both hands.

A QUICK GLANCE THROUGH the scope told Ryan the machine gun belonged to the good guys. A bullet from his own front thunked into his protecting mound as he flopped down behind it once again. He got the piece braced again and began to sweep the pass for targets.

The scope suddenly went dark.

There was one right answer and Ryan gave it. He squeezed the trigger on the spot. The SSG roared and bucked. The Chichimec who had jumped up right in front of its muzzle, raising an ax with a yellow synthetic haft two-handed to split Ryan's skull, instead screamed as the heavy boattailed bullet punched through his pelvis. He fell onto his face across the gun, dropping the ax.

Ryan was already out from behind the Steyr, rolling hard to the left, hauling out his SIG-Sauer. He got the weapon free as a Chichimec came leaping over a bush at him, jabbing with a spear. Lying on his back, Ryan pumped two slugs through his attacker's belly. The man went down shrieking and flailing right next to him. More to keep the wounded man from fouling his aim with a thrashing arm than from any kindness, Ryan put the muzzle up by the raider's ear and quick-bored a hole through his head.

He came up on one knee. To the left and right of him shots were cracking, screams were ripped from sundered bodies, men struggled and cursed and smelled the breath and body reek of the man they were going to kill or who would kill them.

The Chichimecs had played it cagey. They had run up against rapid-firing blasters often enough to know that a balls-out charge across a couple hundred yards against a firing line waiting under cover would result in their getting chilled without ever getting in spear-cast range of their enemies. The few who had forgotten that lesson and tried trotting down the road had quickly been served up steaming and stinking of ruptured guts as an object lesson to their brothers.

So they had infiltrated under cover, squirming on their bellies with astonishing speed to close with the scavvies and then rush them from close range. The problem was the scavvies, even the pudgy soft-handed ones who got all cloudy and sniffly reading some poignant scrap of poetry in a moldy scavenged predark anthology, were accustomed to fighting like tigers one-on-one. The city was a hard place. It would kill you. Not just the careless; it just got you sooner if you were. Soon or late, it killed everybody presumptuous enough to invade its waterlogged fastnesses. Everybody on the fighting line had come to terms with that. And so far survived.

So most of the Chichimecs got blasted when they sprang. The others managed to leave some marks—the scavvies lost three killed and five wounded and bundled on the wags, excluding Claudia and the Jaguar Knight shot up on the ridge, and also not counting Claudia's squeeze Ricardo who marched and fought on despite a busted jaw. But the marauders were quickly beaten down, especially once J.B., Jak and the scooter scouts began flaying them from their own ambush site up on the hogsback.

Ryan chilled two more with his handblaster, a human with a break-action shotgun and a mutie with pebbled gray skin who wasn't holding a weapon at all, but crossed Ryan's sights and so had to die.

And it was over just like that.

Chapter Twenty-One

"You're late, Señor Cawdor," Don Hector told Ryan caustically as the Hummer pulled up to the command post, which was a recreational vehicle on a hilltop.

It was noontime, and he hadn't eaten since a handful of something he couldn't even remember, gulped down before sunrise, but Ryan's appetite for the *cacique*'s bullshit was strangely nil. "Chichimecs tried to bushwhack us two miles back, where you promised us we'd have a clear road. Took us a while to scrape them out of our way. Maybe you oughta chop the hearts out of a couple of your recon people to smarten them up a bit."

Hector's big square jaw jutted a bit more and the crow's feet outside his eyes—that showed if you looked close he wasn't as young as he liked to play—cut a little deeper into his dark skin. But he was good; he didn't let anything show past that.

"Perhaps you are right," he said smoothly and turned away. "Perhaps I shall."

Don Tenorio appeared out of the command RV with Doc behind him. Tenorio had on an open-collared white shirt and was wearing his .40-caliber handblaster holstered. He looked fresh. He made a conspicuous point of embracing Ryan.

"It is good to see you, my friend," he said. He already knew of the ambush on the road by radio. Radio communications were unreliable, and nobody was relying on them much, but made use of them as proved feasible.

"I was a little concerned about you and our friends," Ryan said, nodding slightly at Hector, who had strutted over to speak to some of his Eagle Knights.

Tenorio had ridden up with Hector and his forces to this staging point, agreed on the day before, about five miles north of the lake. Supposedly it lay directly in the path of the approaching Chichimec horde. Ryan didn't know how Don Hector knew that. There were a lot of things he didn't know about this setup, a fact he could basically like or lump.

"We were in no danger," Tenorio said. "Not even Hector's so big a fool as to act against us *before* the great battle."

He slapped Ryan on the shoulder. "Come, let me see to my people."

WHETHER THE CHICHIMECS had jumped the gun, or keen-eyed Claudia had spotted their ambush, or whether they had simply misjudged the psychology of the scavvies and miscalled the way they'd react to seeing one of their own torn to pieces in front of their eyes, Ryan never knew and never would. As gentle and peace-loving as the scavvies were in everyday life, they weren't loaded up with notions of mercy to foes. "Come for us and ours, you die" was the law they had lived by since Don Tenorio had led them or their parents into the half-sunk ruins a generation before. If any Chichimecs had tried to surrender, they'd been turned down terminally.

The scavvies' notion of first aid to fallen foes was administered with knives, rifle butts, handy rocks, or in the case of a couple of wounded who dragged themselves into the roadway as the column moved out—one trailing his guts behind him along the ground—the tires of their support wags. Conserving ammo. No skin off any part of Ryan's anatomy. It wasn't all that different from the rules he'd grown up playing by.

The city contingent rested in a hollow near Hector's war RV, not very well drained and so somewhat marshy. They were bitching about Hector sticking them there but were in generally good spirits. They were telling the story of the abortive ambush to their buddies who had come up with Tenorio's and Hector's bunch, and affecting to be matter-of-fact about the whole thing.

While Tenorio saw to the wounded and went among his people, speaking to them as if they were members of his family, Ryan, with Doc, J.B. and Jak, took stock of the forces assembled. Aside from his groundpounders Hector had three big wags mounting Browning M-2 .50-calibers, and several tripod mounted M1919A4 machine guns in .30 caliber, heavy suckers that needed to be carried in several pieces, then had to be assembled to be ready for action. Once they were properly emplaced, they were deadly. Ryan was glad he wouldn't be trying to fumble one of the beasts together while muties were jumping out of the bushes at him with obsidian daggers in their teeth.

For the first time Ryan saw the multiple-rocket launchers, home-built on the beds of converted pickups, which Five Ax's patrol had fired into the abandoned ville to spring the companions from Two Arrow that first day. The projectiles they launched were likewise improvised—not terribly accurate, but all the artillery the entire army had. Hector didn't believe in it, himself. It wasn't macho, apparently. There were also two more city supply trucks mounted with .308-caliber MGs.

"How did our friends bear up under their first trial of fire, Ryan?" Doc asked.

"They're not true coldhearts, but they'll do what needs to be done," Ryan said. "They don't fear the sight of blood, theirs or anybody else's. Whether they can stand up depends on what the Chichimecs throw at us."

"What about Hector's gang?" J.B. asked.

"Less impressive than their leader's bombast or the barbaric splendor of his bodyguards," said Doc. "Still, some are well-seasoned. The rest will stand so long as they fear Hector more than the invaders."

"And there you have it," J.B. said, cleaning his glasses.

THE CITY TROOPS WERE set on the right wing of the army, such as it was, and the whole mob was sent on its way north, led by Eagle Knight pathfinders on motorcycles. Ryan kept his own motorcycle scouts deployed close to their own front and covering their own right, which was otherwise open all the way to the eastern mountains. Don Hector was apparently the executive sort of leader who watched the battle and directed it from well behind the action, rather than a follow-me type. Ryan suspected that was the only way to manage a force of this size.

Still, he wasn't sure that was the only reason Hector was trailing along well behind the advancing force. The *cacique* was probably as bold as any man, one on one. But the prospect of being laid low by a blaster fired by some distant peasant would horrify him beyond endurance.

Tenorio was still back with his fellow baron, mainly to keep an eye on him. Doc had once again stayed at the *alcade*'s side. Ryan was just as glad. It wasn't as if one blaster more or less was going to make much difference in what was to come, and the old man didn't really need to go through the panic and exertion of someone else's fight.

The country rolled gently away from the lake, broken up by fewer lava flows than were common further south. Once they had a couple hills between them and Hector, Ryan summoned Five Ax, Miguel and a couple of the other English-speaking city folk.

"Spread the word to start dragging heels, just a bit. We want to let the main force get at least a couple hundred yards ahead of us."

"What for?" somebody he didn't recognize asked.

That was the price he had to pay, Ryan reckoned, for not having any official status. His orders could be questioned, because, after all, he had no standing to *give* orders. Of course, given what an independent bunch the scavvies were, they might've questioned him even if Tenorio had given him a shiny new uniform and a chestful of medals.

"I don't like advancing blind like this," he said. "Chichimecs already tried to trap us once. They might spring a bigger trap, try to bag the whole army. Whatever we run into, I want Hector's people to run into it first."

The scavvies spoke to each other in Spanish, but it was quickly apparent they agreed with his reasoning.

"But what will *they* say?" Miguel nodded toward the larger body of troops tramping along to the west. Their own officers were yipping at them like sheepdogs, trying to urge them on faster to the unseen foe.

"They're such machos they'll never notice we're not keeping up," Five Ax said. "Or if they do, they'll just sneer at us for a pack of cowards."

The scavvies laughed and spread the word. They didn't shrink from a fight, but they weren't going to go running to look for one, either. And it seemed the notion of letting the first blow land on the forces of the arrogant Don Hector struck them as a fine joke.

The look J.B. gave his old friend, though, was even blander than usual. "You sure about this, Ryan? Those Eagle Knights and sec men don't mean a spent shell case. But what about when the big boys, the dons, tumble-wise?"

Ryan heard his friend. What he had done was nothing shy of revising the whole battle plan on his own hook.

"This isn't really our fight," he said, "but since we

made it ours, I figure we should win. And I can't go against what my gut tells me."

"Never saw anybody turn down a victory once it's won," acknowledged the Armorer. "Not even a pissed-off baron."

THE DAY REMAINED FINE, bright, warm but not oppressively hot. They made their way north a mile across green land and fields of crops, now sadly trampled, either by the defending forces or by the raiders. They had passed a burned-out ville maybe a mile to the east of them. Ryan kept the Hummer purring along slowly, pacing his troops, winged out maybe twenty yards to secure their own hanging right flank. The valley troops had moved out maybe three hundred yards in advance of the city contingent. As Ryan anticipated, nobody said anything to them about their tardiness. Don Hector was still in his manic phase, no doubt strutting and blustering for Don Tenorio's benefit and his own, back on the hill by his RV. His subcommanders with his actual army were too busy snarling and screaming themselves hoarse urging on their troops, whose pace was noticeably slacking.

"Surprised he doesn't just give his sec men whips to drive the draftees into battle," Ryan said.

"No doubt he'll think of it next time," J.B. said.

"Notice our boys're slowing to keep pace with them without my having to say so."

"Wearing down," J.B. observed. "Only thing runs a man's battery down faster than marching toward a fight is actually being in it."

"You got that right."

He had three MG wags now, the fourth having stayed back with the mobile command headquarters along with about thirty city fighters, with half a dozen of Tenorio's small corps of elite Jaguar Knights among them. They were serving as bodyguards for the *alcade,* and likewise a mobile reserve, that being something else Don Hector didn't believe in. Between them Tenorio and the canny Doc surmised that Hector might have left as much as half of his armed strength back at his palace on Chapúltepec and among his subject villes, to keep the peons from getting notions about playing while the big cat was away. But everything he brought to the dance he was throwing straightaway at the invaders.

Ryan had two machine-gun wags up at the front, right now winged out twenty yards each, as far as he dared given the Chichimecs' propensity to lurk under cover and swarm. His scooter scouts circulated in front and to the flanks in hopes of spotting any infiltrators and ambushers, but staying close by so they wouldn't get wolf-packed without hope of rescue as Claudia had. When the city fighters deployed into a rifle line the machine-gun wags would this time deploy properly, to anchor either end and cross fires to the front. That was the theory, anyway; whether the Chichimecs would give them time to deploy was a whole other smoke. The third MG truck brought up the rear. When the hammer came down, it would be Ryan's reserve, which he could send to where its firepower was most urgently needed.

Also at the column's rear, just in front of the machine-gun truck, were the two multiple-rocket-launcher wags, which could shoot over the heads of the foot soldiers. All told, while he would naturally have preferred to have the hard-forged and tough-tempered chillers from Trader days with him, Ryan was as well set up as he could hope to be in terms of his own forces. The kicker was that he knew nothing at all about the enemy, except there were thousands of them, fanatical cold-hearts every one, that he didn't know where they were other than out there somewhere—and that they disposed of some kind of fearsome mutie powers.

Off to the right maybe sixty feet a metal post jutted at a crazy angle from the grass. It might have been a fence post, or a sign post, in predark times; he couldn't know. A meadowlark was perched on it, yellow breast with the deep black V-shaped collar glinting in the sun. He sang his distinctive trilling song as if nothing could go wrong in the world.

As Ryan watched him he took off and flew away south as if a devil were on his tail. From up ahead to the left came faint cries and the distinctive thump of shots.

"Here it comes," J.B. said, jacking the charging handle of his BAR and shoving it out the rear right-hand window.

"Look," Jak cried from the pintle.

A black shape in the sky to the northwest. A big shape, wings spread impossibly wide against the bright clouds high-piled above the horizon. It was bearing down on the valley force. Something in the way it moved told Ryan it was a beast, a mutie horror, not some kind of sky wag.

Coming to kill them.

Chapter Twenty-Two

They heard a distinctive, slow, deep rapping, joined instantly by another voice, and another. The flying mutie's wings suddenly went straight up and it dropped out of Ryan's sight to the ground, well in advance of the valley ranks. Jak whooped in triumph, although he hadn't busted off a round from his M-60.

"What in the name of blazing nuke death was that?" Ryan asked.

"Ma Deuce," J.B. said fondly. "Whatever the mutie was, it's cat food now. Flying fuckers don't stand a chance, this day."

No matter how dubious Ryan was of the bulk of Don Hector's forces, his machine gunners had seen a pack of hard fighting. They'd be steady as norms could be at the work they had to do. What remained to be seen was if that would be enough against what Howling Wolf and the Holy Child could throw at them.

"Wouldn't mind having a few myself," Ryan said. That had been Don Tenorio's own point of stinginess: the limited number of the big .50-cal MGs he had access to, he'd chosen to leave to guard the city, mostly on his handful of patrol boats, including the *Paloma*

Blanca. While he was serious as a sucking chest wound about concluding the war with this day's fight if at all possible, he still chose to hedge his bet. It should prove no big disadvantage. The Chichimecs had never shown sign of having war wags, and if they used powered wags at all for transport they never let them slip into sight of enemies.

Ryan honked his horn and waved his arm out the window. The column had stopped at sight of the giant flying mutie. At his signal the men began to spread out into a rough line. Ryan wasn't sure what kind of command structure he had under him, but the city fighters seemed to handle simple tasks and maneuvers well enough for the work at hand, so it was one more thing not to stuff his head with. He got on the squawk box to Five Ax. Miraculously it worked. He wasn't quite up to getting what he needed to across purely by speech, but he let the Jaguar Knight know he needed a palaver now, and here he came, bent low over the handlebars of his dirt bike, grinning.

"Make sure everybody watches the sky," he communicated. He had no idea how to say "screamwings" in Spanish so he didn't try. "Fliers. Bad."

Five Ax bobbed his head, threw up a wave of dirt that thunked against the door of the Hummer as he slewed his ride around and rode away.

"You, too, Jak," Ryan called. "We might have more flying friends come along."

"On it." The albino youth sounded aggrieved. Well, hell, this was battle. If there was an appropriate time to be pissed, this was it.

The battle noise from Hector's troops was coming fast and loud now. Apparently the flying mutie's appearance had coincided with contact with serious Chichimec forces. While he was still able to, Ryan took a swallow of water, recapped his bottle and slung it back to his belt.

He accelerated the wag and drove to a position just east beyond the end of the line that was forming. He waved to the city fighters to keep moving. They did, and he didn't have to tell them to be cautious.

A gentle swell of ground hid the developing battle from their sight. Ryan moved out deliberately in advance of what had become a skirmish line. "Jak! Sing out the second you see anything. I want to put us hull-down."

The Hummer purred upslope. "Now!" Jak shouted.

Carrying his Steyr, Ryan got out and climbed onto the hood. His Simmons hung by its lanyard around his neck. He raised it and surveyed the ground ahead.

The land fell away to a broad basin, apparently flat. The key word was "apparently." It was veined with low lava flows and greened-over rills that may have been drifts of ash long condensed into soil and rock by rain and sun, transversely cut by at least one shallow stream. Dead ground heaven, in other words, the kind where, with no obvious cover at all, you could hide an army.

Sure enough, the Chichimecs had.

"Called it right again, Ryan," J.B. observed, clambering up and standing on tiptoe beside him to see what the taller man could see. "Don Hector pissed away most of the advantage his blaster power gave him and walked his men right into the bastards. But what's this?"

Ryan was already looking, not off to the left, where battle was marked largely by writhing, wrestling bodies where the raiders had already come to grips with the front ranks of Hector's men, but directly in the path of his own force.

"Chichimecs," J.B. said, "swarming like maggots on a two-day-dead stiff. Least a thousand of them. More."

He looked at Ryan. "Damned good thing we hung back. They'd be on *us* right now like stink on a sec man."

Ryan nodded. There was something wrong here, bad wrong. If they'd kept up with Hector's men, that pullulating mass of human and mutie flesh would have crushed them like a bug, for all their machine guns and rockets. But pondering would have to wait.

It was time to chill. The city fighters were flopping down along the hilltop, using its mass for cover. The scooter scouts were chivvying the blaster wags into defilade positions like the one Ryan had parked the Hummer in, with only their gun mounts showing. Five Ax had his talkie to his mouth, feeding range and bearing data to the rocket wags.

The mass of warriors on the horde's left had struck at what was supposed to be the city force. Hitting only air, the invaders then did the natural thing, swarming like locusts over the bare right flank of Hector's main force and wrapping around behind it. It was a classic outflanking maneuver, and was about to have the classic result. Hector's battle line would be rolled up, his men would break and flee in screaming panic, throwing away their blasters as the Chichimecs ran them down and butchered them like hogs. The battle would be over in a rout.

But in turning to rat-pack Hector's lines, the Chichimecs bared their own flank to the late-arriving city forces.

It was slaughter. In their eagerness to deliver the kill shot to Hector's army, and probably to tear away the first mouthful of blood-pumping man-flesh, the mutie-norm mob had thrown away all thought of stealth. They were rushing forward in a wave, some actually trampling down and crushing those in front of them in a feeding frenzy.

It was like shooting babies in a barrel. Even the few city fighters armed with nothing more than handblasters couldn't miss, though the swarm was two hundred yards away. The machine guns cut swathes of flying limbs and spewing blood like invisible chainsaws. The rockets, after a couple of volleys threw up divots out in the weeds and the launcher crews found the range, blasted bodies spinning into the air.

"Ryan!" Jak shouted.

Ryan lowered his monocular. Chichimecs had appeared at the foot of the rise they were forted-up behind and were charging up at them. Too many and too close to make throwing the bolt and hunting in the narrow vision field of his scope a very survivable pastime. He slung the rifle, jumped to the ground, started reaching into his backpack for frag grens, pulling the pins and lobbing the bombs over the hill. He threw three in rapid succession, releasing the third as the first cracked off. A satisfying chorus of screams answered the blast.

Even with onrushing danger to focus his mind, it took a certain effort to concentrate against the storm of noise and muzzle-blast erupting from Jak's M-60. He could feel its hot breath on the back of his head and neck; the shock of the blasts buffeted him, made his hair fly and seemed to be trying to tear off his right ear. J.B. was up on one knee now, firing his BAR in short savage bursts not twelve feet away, but even though it wasn't any quieter than the 60, Ryan could barely hear it; he wasn't in front of its muzzle.

Ryan drew his SIG-Sauer and his panga. A human raider sprang over the hill and hacked at him with, of all things, a samurai sword. Ryan threw up his panga to block; evidently the *katana* was a cheap reproduction, since it failed to cut through the panga's broad blade. With the muzzle of his SIG-Sauer an inch from the Chichimec's breastbone, he shot the man twice. The man staggered back a couple of steps up the slope and sat down. He touched his chest, looked in horrified surprise at the blood on his fingers, looked up at Ryan. Then he fell over.

Another human wielding a spear came charging over the hilltop and promptly tripped over his dead comrade. Before the attacker hit the ground, Ryan had drilled a hole through the top of his head. His entire body spasmed repeatedly and then lay still.

The Armorer was nowhere to be seen. Ryan looked frantically around. Then from just over the hill he heard the staccato snarl of the Browning automatic rifle. J.B. had hopped the crest to pour fire into the flank of the muties charging the city line.

A cheer unfurling along the hilltop told Ryan the sudden desperation charge by the Chichimecs had been driven off. By chance the hill's north face offered virtually nothing by way of cover. In just the twenty yards or so of clear ground the invaders had to charge across, the city fighters had been able to shoot them all down, with help from J.B.

The Armorer jumped back over the rise, holding his BAR in one hand and clamping his fedora to his head with the other. "Cannies're shooting back," he said, and Ryan felt the thumps of bullets hitting the far side through the soles of his boots. "They've pretty much had it, but a man could still get dead."

The cheering turned to screams.

Chapter Twenty-Three

The huge mob of invaders in front of the scavvies' position was milling in confusion. The missile wags had continued to punish the Chichimecs, the rockets drawing corkscrews of white smoke overhead before arcing down to burst among the enemy with bright red flashes and puffs of black smoke. J.B. and Jak added their firepower to the slaughter once more.

Although it was still beset on two sides, Hector's force had solidified and was pouring fire into the Chichimecs. As many as a third of the valley men had been killed or routed off, but now the rest fought briskly. Ryan cinched up his shooting sling and began to seek out any invaders who looked as though they might be in positions of command. When he found them, he chilled them.

Already huge piles of dead and writhing, groaning wounded lay out in front of the scavvies' hilltop. Ryan was amazed at the fanaticism—or sheer desperation—that kept them hanging on in the face of such a terrible bloodletting. It was as great a slaughter as any he had seen.

As he watched, it became too much. The Chichimecs broke. First a few clumps broke away and began running to the north. Then the whole mass seemed to fray and then disintegrate like a clod of earth caught in a torrent, streaming away from the terrible blasters that flayed them with relentless fire.

Again the scavvies cheered. Some of them started to rise up as if to pursue. Ryan yelled at them and waved his arms. Cooler-headed comrades dragged them back down. The headlong retreat might be another ruse, designed to draw out the defending forces in a pursuit that would destroy their own cohesion, scatter them so they could be bushwhacked in convenient bite-size chunks.

And then the flight stopped. The running Chichimecs slowed, halted. Then, turning, they began to run back at their tormentors at the same mad speed, shaking their weapons and screaming with rage.

"Fireblast!" Ryan said.

"Ryan! Watch it!" J.B. shouted. He rose and fired a burst from the hip, into the ground right in front of his friend.

Ryan jumped back. The bullets had cut a rattlesnake clean in two. The halves writhed in a final frenzy. As Ryan watched, a second snake slid from the grass, headed right toward him. It was a standard-size rattler, maybe four feet long, and looked normal. But it wasn't acting normal. There was nothing normal at all about a rattler emerging from the grass to charge a human.

Ryan blasted the snake with his Steyr. J.B. vaulted onto the hood of the Hummer. "Bastards're all over the place!"

They seemed to be all over the line, as well. Scavvies were jumping up and away from their positions with frantic haste. A few who hadn't been alert or quick enough screamed as fangs pumped toxins into bodies or limbs or pain-contorting faces.

A clump of scavvies not thirty yards from the Hummer began to holler and slap themselves and run the way the crew from the valley gun wag had. Ryan saw small flying shapes swarming around them.

"Wasps," Jak said. "Wasps and snakes. Animals fight us now."

Ryan had joined J.B. on the wag hood. They looked at each other.

"The Holy Child—" J.B. began.

"Can control the emotions of men and animals," Ryan finished.

The onslaught of vermin were breaking the scavvie line. Behind the creatures came hundreds of Chichimecs, yelling their bloodlust—bloodlust that, Ryan knew with sudden conviction, had replaced the panic that had driven them to rout because of the mutie powers of their prophet, or god, or whatever he was.

One of the scooter scouts was forking his stationary bike off to the right of the Hummer, firing an M-16 into the onrushing muties. Ryan shouted, waved at the man. When the scout looked up, Ryan beckoned furiously with an arm. The man looked puzzled, but slung his longblaster and rode over to the wag.

Ryan jumped down. "I need your ride." He grabbed the man's arm and all but threw him off the dirt bike.

"Better hump it on up here," J.B. said helpfully to the

scout, who stood staring wildly after Ryan as the one-eyed man jumped on the bike and gunned it off to the northwest, angling away from the charging Chichimecs. "Snakes."

RYAN HEARD a shout from behind him, looked back over his shoulder. A lone biker was riding in his wake: Five Ax. For a moment Ryan wondered if the Jaguar Knight was trying to recover his comrade's stolen property.

The other bike came up alongside. Five Ax grinned and flashed Ryan a quick thumbs-up. Realizing the other had followed to watch his back, Ryan nodded and grinned.

He was several hundred yards wide of the screeching, racing mob of Chichimecs. Beyond them he could see Don Hector's men streaming back away from the battlefield in droves. Maybe monsters had gotten in among them, or maybe it was something as mundane— but still dangerous—as hornets and rattlesnakes. He could still hear machine guns, both the slow deep thump of the .50s and the higher-pitched rip of the .30-calibers and rockets continued to snake across the sky, although they were now falling behind the main crush of invaders as they charged for the scavvies. The defenders were still fighting back, still bringing some pretty awesome firepower to bear. But he knew that couldn't last.

A pair of figures loomed up in his path: Chichimecs, one of them a mutie with sheets of skin hanging from his chin and torso and limbs like bloody moss. Ryan yanked up on his handlebars. His front wheel came off the ground and bit into the mutie's chest like a circular saw. The mutie screamed and fell backward as blood and tissue flew. Ryan felt bones break as his weight combined with the bike's landed on the man. He kept riding.

Ahead of him and a little to the left rose a small hill. By its near-perfect conical shape he guessed it was a baby smoky. Hopefully a dead one, although since it wasn't spitting hot gas and molten rock right that moment its actual state was the last of his worries. He swung wide and then ran the bike up it almost to the top. He laid the machine down, unslung the rifle, began to scramble to the crest. Five Ax laid his bike down next to Ryan's and immediately began to fire single-aimed shots from his FN FAL.

A glance back told Ryan why: Chichimec stragglers were running toward them from all directions.

Good thing he tagged along, Ryan knew. The Jaguar Knight had followed to watch his back. He'd just have to trust him to do it long enough.

Ryan unslung the Steyr and went to his belly. A bullet whanged off a rock a yard to his left; a muscle in his cheek twitched.

He crawled upward, peered over the top. A knot of invaders stood four hundred yards away. He pushed his Steyr in front of him, pulled the butt into its shoulder, peered through the scope.

A bullet from somewhere behind cracked overhead. "Fast, fast," Five Ax urged in English. He swapped mags.

After a moment of near panic when he saw no targets—the earth is wide, the field of view of a telescopic sight very narrow—Ryan found the group he had seen before. There were a dozen Chichimecs, human and mutant, and a figure he guessed was human, although it seemed to be wearing the skin of an animal, complete with the animal's head draped over his own. But even that bizarre sight wasn't what commanded his attention.

In the midst of the group stood a figure that was maybe four feet tall and maybe three feet wide. Its skin was chalky white, the lank hair on its round skull was silvery-white. It looked something like old, faded ads Ryan had once seen, featuring what he'd read was the Michelin Tire Man, with fat hanging in folds around it. It was standing where it could just peer south over the top of a rise.

A full-auto burst roared out from behind Ryan, a very bad sign. He laid the crosshairs on the middle of the body. Even he, hardened chiller that he was, felt a tiny pang at dropping the hammer on a child. But not enough of a pang that he didn't take a deep breath, release some of it, hold, gently squeeze the trigger as if it were one of Krysty's perfect snowy breasts….

Something slammed into his back at the instant the shot broke.

A wave of agony and terror washed over Ryan and knotted his guts. Desperately he rolled onto his back. Or tried to; he got halfway and something jammed him, stopped him cold. A Chichimec was standing right over him. Five Ax had the long FN FAL across the invader's throat like a bar and was trying to choke him with it from behind.

Still almost sickened by repeated electric shocks of emotion, Ryan struggled and with a convulsive heave of effort brought out his SIG-Sauer. Five Ax's eyes got wide as Ryan raised the blaster; copper-jacketed nines would punch right through the Chichimec's skinny body into his.

Ryan fired twice. The noseless mutie who had been about to plunge a spear into Five Ax's back fell.

Five Ax released the raider he was holding with his longblaster. The man dropped to his hands and knees across Ryan's legs. He tried to get up. When he looked back toward Five Ax, the Jaguar Knight's *macahuitl* struck him in the center of the forehead and split his skull.

Hot blood pulsed over Ryan's legs. Ignoring it, he pointed his SIG-Sauer past the Jaguar Knight. He could see four or five Chichimecs. But they were no longer trying to attack the pair. As Five Ax wrenched his weapon free and turned, the raiders began to back away. Their faces began to twist as from unbearable agony or fear. Tears gushed from their eyes. Crying out as though in pain, they ran away to the north.

Ryan's own strange sourceless panic had ebbed. He rolled over onto his stomach again, got behind his rifle and looked through the scope. The group of raiders he had seen before was now gathered tightly around what he could only glimpse as a supine white form. He had tagged the Holy Child. Now he'd finish the job, if only one of those bastards down there would move just a little out of his line of fire....

He felt an odd wrench at his back. He yanked around

to find himself looking up at Five Ax. Five Ax held up the obsidian-tipped spear he had just pulled out of Ryan's backpack.

"Spoiled my shot," Ryan said accusingly.

Five Ax grinned. "Better go now." He jerked his head to the south.

The surviving Chichimecs were all headed north at a brisk pace. That meant hundreds of them were headed, if only incidentally, right at this hill. The Holy Child had obviously broadcast his pain and terror when Ryan's bullet hit him. Fortunately he was tuned more to his followers' wavelength, or whatever you'd call it, than Ryan's. The one-eyed man had almost been unmanned by the psychic blast as it was. The invaders were still feeling their leader's pain, or so Ryan guessed. They were obviously no longer interested in fighting.

But Ryan couldn't but think it would be unhealthy to just sit here and let them flow past. And if they caught the notion the two enemies on the hill were the ones responsible for their holy one's anguish…

"Yeah," Ryan said, "reckon we better do that thing."

Chapter Twenty-Four

The moon hung low over the mountains to the west. Down south the smokies were hardly making their presence known.

"Tenorio's heading back to the city," Ryan said into the mike from the Hummer's radio. "He's got about twenty wounded with him. Couple won't make it, no way. Three, four more, mebbe. Rest're basically patch-up jobs."

"I'll be glad of something to do." Mildred's voice came back. "Been getting antsy, sitting here watching Krysty and fretting about you boys being off in the middle of some battle. Is that crazy old coot coming back with Don T.?"

"Doc? Yeah. He'd rather sleep in a nice soft bed tonight than in the back seat of the wag." He glanced toward the big bonfire at the main camp a hundred yards away. A ring of city fighters was attempting a drunken dance of celebration. They kept weaving perilously near the flames. "Can't say I blame him. Are you sure Krysty—"

"Ryan, I told you, I'm not sure of anything except that her life's not in danger, and that's mainly because she's so tough. Her fever's mostly gone and she seems to be sleeping normally right now. I still have no idea what's hit her. And if there's any change in her status I'll definitely call you right that instant."

"All right."

"Now, quit fussing and go back and play the hero. Get drunk, unwind, live a little. You've earned it, from what I hear."

"All of us. Jak and J.B. were right in the thick of it—you know them, no way to keep them out. And I'm not sure Doc wasn't in as much danger as any of us, back there at HQ with Don Hector on hand."

"You were the one who turned the tide, though, Ryan."

"Yeah." He turned away from the fire and the noisy celebration. "I shot a kid."

"What's this? Regrets?"

"Well, not really. I mean, I try to do what I have to do—"

"Just nail that down right there, Ryan. You do what you have to do. Shooting a child doesn't come easy to you? Well, congratulations on still being part of the human race in spite of being Deathlands born and bred. But that child was turning the whole battle against you, fixing to wipe out the whole army. Maybe this isn't our fight, although you know I agree with your reasons for making it ours. But at that point you were saving your life and J.B.'s and Jak's and Doc's, as well, and maybe Krysty's and mine, too. It's a bad old world, Ryan."

"Yeah. Okay. And if Krysty—"

"I'll keep her near me so I can keep an eye on her

while I'm helping with the wounded. And I'll call you. I promise. Bye."

For a moment he stood looking at the microphone in his hand. It was usually this way after a fight. Once that old adrenaline quit holding you by the neck, a body started to feel wrung out and empty.

"Rye-on," a voice called from behind him. "Amigo."

He turned. It was Five Ax, carrying a heavy earthenware bowl. With him came J.B. Neither was too steady on his pins. The Jaguar Knight pressed the bowl on him. He looked into it and by reflex wrinkled his nose.

"Pulque," the Armorer said. "Local brew. Our city friends trade the valley folk for it. Looks like snot, smells like a horse. Don't taste half bad, which isn't to say it tastes good. But it'll knock you on your ass."

Ryan raised his eyebrow. "This is a good thing?"

"This is a good thing." The Armorer laid a hand on his friend's shoulder. Ryan noticed there was no tremor to the grip, and it came to him he'd seldom seen his friend anywhere near incapacitated by drink. "Sometimes a man needs knocked-on-his-ass for a spell. *Comprende,* like they say in Mex-talk?"

"Yeah." Uncertainly he accepted the bowl from Five Ax, who grinned like a goblin and slapped his shoulder.

"Helps if you hold your breath when you drink it," J.B. said.

So Ryan did.

THE MOON ROLLED UP the sky, getting smaller but more intense. The volcanoes away off to the south emitted a loud fart or two. Their hearts weren't in it. The celebration broke up into smaller gatherings.

Ryan, J.B. and Jak were hanging out by the Hummer with Five Ax and a couple of his Jaguar Knight buddies. They'd made their own fire out of dried cow chips and grass. There wasn't a lot of wood to be found in the valley. Trees weren't common. It was kind of a small, pallid fire, but that suited a more intimate, wound-down kind of gathering. It didn't smell bad, which might have surprised Ryan if he hadn't encountered the primary fuel source before. The key was getting properly cured cow crap, which mostly meant dry.

J.B. was laid out under the wag, snoring like a dirt bike with an out-of-tune engine. His lack of consciousness owed far more to postcombat exhaustion than alcoholic intake, Ryan felt sure. Jak squatted on his haunches on the far side of the fire. His eyes glittered like rubies with reflected flamelight. Ryan had made himself relax about the youth, although he was still keeping an eye on him. Jak and alcohol could sometimes be a volatile mixture.

There was another potential worry. Some of the people from the valley villes, especially the ones burned out by the Chichimecs, had come around the battlefield to gloat over the dead bodies of their tormentors. They had plenty to gloat over. Don Tenorio estimated on the basis of reports from his people who'd scouted the field after the action that there were over two thousand dead invaders strewn across the green grass and black lava. Don Hector, who had been in full manic glory after the battle, had been strutting around making far higher claims. Even if the valley *cacique* hadn't been a few rounds short of a full mag, Ryan would've credited the city *alcade* over him where it came to counting.

The defenders hadn't exactly escaped unscathed. The scavvies had lost a total of thirty-one dead and a couple more than that wounded. The valley army, almost half its strength, well upward of two hundred dead, wounded or gone on what Doc termed "French leave." For the city force it was a big bite of their total strength as it was. But in lasting terms it would gouge a disproportionately huge cavity out of the small, tight-knit scavenger community. The victors celebrated this night with single-minded purpose in part because they knew tomorrow the serious grieving would begin.

The valley ville folk and refugees had other ideas in mind, as well. They wanted to express their appreciation to the victors who had laid such a powerful hurt on the brutal invaders from the Great Chichimeca. They brought presents of food and drink—Ryan got the impression their *cacique* didn't allow them much by way of personal possessions. Some of the female ones, especially on the younger side, had more personal expressions of gratitude on their minds. Five Ax and his pals had all been off for a couple of trips into the darkness apiece this evening.

On the basis that people find what's really different from themselves exotic and attractive, the paper-pale Jak Lauren with his long white hair and red eyes was as big a hit with the ladies of the valley as he had been in the city. He'd come in for his share of attention, and more than his share. Ryan didn't begrudge the youth the R&R. What gnawed at his vitals was the fact that there might still be vengeance-minded Chichimec stragglers lurking out there in the night—and the still-unresolved question of whether, or maybe when, Don Hector might turn on his allies and their friends from *el norte*.

Still, the albino youth had been looking out for himself for longer than he'd been under Ryan's watchful eye. And he had the outlook and skinned-fine senses of a once-ambushed alley cat. He'd be fine or he wouldn't; which were the same rules Ryan and everybody else on Earth lived by each and every day, after all.

"Shit," he murmured. "I'm getting all philosophical. I need to leave that nukeshit to Doc."

Out in the night a coyote howled. A chorus of voices answered. The coyotes followed the Chichimecs as religiously as if they believed in the Holy Child themselves, so Five Ax had told him. The invaders left a wake of bodies wherever they marched for all that they were cannies; the wolf-dogs ate like kings. Well, they were eating like the baron of all barons this night; the scavvies had policed up their own dead, but most of the Chichimecs and, as far as Ryan knew, Hector's casualties lay where they fell.

But Ryan wasn't wasting mind time envisioning red-muzzled coyotes rooting in the bellies of what had that morning been living men. He had drunk with the others, pulque and some much more palatable stuff the scavvies had brought along with their stores wags, just in case. He had become…relaxed. He had reached a point where he wasn't worrying about whom he'd dropped the hammer on that day, or how close he and his had come to the red roaring edge. He was just warm and comfortable, and even leaning against the big knob-bly tire of the wag felt fine.

Five Ax was talking to his buddies, who seemed to be heading off for the main scavvie encampment. "Wel-come to bunk here if you like, Five Ax," Ryan said. "Plenty of room." But the bandy-legged little Jaguar Knight was definitely the worse for wear.

"Damn," Ryan said. "That means I'm gonna have to rouse my dead ass and take first watch." He wished he'd chosen to head back into the city with Doc, Don Tenorio and the wounded. He wasn't even sure now why he hadn't. Something, maybe, about feeling re-sponsible for the scavvie field force. They deserved somebody to look after them.

"No, that's not right." Had he spoken aloud? The scavvies could take care of themselves. But…Don Ten-orio's place this night was back in his city. Ryan's place this night had been out here with the army he'd helped win a desperate victory, even if it meant a night sepa-rated from Krysty.

He wondered how she was, but he wouldn't call. Mildred would either be asleep or busy treating the wounded. And she would have called him as promised had there been anything to report good or bad. He trusted her for that.

Something seemed to flicker in Ryan's vision. Dark

liquid gushed from the region of Five Ax's chin and splashed hissing and reeking into the fire, half-dousing it. Ryan opened his mouth to chide the commando for getting so drunk he vomited out the campfire. Then he saw brown arms tangling Jak, who, too late, came alive with whirling fury.

It wasn't vomit putting out the fire. It was blood from a slit throat.

All at once the dark and Ryan's peripheral vision were alive with flitting shadowed menace. He grabbed for his SIG-Sauer, sprang to his feet.

As he did, something was descending hard and fast for his face. Firelight danced dimly on thin blades of obsidian, sharp as fate.

A thudding crunch, a flare of agony in his head, a blinding white flash of light. Then falling, falling into dark...

Chapter Twenty-Five

"Krysty! You're awake."

Wearing only a long white T-shirt bearing the name and likeness of some long-dead pop star of the days before the skydark, Krysty sat with her white but hard-muscled legs dangling over the side of the cot she'd been laid on. It sat in an office off the main floor of the cafeteria, which had been commandeered as a receiving ward for wounded from the battle. Her sentient red hair hung lank around her shoulders.

The redhead nodded. Mildred glanced around the makeshift ward. For the moment the situation appeared to be under control. While there were no medical doctors trained as she had been among the scavvies—nor much of anyplace in the world, for that matter—there were people who had read extensively of scavenged medical literature, and some who possessed pretty comprehensive rough-and-ready knowledge. Emergency surgery wasn't really that rare in a community devoted to foraging through half-destroyed and half-tumbled buildings in an incredibly active seismic zone. She had numerous assistants, including friends and family of the injured, many of whom had some idea what they were doing. It was an asset at least as valuable as the relative abundance of med supplies the settlers had scavenged.

Mildred went to Krysty and began inspecting her with professional dispatch. "So that Gaia-powered immune system of yours shook off the infection, finally?" she asked, peeling back an eyelid and shining a light in one blue eye.

"Not infection," Krysty stated flatly. "Drugs. Some kind of plant poisons. Maybe several different ones blended to produce nausea, fatigue and fever."

She tried moistening cracked lips with her tongue and asked for water. Mildred made a sipping gesture. A scavvie girl of ten or eleven named Juliana, with big shiny black eyes and ears whose prepubescent prominence was emphasized to an almost comical degree by the painful tautness with which her long black hair was drawn back in two braids. The girl, who spoke some halting English and professed her intention of becoming a healer herself someday, was serving as gofer. She came bouncing up carrying a plastic sippy bottle. Mildred smiled and thanked her. The girl nodded gravely.

Krysty drank greedily. "Thank you," she said to Mildred and, "Gracias," to the girl.

"You recognize the agents involved?" Mildred asked. Alongside her self-healing powers Krysty was an herbalist of great skill.

Krysty shook her head, drank again, handed the bottle back to Juliana with a radiant smile. "No. The effects on my body—they didn't have the harshness of man-made or mineral poisons, I guess is the best way to put it. They lacked some kind of edge."

"But not potency."

"Not potency. Somebody intended to put me out for a while."

"Not kill you?"

"No." Krysty frowned. "There was something else…maybe it didn't really mean anything."

"Let me at least hear about it so I can pass judgment."

"Nothing medical. At least I don't think so. Several times when I was slipping between a fitful doze and a deep sleep, it seemed to me that I saw a woman standing near me."

"A woman? You mean, like, in your room?"

"No. Not in the room. In the world behind the world. She looked like the pictures we saw. Of the Lady of the Valley."

"I see," said Mildred, who didn't really. Juliana, who had started to lope away with the now-drained bottle stopped and turned back. "You're not going all mystical on me now, are you, honey?"

Krysty shook her head. "I think she was my own doomie power talking to me. She told me…confirmed for me, I had been dosed with a herbal poison. And she told me I would confront some great dark power and I must risk everything to save myself and those I loved." She looked up at Mildred. "To save my soul," she said.

"¡La Dama!" Juliana exclaimed, and rushed away to speak excitedly to the other helpers.

"Probably just a dream induced by your fever," Mildred said, without much hope of convincing her friend. "Probably doesn't mean anything."

Krysty just smiled knowingly at her. The other assistants were all looking their way now. Several of them crossed themselves, a gesture Mildred hadn't seen much for, well, over a century.

"Girl, this is way over my head." She checked her wrist chron. "Well, Osberto should be about ready for me to try stitching his gut back together. I'm glad to see you come out of it, but now you should try to rest—"

From the doorway came a shattering burst of noise.

"Ow! NUKESHIT!"

Ryan heard himself yelp the words. Then he realized he was alive.

Something tinkled almost musically. "For the moment, Barnabas, my friend. Here, hold still."

Ryan blinked his eye. He was having trouble focusing. It was dark all around, except for a blinding white full moon. The moon seemed to move around slightly; his vision must still be swimming from whatever happened. There was nothing wrong with his ears, though.

"Doc?" he croaked.

"One and the same. Hold still, I say!"

Then something crossed the moon, causing it to move even more. The object glinted dull silver. Ryan realized it was some kind of multitool pliers. And the moon was a small intense flashlight.

He felt the pliers grasp…something. Something that

almost felt as if it was part of his head but wasn't. Something embedded in his head.

"What in the name of glowing night shit—ow. Fireblast!" Doc had pulled whatever it was out with a twist of his bony wrist, pale in the artificial light.

"You bore your suffering with much more stoic silence when you were passed out, Barnabas."

Barnabas? Whatever. Doc seemed to be mildly phased out of reality. It didn't seem to be impairing his ability to treat Ryan's wounds, so under the circumstances it was far less pressing than other concerns. Such as…

"I was out. Serious out. Does that mean I've got a bleeder in my skull that's going to implode my brain?"

"I believe you lost consciousness due to wound shock. You had one of those barbaric obsidian-edged clubs buried in your cranium. Some of the stone shards are still stuck in there."

Back into the light swam the pliers. This time they held a wafer of black glass. It had dark clotted stuff stuck to it and a few curly dark hairs.

"Fireblast," Ryan said again.

The tinkle again. Doc was tossing the fragments of volcanic glass from the broken *macahuitl* into a coffee can. "A painful wound and a shockingly bloody one. But superficial for all that. Still, you can be grateful for it."

"Why the hell is that?"

"You're still alive because of it. Or at least free. Your would-be captors thought they had killed you. As they did for our noble red friend Five Ax, there."

He twitched the flashlight. Five Ax lay sprawled by

the fire. His own *macahuitl,* busted off near the hilt, lay near his hand. His body had been gashed and gored horribly. At least three other bodies lay near him—small, dark, almost naked. *Chichimecs.*

"I…saw him get his throat cut," Ryan said. His throat felt as if somebody had been down it with a giant wood rasp. "Or did I imagine that?"

"No. Though his wound was mortal, he fought fiercely. And slew his foes, until he bled out and fell. An epic scene, I should imagine."

"What about J.B. and Jak?"

"They are gone. Marched into captivity. One does not like to think of their fate."

"We'll get them back. Is there any more of that crap stuck in my head?"

"One more piece, which I will attend to, once you cease fidgeting."

Ryan held himself stock-still.

"Very well." Doc plucked the last fragment from Ryan's head and dropped it meticulously in the can. Then he tore open a scavenged packet, poured antibiotic powder into the wound and bandaged it with more supplies from the medical kit the scavvies had provided them for the fight, taking great twists of tape around Ryan's head. "That's the best I can do for you now. It will pull your hair most cruelly when the tape is removed."

"Fine. How about the wag?"

"What do you think it is you're leaning against?"

"Oh."

With Doc's help, Ryan got to his feet. He examined the

wag quickly by the shine of the small flash. The machine gun was gone and the tires were slashed. The microphone for the radio had been ripped away; the cord dangled out the open door like a curiously coiled umbilicus.

"Wonder why they didn't burn it," Ryan muttered.

"That would ill have accorded with the stealth that was needful, to commit murder and kidnap under the noses of a sleeping army."

"A sleeping, dead-exhausted, largely drunk army," Ryan said. "But yeah, a blazing wag would have been a little conspicuous."

He half turned and fell into the driver's seat. He started the engine. Reaching down, he found by feel and pulled a lever. A hissing sound came from under the chassis. The Hummer slowly began to rise from the ground.

"Our friends did their savage best to incapacitate our vehicle quickly and quietly," Doc said. "Sadly for them, they failed to reckon with that apex of technology that was attained in the late twentieth century, shortly before everything blew up, of course."

The Hummer's tires, which were run-flats to begin with, were resealing themselves with a quick-hardening compound and reinflating automatically by means of a compressor powered by the nuke battery that ran the wag itself.

"So how did you come to be wandering around out here to stumble across me, instead of being back safe and sound in the city with Tenorio and the rest?"

"As we made preparation to pull out, I decided my

place was with my comrades, after all. I suppose that I felt guilty for not having shared your danger. So I begged leave of Don Tenorio to remain behind, which he graciously extended. Then I found myself walking in the moonlight, regarding the battlefield and regarding the fugacity of life, rather than proceeding here straightaway. With the result that I did not arrive until shortly after the villains decamped with our comrades. At which point I knelt to examine what I sorrowfully took to be your corpse, and the rest, as they say, is history."

"I'm glad I'm not."

He patted himself down. "They left me my SIG-Sauer and my panga."

"They got the other weapons, including the BAR that our hosts lent to John Barrymore." The Armorer had left his pet Uzi and shotgun safely back in the city. "I believe your splendid rifle, as well."

Ryan shrugged. The Steyr was a fine blaster for a fact, but it was just a blaster; if he lost it, he lost it. He didn't feel the same about his friends.

"You still got your swordstick and that giant old horse pistol, don't you?"

"Most assuredly."

Ryan nodded. "We got all we need and mebbe a hair more. Let's go."

"To the rescue of our compatriots?"

Ryan had drawn his handblaster, pinched back the slide to check for a chambered cartridge. Brass gleamed yellow in the moonlight.

"Damn straight."

SCREAMS. Mildred and Krysty looked out of the cubicle. Two men in dark green camou flanked the door, their faces painted in black-green gray. One held a 9 mm Colt Commando carbine, the other an MP-5.

Between them, dressed the same but with face unpainted, stood Felicidad Mendoza. She was holding up a short-barreled AK-74 Sov-made assault blaster from which she'd just fired a burst into the acoustic-tiled ceiling. Little wisps and dust particles were floating down around her.

A scavvie whose leg Mildred had set and splinted after a Chichimec had broken it for him with a three-foot-long pipe came up to a sitting position on one of the tables with a Beretta in hand. Smiling tightly, Felicidad snapped down the blaster and shot him with a burst of 5.45 mm before he could get off a shot. Then pivoting slightly to her right she began to spray the room from side to side with an ear-imploding roar.

Mildred threw herself over Krysty, expecting to feel the sledgehammer impacts of bullets burrowing into her broad back. None came. The chattering roar stopped for an instant, then commenced again.

When it ended, Mildred dared to look up. The copper-haired woman was feeding a fresh red plastic banana magazine into the well of her weapon. Moans and the stink of burned lubricant and propellant and spilled blood and guts filled the room. At least half a dozen scavvies, wounded or healers, had been hit. Little Juliana stood by one wall with blood spraying in a wide pink fan from a severed carotid artery. She pressed one small hand to the side of her neck and collapsed.

"You psycho bitch," Mildred raged, "what the fuck do you want?"

Felicidad smiled. "You," she said. "And even more, that red-haired bitch behind you."

More of Hector's sec men, painted up and armed to the gills, had crowded in behind her. "Take them," she ordered, nodding at the two outland women. "If they resist, shoot them in the legs. But don't kill them.

"Their deaths will greatly please the gods—but not now."

"DOC," RYAN SAID gently as he drove through the darkness, "who am I?"

The older man blinked at him. "Why, you are Ryan Cawdor, our fearless leader and faithful friend."

"Who did you think I was back there when you were pulling obsidian splinters out of my head, if you don't mind my asking?"

"Why, whatever do you mean?"

"You called me 'Barnabas.' I don't know any Barnabas. Friend of yours from the old days?"

Doc drew himself up as best he could sitting down. "I fear your injury impaired your perceptions. I wasn't calling *you* Barnabas. I was merely recalling—out loud, as sometimes I do—a favorite television show from my sojourn in the twentieth century."

"*Television* show?"

Doc nodded. "'Dark Shadows.'"

Ryan shook his head.

Doc turned ostentatiously to peer out the windows. "At least your attackers were considerate enough to leave a few traces to track them by."

The Chichimec trail was anything but hard to follow. The bright moonlight was a pure luxury. Hundreds of bare horny feet had trampled the grass in a swath a hundred yards wide. Here and there the bodies of stragglers lay, dark and still.

"They say the Chichimecs eat their dead, which to them apparently includes those too badly wounded to fight or keep up," Doc said.

"Reckon they got all the meat they can carry as it is," Ryan said grimly. He was behind the wheel, periodically poking his head out the window to make sure of the trail and terrain. They didn't dare use headlights, which the Chichimecs would spot miles off, so the moonlight was useful in helping him pick a safe path without bogging the wag or dumping it into an arroyo even it couldn't negotiate. The Hummer was equipped with infrared headlights, but unfortunately not with IR goggles, so they were useless.

"You seem confident that our boon companions are not to be found among the sad relics lying by the way."

"Yep. Unless they were bad hurt they'd keep up with a bunch of raiders worn out from marching and fighting all day. And I got a definite hunch the Chichimecs mean to keep them alive. For now. After all, they went to considerable effort to target us, cut us out from the rest. If they'd wanted J.B. and Jak dead, they'd have left them there in their blood the way they did me."

Gingerly he fingered the bandages wrapped around his head with his free hand. To Doc's horror he had insisted on rubbing dirt onto them to darken them up some. He was damned if he was going to try to sneak up on a campful of cannies with a pristine-white bandage shining on his head.

"Their behavior suggests you were specifically targeted. Which suggests knowledge on the raiders' part. Which in turn suggests we've been betrayed. And why then does the name 'Don Hector' spring so readily to mind?"

"Not proved," Ryan said. "Although, truth to tell, if the crazy son of a bitch was to cross my sights right now, I'd hammer down on him, just on principle. But who and why don't matter right now. Getting our friends back does."

"And what of Krysty and Dr. Wyeth, back in the City in the Lake?"

His guts gave a jerk. He ignored it. "I don't reckon Hector will make his play for the city just yet. He might've seen an opportunity to get us in particular out of the picture and jumped on it. But a move on the city means war. And while we laid some savage hurt on the Chichimecs this afternoon, we got no reason to believe they're out of the picture."

He shook his head. "He's nuts. But he's not so nuts I can see him picking a fight with the city before the invaders' asses are kicked out of the valley for good and all."

"I certainly hope that you are right."

"If not," Ryan said, "we're going to want J.B. and Jak with us when we go to spring Krysty and Mildred, anyway."

An hour and several miles later, Doc sat with his head lolled back and his mouth open, snoring gently. "Doc," Ryan said.

No response. "Doc," he said again. When the old man failed to respond, he reached out to shake him gently by the shoulder.

"Not the sows," Doc moaned. "Please don't put me in with the sows again."

"I don't know about the sows, but the people who used to put you in with them are all worm food, long since. Time to wake up and join us in the present."

Doc raised his head and stared wildly around at the night. "Where are we?"

Ryan nodded at a yellow glow in the sky above the rise ahead. "We're there. That's the Chichimec camp. Grab your swordstick, Doc, 'cause we shag it from here."

HAVING OVERSEEN the wounded being unloaded and carried into the makeshift infirmary, Don Tenorio had retired to his office. He sat writing by the light of a kerosene lamp when the door opened. He looked up mildly.

"Ah, María," he said. "What is it?"

"Someone to see you, *alcade*," the diminutive woman said.

The baron stiffened as a tall, cloaked figure strolled through the door.

"Good evening," Don Hector said.

Tenorio tensed to spring up. Then he relaxed, accepting the inevitable, as four Eagle Knights strode in, each wearing a laser armlet, and fanned out to either side of their baron. He rose deliberately, stood straight.

"Whatever your plan, it won't work," he said calmly. "My people will never submit to your rule. Kill me if you will, but they still won't yield."

Hector nodded, smiling. "Kill you I shall, Tenorio, my old friend. But for now you shall serve as a hostage against the behavior of your subjects. And so shall your wounded and medical personnel, whom we have secured."

"You seem to be overlooking my allies from *el norte*."

Hector shook his head. "Not at all. I have captured the witch-woman with the red hair and the black woman. The Chichimecs have taken your allies, I fear, and will sacrifice them to their own barbaric gods. A sad waste, I agree. They are heroes, to be sure, worthy of the flowery death as sacrifices to my own lord, Huitzil-opochtli. Still, the Hummingbird on the Left should be well pleased with the hearts I give him at the apex of his pyramid tomorrow."

"My people will resist you," Tenorio said. But he spoke without complete confidence.

Hector picked up the polished stone globe of the Earth from Tenorio's mahogany desk, turned it over in his big scarred hand, then tossed it up in the air and caught it.

"They will die like rats if they do," he said. "The survivors will eventually learn to be grateful for the discipline I teach them. And they shall know glory. For once I have become immortal, I shall lead the peoples of this valley on a campaign of conquest the likes of which the world has never seen, combining the technology of the predark days with the spiritual powers of our ancestors."

Tenorio cocked an eyebrow. "Immortality? You really believe so?"

"I know so. And you will know the folly of having turned your face from our gods, the true gods, when you behold your own heart, smoking, cut from your chest and held up in offering to Huitzilopochtli."

THE WAG ROLLED west along the causeway from the city. From the south came a low mutter, angry and growing. In the sky above the volcanoes, a red glow had begun to spread like a bloodstain.

A crew of three occupied the strongpoint guarding the landward entry to the causeway. Two of them emerged from the small tower as the wag slowed to a stop in front of the mobile barrier.

"What a glorious evening, no?" one called cheerfully to the driver.

"The only thing wrong is we have to wait for our relief at midnight before we can celebrate properly," the other said. "Unless of course you boys are truly friends, and thought to bring us a bottle or two?"

"I fear not," the driver said. He put his left arm out the window. It was encased in a bulky plastic molding.

An almost-white lance of brilliance flashed from the

armlet to the sentry's chest. Ruby glare underlit an expression of uncomprehending astonishment as the laser flash-boiled the fluid in his lungs, causing his chest to explode.

As the crack of air rushing back into the vacuum created by the laser beam's intolerable heat echoed out across the black uneasy waters of the lake, the other sentry turned to run back into the tower. A second Eagle Knight stepped out of the cab, raising his own arm. A second ruby spear struck the sentry in the back, split him open, sent his corpse skidding along the gravel with his clothing in flames.

The man still in the tower was of sterner stuff. The machine-gun mount was never made to bear back along the causeway toward the city. But he was trying to wrestle the wep around when the second Eagle Knight took aim. The sentry's head exploded at the touch of a laser finger.

As the dismounted Eagle Knight removed the barrier from the roadway, the driver flashed the wag's headlights: once, twice, three times.

A dozen sets of headlights sprang to life in the darkness of the shore. With a rumbling of engines, the force of sec men and Eagle Knights rolled down to the now-undefended causeway.

Chapter Twenty-Six

The dirt bike's engine revved to a frenzied scream. Then the human Chichimec mounted on it let go the brake and let in the clutch. The bike shot away across the hard-packed earth of the little ville's plaza. The captured scavvie tied to the pole behind it screamed louder than the engine as his intestines were unreeled from his slit-open belly behind it.

Glistening greasily in the light of a great central bonfire and numerous torches, the gut stretched out until the tie that fastened one end to the license holder snapped. Then it dropped into the dust, recoiling slightly with natural elasticity. Several figures with matted hair that trailed red stains of fresh blood down their faces, shoulders and torsos came forward to inspect it as the disemboweled man howled and writhed. Next to the drawn-out viscera lay three similar strands, whose erstwhile owners had mercifully bled out and expired.

"Nope, Doc," Ryan said, watching the proceeding through his Simmons monocular. "This one didn't win. Damn, but I can't get over how much gut a person's got inside him."

"Forgive me if I fail to share a sporting interest in this particular diversion."

"Just taking stock of the situation."

The ville was small, no more than twenty or thirty small square adobe huts scattered in a low spot where a stream that had been running underground emerged for a quarter mile or so before going subterranean again. There were at least a hundred Chichimecs, human and mutie, ranged around the plaza on the settlement's south side, squatting on their haunches, drinking from clay pots and eating. Apparently the rumors Doc had heard about the intruders eating their dead weren't lies: at least as many dead Chichimecs were stacked off on the east side of the plaza, to Ryan and Doc's right.

The smell of death and rotting bodies was as thick as cheese.

"What about our friends?"

"Still where we first spotted them, Doc. Tied to some poles over to the right and back away from the main action."

"How do they look?"

"Hard to tell in this light, with a bitty little glass like this. They been beat, mebbe medium tenderized. Don't reckon anything's broke."

"You do not feel perhaps a certain amount of expedition—haste, even—might be in order?"

"Relax. Still got a dozen or so prisoners to play with. Obviously, J.B. and Jak are being saved for something special. From the looks of things, the Chichimecs'll be hours before they get to them."

"You have worked out a way to slip up to them in the excitement and cut them loose, of course?"

Ryan shook his head. "They're too much out in the open, and there's too much coming and going. I think the raiders may have some captured local women stashed in that hut mebbe twenty yards back of them. Traffic seems pretty regular between there and the plaza."

He lowered the monocular. "We're going to need a diversion."

"May one hope that it might entail standing off at a goodly distance doing something to attract the dacoits' attention? Honking the horn, perhaps?"

"One might." Ryan grinned tigerishly at the older man. "Won't do no good hoping, though. We need something better, and for that, we're going to have to creepy-crawl the ville and get a closer look at things."

WHILE DOC FRETTED at the delay, Ryan drove the Hummer in a wide arc to the east of the ville, then around to come in from the north. They found a rare stand of trees by a little stream that ran along the far side of a rise a couple hundred yards from the farthest outlying house and stashed the big wag there.

The crickets sang. The rumble from the smokies, almost subliminal, was constant and seemed, if you concentrated on it for a spell, to be growing. Out among the lava flows and grown-over ash drifts a litter of coyote pups yammered and their mother yipped them sternly into silence.

As with most of the valley they'd passed through, what looked at first glance like easy-rolling land hid lots of pockets and dead ground. The two men were able to slip into the ville without exposing themselves to possible view for more than a few steps at a time. Not that anybody seemed to be looking.

They reached the rear of the northernmost hut, hugged it briefly as they looked around. It had been trashed for no visible reason except mean spirits: doors and windows smashed, and a glance inside showed even by the light of the stars and falling moon that filtered in that what simple furnishings it boasted had been wrecked.

"Deserted," Ryan said in a low voice that carried much less distance than a whisper. "If it wasn't for all the sounds of partying from the other end of the ville, the whole place would seem dead."

"I cannot understand why we have seen no signs of vigilance. Normal prudence would dictate patrols around the settlement, at the very least."

"May've escaped your attention, Doc, but these Chichimecs don't much play by the rules other people do, even coldhearts." Ryan paused, listening, watching, tasting the wind. The latter task was made more pleasant by the fact that the prevailing breezes blew the stench of the corpse mound, and whatever grotesque defilements and putrefactions might remain to be found in the rest of the ville, away from them. Even with the wind blowing away they could plainly hear the shrieks of the victims and the uproarious approval of their tormentors.

"Besides, they probably left scouts to keep an eye on the defending forces. We know they sent somebody back that way, obviously. So they know the scavvies and Hector's mob were a lot more interested in hunkering down and getting blind and getting their ends wet than pursuing them. And they don't reckon on any danger coming down from the north, 'cause basically, between here and the impassable rad bands and chem storms, they're it."

He eyed the hut. It wasn't a very tall structure, and it had a flat roof, as did almost all the buildings they'd seen in valley villes outside the city. "Give me a hand up," he said.

Looking doubtful, Doc carefully propped his sword-stick against the wall. Then he squatted and made a stirrup of his interlaced fingers. Ryan put a boot into it and boosted himself up to seize the projecting end of a roof beam, then clambered up and over the low parapet.

"Mind you do not silhouette yourself, lad," Doc said softly.

Not bothering to respond, Ryan slithered forward on his belly. The roof consisted of earth spread across the planks of the ceiling. Grass, weeds and wildflowers grew on it, providing just a touch of additional concealment. Ryan was grateful for anything he could get. But with the moon well past the zenith and no lights in the immediate vicinity, he was near invisible.

He reached the far side of the roof, peered cautiously over. Nobody was outside anywhere near him. He took out his monocular and studied the scene.

Off across the ville, set back not too far from the plaza where the prisoners were being tortured, a hut was surrounded by Chichimecs. Some seemed to be praying, others simply to be squatting or kneeling. Safe guess that was where the injured Holy Child was being cared for.

Closer to the roof where Ryan lay, a multiroom hut, the largest he could see in the ville, had a pair of sentries squatting on the roof with longblasters across their bare thighs. Even more intriguing was the motorcycle parked out front. Ryan had spotted it first from his vantage point on the hill. A single Chichimec, whose body seemed to be covered in fur, squatted disconsolately at the rear of the house holding what was either an M-1 carbine or a Ruger Mini-14; he was in darkness and Ryan couldn't be sure if it had a squared-off forend like the Mini or a rounded one like the M-1.

Still nearer, off to Ryan's right maybe fifty yards, a couple more bored Chichimecs stood guard over the door of an unlit hut. Might be worth checking, he thought. But he felt strongly drawn to the hut with the bike. He eased back, then crawled to the rear, flowed over the edge, let himself lightly down next to Doc.

"We proceed?" the older man asked.

Ryan nodded.

Doc drew his swordstick with a quiet song of sliding steel. "Mind the shine on that," Ryan said.

"Indeed." Doc stooped, rummaged up a handful of dust from the yard, rubbed it along the slim blade to dull it out. Then he stood straight. "Shall we?"

THEY SLIPPED between the dark blocky huts like splinters of the night itself. Their stealth seemed almost wasted. All of the Chichimecs in evidence were at the plaza, gathered in the vigil around the Holy Child's hut, or standing sentry duty. Without incident Doc and Ryan reached the back of the hut just before the house where the motorcycle was parked.

Ryan led off along the side wall, holding the SIG-Sauer ready in both hands. Where he got to the point he was about to come into view of the guard at the back of the house he took a step sideways, extended his arms and squeezed off a round. The mutie's head snapped back. He seemed to melt sideways to a pile on the ground.

Ryan sidestepped back to the corner of the house, continued to hold his weapon online while he watched with eye soft-focused for any sign of reaction. None came. The sentries on the roof seemed to be paying all their attention to the festivities around the bonfire. They had to have been reaching another climax, because there came a fresh crescendo of screams and roar of approval from the crowd.

The rear door was unguarded but closed and locked. The window in back had been boarded shut. Doc grabbed up the dead mutie's Mini-14, eased back the charging handle to confirm a round was chambered, let the spring carry it slowly forward again to seal the breech. Holding the carbine in his left hand, swordstick in the right, Doc nodded to Ryan.

The one-eyed man crept to the side of the house,

peered around. No one was in sight between the house and the plaza. He slipped silently around the corner, followed by Doc.

A yellow blade of light fell from a boarded window of what should be the front room. Signaling Doc to keep lookout, Ryan stole up to it, peered inside.

The room was simply furnished: a couple of scavenged tubular-steel-and-plastic chairs, a folding card table with a lantern on it. There was a picture of the Virgin of Guadalupe on the wall in an ornate frame that looked like gold and was no doubt painted plastic.

A tall figure wearing a foul loincloth and the head and cape of a wolf stalked back and forth across the floor, which had been formed by pouring blood into the dirt; constant foot traffic had compacted and then polished it so that it looked almost like seamless maroon tile. Howling Wolf was gaunt, almost emaciated. The hollows of his face and between his ribs were accentuated by the streaks of blood, now dried and black in the lantern light, that he had apparently poured over himself. Ryan could smell the stench of the rotting blood, and hear the buzz of flies around him. As startling as it was, the bizarre apparition of the Chichimec prophet wasn't what caught his attention. Nor were the two bodyguards in his field of vision, a giant mutie with no hair, small pointed ears and slits in a muzzlelike face in lieu of a nose who held a Browning autoloading shotgun, and a human armed with some kind of machine pistol with an extended tubular-steel folding stock and front and rear pistol grips.

What grabbed his eye instead was Felicidad Mendoza, trim and cool in camou blouse, shorts and hiking boots, her copper hair drawn back in a severe bun and glinting like wire. She sat behind the table watching Nezahualcoyótl with a bland expression, as if he neither looked nor smelled the least bit out of the ordinary.

Their voices were clearly audible. They were speaking in Spanish, however. Ryan tapped whatever part of Doc it was that was close enough to reach.

When the old man turned, Ryan said softly, "Translate. Keep it down, though, or we're both catching the last train for the coast."

"Surely, my boy. Ahem. The frightfully bedizened specimen is saying 'Passed right through his flab. He should recover fully.'

"'Especially with the antibiotics I brought,' the brazen hussy—highly appropriate term, given the color of her hair—says."

Ryan was keeping watch now, his blaster ready. There were still no signs of movement in the crooked streets nearby. Felicidad was apparently trusting her host to make the security arrangements, and he in turn was sloppy. Well, Ryan guessed, there was nothing like being surrounded by hundreds of literally bloodthirsty fanatic followers to lull a man into a sense of complacency.

"You trust your whitecoat technology more than our ancestor's healing wisdom?" the false prophet asked.

"Absolutely," Felicidad said, "where matters like preventing infection are concerned. That's how Don Hector will conquer all, by taking the best and strongest of the old ways and the new and bending them to his will."

"As you say. We shall continue to have use of the boy for so long as we need him. I cannot say the same for his uncle, though. The old man has grown querulous. I think it is time for our gods to accept his flowery sacrifice."

"That's your concern—*if* you can control the boy without him."

"The boy is used to obeying me. I'll tell him his uncle grew sick and died unexpectedly. It won't enter the brat's simple mind to doubt my word."

"So long as you're willing to stake your life upon it," Felicidad said, and Ryan could hear the heavily affected boredom in her voice, "since that's exactly what you're doing."

"Do not try my patience. Bad enough Don Hector dishonors me by sending a mere woman to dictate to me, without my suffering your impertinence."

"I'll have you know I'm now Don Hector's sec boss, my dear father having earned his own flowery death. And don't forget, you are nothing but Don Hector's creature."

"Enough! Do you forget that Don Hector is far, and my followers are close at hand? Did I give the word they would tear your harlot's carcass limb from limb."

"Maybe," Felicidad said, inspecting her fingernails. "But if they did, I'd be sure to inform them, loudly, how you've been betraying them to Hector from the start, and how today they were supposed to be slaughtered—*after* destroying the weak fools from the city, which I note you failed utterly to accomplish."

"The cowards hung back. I deployed the bulk of my men to fall upon them—as Don Hector directed. But when we struck the ranks of your valley troops the city scum were nowhere to be found. Only when my men had turned to fall upon the flanks of Hector's force did the he-goats fire treacherously on us from ambush."

"It doesn't matter how you failed, only that you failed. Fortunately, for you, your failure wound up costing us little. Don Hector and his Eagle Knights have slipped into the city and captured the fool Tenorio. I myself took prisoner the red-haired witch woman and the black bitch before riding here."

Ryan gritted his teeth. He raised the SIG-Sauer to press its muzzle to the crack. Doc checked the motion.

"Not if you would live to rescue Krysty and Mildred, my dear boy."

For a moment Ryan's eye blazed like a lethal blue star. Then he swallowed and nodded.

Doc resumed translating the copper-haired woman's words. "—notice only two of the outlanders tied up outside. You were instructed to capture all four who remained encamped with the army."

"The leader resisted and was slain. The commander of the raiding party has already given his heart to the gods for his ineptitude. The other, the older man, could not be found. My spies say he is given to bouts of confusion. Without doubt he's wandering the night, befuddled." Doc's eyebrows rose in indignation as he translated.

"He is surely of no consequence. What would you have me do with the captives we did obtain?"

"Hector wanted that arrogant one-eyed-dog Ryan to watch his friends tortured to death for the gods' delectation, before he made his own sacrifice. Since he's dead, it doesn't matter what you do with the others. The important one is the witch with the red hair that moves like so many snakes. There's great power in that one. Her sacrifice alone should be enough for Huitzilopochtli to grant Hector immortality!"

"And what of me?"

"Don Hector will see you get what's coming to you. But beware of failing him again!"

"My Chichimecs were to lose to his triumphant army today. And so they did. Can I be blamed if every detail isn't exactly right?"

"Oh, yes," the woman almost whispered.

There was a pause. "What does Hector want of me now?"

"Hold your people in check. They can continue to ravage the countryside north of here as they will. Hector will no doubt wish to lead his forces in a triumphal final battle, after he's brought the city to heel."

"I will try. There is great dissatisfaction after today's huge losses. The prisoners will assuage their grief and rage for a time, but will soon be used up."

"Then I'd advise you to concoct something extra special for the outlanders. Tell your savages they're the witches responsible for your defeat. Use your roly-poly Holy Imbecile to twist their passions. I can't work out every detail for you. I need to get back."

Ryan thought about trying to snatch her as she left,

or simply chill her. He dismissed the notion as soon as it entered his head. No opportunity in the ville, and as for racing back to the wag and trying to intercept her…. Though hatred for her boiled in his blood, it meant nothing in comparison to his need to save Krysty and the other companions. Payback would be sweet, but would have to wait.

Chapter Twenty-Seven

"I wish our relief would get here," Three Feather said. His name, like Two Arrow and Five Ax, was typical of the names traditionally used by the people of the valley of Mexico and its environs, or at least so far as the wretched survivors who crawled out of their caves after the end of skydark a hundred years before could make out. In his case it was unusually appropriate: he was a mutie, a *brujo* or witch as the Chichimecs called his kind, who though mostly norm in appearance had a crest of three feathers of increasing length growing back to front over his skull.

"I know what you mean," his companion said. Both were guarding the hut on the ville's outskirts. He was a normal human, short like almost all the Chichimecs, potbellied. "I haven't eaten all day."

"That's all you think about, stuffing your gut."

"At least we have enough to eat for a while."

Frowning, Three Feather said, "If you keep eating like you do it's going to slow you down. Then it's you for the pot."

"I keep up! I ran back here as fast as you did today. Besides, if you aren't hungry, why are you so eager to be off?"

Three Feather bobbed his head in the direction of the plaza, from which screams and applause continued to rise into the cloudless night sky. "I want to watch. Those bastards hurt us today, killed many of my friends. I want to see them get what's coming—"

There was a strange popping sound. Something splashed against the side of the mutie's face. "Did you spit on me?" he demanded, turning in outrage.

But his companion had collapsed on the packed dirt in front of the hut. Dark fluid was gushing from of the side of his head.

Three Feather opened his mouth to scream an alert. But what emerged from his mouth was a bloody thin tongue of steel.

"BLAZES!" DOC HAD his boot on the neck of the fallen mutie and was trying to unstick his sword from the dead sentry's head. "It is wedged!"

"Hurry it up, Doc," Ryan said, looking around cautiously, SIG-Sauer still ready in his hand. "It was your bright idea to poke him through the headbone."

"Well, you must admit it dispatched him quickly and, of paramount importance, silently. There!" The blade came free with a pop. He flourished it triumphantly in the air.

They dragged the dead sentries around to the back of the hut and left them by a pile of debris. Better that passersby see no sentries at all than stiffs on the doorstep.

The door had no visible lock. With both men standing clear, Ryan pushed at it gingerly. It opened with a groan of rusted hinges that sounded horribly loud and made his heart jump into his throat.

Again, no outcries of discovery. Doc took out his flashlight and shone it inside.

A man sat in the midst of the bare floor with his knees up and his head between them. His heavy black hair was shot with gray. He raised his head and glared at them defiantly. Then as his eyes, accustomed to the dark, made out their vague figures past the dazzle, his look changed to one of surprise.

"You're foreigners!" he exclaimed in Spanish.

"You the Holy Child's uncle?" Ryan asked. Doc translated.

The man had gotten to his feet, slowly, as if his joints pained him. Ryan guessed he'd been sitting on the floor for many hours. His seamed badland face was impassive, but Ryan guessed he was going through a fierce internal debate.

"I am," he said. "I am he called Raven. Have you come to kill me?"

"No. You're free to walk out of here. But we need to talk. There's some things you ought to know. But first we need to get out of here before somebody comes along. Will you come with us and hear us out?"

Without hesitation the older man said, "I can do that much."

The three left the hut, moved out of the ville with more concern for speed than stealth, to a brushy lava outcrop from behind which they could keep an eye on pursuit. Unsure of the Chichimec, Ryan had no intention of leading him to their concealed wag or even betraying its existence.

Quickly he recounted the conversation he had overheard between Howling Wolf and Felicidad Mendoza. Raven squatted, listened without emotion.

"So there has been a battle. I have been imprisoned for several days. What of my nephew?"

Ryan looked at Doc, who shrugged. "He was injured. Not badly, they say. He'll recover. I shot him. It was the only way to save myself and my friends from your army."

For a moment Raven stared at him with eyes that glittered like glass in the starlight. "In hard times a man does what he must. It is the way of this world. If my sister's son lives, I bear you no ill will. But what do you want of me?"

"First tell me how you got wrapped up in this." For a fact Raven struck Ryan as a basic hunter-warrior type, a man of dignity and honor. Not the sort of crazie or dreg he'd expect to find taking part in a cannibal crusade.

"The man Nezahualcoyótl came up from the south speaking to us of destiny. He called my sister's son a great gift of the gods, and claimed that the gods had guided him, Howling Wolf, to us to show us how to use that great gift."

For a moment Raven sat silent. The wind had picked up. Over it Ryan could hear the demonic festivities from the ville and the deep sullen voices of the volcanoes.

"Times had turned bad. The death winds were blowing ever farther south, and the rains that strip the meat from a man's bones. Game grew scarce. Our shadows dwindled with each sun. We should not have listened to him—I should not have listened to him—but his words were honey to our ears. I in particular was touched by destiny, he told me. For I was always the one closest to the boy. In turn I was the one the boy listened to, although in time he began to heed Howling Wolf, as well."

He shook his head. "My heart began to turn bad almost from the start. All the torture, the eating of human flesh. If an enemy does you great hurt, you give him a hard time before he dies—that's the way of the world, too. But Howling Wolf has a great hunger for human pain, which he has passed on to the others. All to please the gods, he preaches, but I think it is mostly what pleases him."

"And speaking of which," Doc said with a meaningful nod toward the wavering glow from the ville, "if we wish to avail our friends, we'd best act with expedition."

"Um, right. Will you help us, Raven?"

"You mean no further harm to my sister's son?"

"None unless that's the only way to stop the invasion."

"Removing Nezahualcoyótl will stop the invasion."

"That's what I reckon."

"You will slay the false priest Howling Wolf?"

"That's the general plan."

"You will not try to destroy my people?"

"Don't care about your people one way or another as long as they leave my friends and me alone. We're probably going to have to chill a few to free our pals and put Howling Wolf on ice for keeps, though."

"I will help you as best I can."

"Then all that remains to us," Doc said, "is to determine how."

"HOW YOU HOLDING UP, Jak?" J.B. asked.

"Alive. Till dead." The albino youth spit bloody phlegm into the dust at his feet. "Not crawl for bastards."

"That's the spirit. Spit in the bastards' eyes when they come for you." He shook his head. His face, like Jak's, was crusted over with blood. His left eye was swollen almost shut. Improbably, his spectacles had survived, and one of their captors had placed them carefully back on J.B.'s face when the two were lashed to the poles.

"And here they come," the Armorer said as a group led by capering blood-soaked figures started across the naked earth toward them. "Always intended, when came time for me to chill, to show whoever did me just how much guts I had. But I gotta admit, I never meant it quite so *literal*."

From right behind them headlights came on, striking the pair with an almost physical impact.

"I THOUGHT," DOC SAID with asperity as Ryan drove into the ville from the north, lights out, at a slow pace for a wag, but faster than a man could walk, "that you intended to create a diversion."

"Circumstances changed, so the plan changed. Be pretty diverting, though."

"Was it truly necessary to throw stealth out with the bath water?"

"Time's blood, Doc. It's running out fast for our friends here, and who knows how fast for Krysty and Mildred back in the city?"

Doc rode in back. Raven was up front where Ryan could keep an eye on him. The Chichimec cradled the weapon the feathered mutie guard had carried, a nice lever-action Marlin 94 in .30-30, complete with a box and a half of cartridges for reloads. Mostly he seemed to be trying to maintain his stoic front and hide the fact he was as delighted as a kid at riding in the wag, no doubt for the first time in his life.

Doc had the other guard's weapon, a 20-gauge Winchester Defender pump shotgun. Between Ryan and Raven rode the Mini-14 off the sentry he'd chilled at Nezahualcoyótl's hut. The two had their handblasters in reserve, as well.

Yet again, no one paid the least attention as they rolled right up toward the plaza. They could see their friends clearly. Beyond them the games were suspended; a dozen or so Chichimecs were approaching J.B. and Jak even now. Their turn was imminent.

"We should have guessed Don Hector was never serious about fighting these crazies. Their security's so bad he could have wiped them out any time he felt like it."

"Which is the very fate he intends, according to that remarkably wicked young woman," Doc said, "To make himself fully the conquering hero once he has no further use for these poor deluded fools."

"Well," Ryan said, "we'll just have to piss on his parade."

He rolled the Hummer to the edge of the plaza, barely fifteen feet behind the stakes to which his friends were tied. He switched on the lights.

The group making for the captive pair stopped, their faces frozen in comic parodies of surprise.

Ryan got out and clambered up on the wag's hood, then helped Raven up and onto the roof. He then raised the Mini-14 above his head and fired off three quick rounds. The short-barreled longblaster made a satisfactory amount of noise.

It definitely got the undivided attention of the several hundred blood-drunk celebrants. Everybody stared; nobody moved.

With all the immense dignity of which he was capable, employing his again-sheathed swordstick with a grand flourish, Doc marched forward to the torture poles. He pulled out his pocketknife and slashed the bonds of first J.B., then Jak.

Both men dropped to their knees, groaning with the aches and pins-and-needles agony that flowed with blood back into their arms and hands. "What took... long?" Jak demanded.

"Never thought I'd want to kiss that mug of yours, Doc," J.B. said, rubbing his wrists and getting one knee up.

"Keep your expressions of gratitude in abeyance, John Barrymore. We are not out of the woods yet."

The Armorer nodded to the execution squad, which still stood frozen sixty feet away. "Yeah, we are."

Jak got to his feet, reached out a hand to help J.B. up.

They limped together back toward the wag as Doc stood facing down the mob with sheer presence.

Through all this, Raven stood like a clay statue atop the Hummer, arms folded, Marlin jutting at an angle from one hand. As the two freed captives approached, he tossed the longblaster toward J.B. Though his hands felt like vast pincushions, the Armorer fielded the weapon without dropping it.

Raven raised his arms above his head. "People!" he shouted. "You know me. I am Raven, uncle to the Holy Child." Or so Ryan reckoned, based on the smattering of Spanish he'd of necessity absorbed the past week and what he'd have said under the circumstances. The Chichimecs gaped at the man.

Doc turned grandly on his heel and strode back to the wag. "Shotgun, Jak," he said out of the corner of his mouth. The white-haired youth nodded and took up the Defender the older man had left leaning against the Hummer's front left tire. Doc walked to cover the right side of the wag. As he turned back to face the mob, he drew his bulky LeMat as discreetly as possible, held it down by his trouser leg.

As Ryan had anticipated—bet his life and those of his friends, to be more precise—the prestige of the Holy Child's uncle and guardian was sufficient to hold the mob back and win him a listen. His speechifying had long since outstripped Ryan's comprehension, but it seemed to be making an impression.

"He is displaying oratorical skills of an unlooked-for degree of advancement," Doc said admiringly. "Would you like me to translate?"

"He keepin' to the script?"

"Substantially, yes."

"Then no."

Of course, the spell couldn't last. A strapping mutie pushed to the head of the mob. He was broad-shouldered, thick-muscled, with a fist of cartilage for what passed as a face. Ryan had seen him helping supervise the evisceration of the prisoners, and guessed he was one of Nezahualcoyótl's chief enforcers. He raised his massive arms above his head and began to bellow at the crowd, for all the world like a common everyday Deathlands sec goon bullying the masses.

"He says, 'Do not listen to this traitor, his head and heart have grown soft, he has turned his face from the gods, only Nezahualcoyótl knows the heart of the Holy Child,' so on, so forth," Doc translated in a monotone.

"Right." Ryan whipped the Mini-14 to his shoulder, centered the mutie's head in the peep rear sight, squeezed off a round. The carbine might have been loaded with some kind of soft or even hollow-pointed hunting rounds—Ryan hadn't bothered to check beyond insuring it had a full mag and one up the spout—because the mutie boss's head popped like a zit. He fell right over backward in the dust with his arms still rhetorically up-flung and the last convulsive clench of his heart ejaculating blood from his lower jaw and neck stump.

"Ryan!" Doc exclaimed.

"We ain't here for debate, Doc."

Doc eyed the crowd with eyes like boiled onions. "Surely that was a touch precipitous?"

But the Chichimecs, having watched the spurting corpse drop with avid interest, had turned their collective eyes back to the small man with the silvered hair who stood atop the wag. "It's results I'm interested in," Ryan said.

"Think about it, Doc," J.B. said. "Do you really want our fate decided by democratic processes among cannies?"

But Jak swore bitterly. "Fuck, Ryan. Wanted that one!"

"Uh-oh," J.B. said. "We got company."

From the street to their right appeared a wedge of big Chichimecs carrying blasters and flame-streaming torches. Behind them came several of the blood-drenched men, wearing things that looked like shiny shower caps on their heads. Finally came Nezahualcoyótl himself, stalking more like a big cat than one of his namesakes.

Ryan had to admit the old devil was cool as concrete in a Laska midwinter. He'd not just gathered his chillers around him but had rounded up torches for them to tote, to make his appearance that much more impressive.

J.B. raised the Marlin. "This one's mine."

Ryan held his hand out to stop him. "No. We can't chill him. Watch the mob and the main man's hitters. If they look like they're thinking about moving on Raven or us, chill them. But if we drop the Wolf, the mob eats us."

J.B. gave him a "hope you know what you're doin'" frown, but lowered the wep.

The prophet's procession marched into the middle of the open space, which still separated his followers from the interlopers. Turning his back on the wag, he began to address the crowd in a shrill, piercing voice. The bloody men screeched approval and reinforcement at what were apparently key utterances.

"What's with those crazies?" Ryan asked. He held the Mini-14 gingerly, not aimed, but pointed and ready to raise and snap off a shot. This was the tricky point.

"Priests." Jak spat.

"They added little details to the fun," J.B. said. "Like cutting one dude's man parts off and shoving them down his throat before they pulled the guts out of him."

"By Jove, I believe those are human heart cauls they're wearing on their heads!' exclaimed Doc. "Just as Prescott described the ancient Aztecs as doing."

"If you mean a kind of membrane bag your heart comes in," J.B. said in a guttural voice, "you got that right. Fresh cut."

The Chichimecs were starting to rumble deep in their throats, a sound like the noise of the smokies away off to the far side of the lake, but under the circumstances far more menacing.

"What's he saying, Doc?" Ryan demanded.

"The expected. He alone is the prophet, sent by the gods to aid the Holy Child. Raven is a heretic rebel and must die."

A snarl issued from the throats of the mob. "Ah," Doc said in dismay. "He just told them Raven has disgraced himself by making common cause with the very infidel who struck down the Holy Child. He scored points with that one, I very much fear."

The priests began to dance in front of Nezahualcoy-ótl, chanting shrilly.

"They say, 'Take their hearts, their hearts to the gods, their blood for the blood of the Holy Child,'" Doc said.

First one Chichimec took up the chant, then another. Suddenly the whole mob was chanting along with the capering priests.

It began to surge forward.

Chapter Twenty-Eight

"What is our plan now, Ryan?" Doc asked.

Ryan shouldered the Mini-14. "We get ready to die a lot."

The crowd stopped. Silence fell like a hundred-ton nukeproof door.

A short figure limped painfully into the glare of bonfire and torches. A large round head propped atop a near-spherical body, one pudgy pasty arm pressed to a poultice taped onto the side of its vast belly.

"*¡El Niño Santo!*" the horde gasped.

"*¡Mira!*" cried Howling Wolf. Ryan understood it to mean "Behold!"

The boy raised the arm that wasn't clutching his gut wound. He pointed a chubby finger at the tall gaunt figure in the wolf's head.

The prophet sensed his luck had just caught the last train for the coast. "*¡Mátalo!*" he screamed. *Slay him!*

The big bastard turned and drew down on the boy with his Browning autoloading scattergun. Ryan already had the Ruger aimed. He fired three quick shots into the muscle-sheathed rib cage beneath the massive right arm. The mutie went down trailing blood from nose slits and mouth.

Howling like coyotes, the crowd charged. They swarmed up the big torch-bearing guards like soldier ants, tearing, biting. Several of the bodyguards blasted full-auto bursts into the crowd. It didn't win them so much as a second.

The priests shrieked in terror and turned to run. Most were taken at once, disappeared under flailing limbs. The Chichimecs who had weps seemed to be disregarding them in favor of the equipment nature had gifted them with. A couple of the priests broke away to be hunted through the ville by baying packs of Chichimecs.

For a moment Nezahualcoyótl stood alone, with a sea of humanity and near-humanity surging around him like surf. His eyes blazed forth from a face streaked with other men's blood. Later Ryan decided he simply couldn't believe that everything had deteriorated so quickly for him.

For a moment, though, it seemed as if he would repel the horde now lusting—with the Holy Child's guidance—for *his* blood by sheer force of personality. Then a muzzled mutie leaped on his back and, leaning forward, ripped away the whole of Nezahualcoyótl's right cheek with his fangs.

The prophet became the nucleus of a hill of writhing figures. Horrific screams emerged from the midst of it, and jets of blood. Slowly the mound dwindled toward the hard-packed soil.

Then the struggling ceased. The mob fell back, humans and muties alike looking as if they had bathed in fresh blood. In the space they suddenly cleared, nothing remained but a blood-soaked wolf's hide and a crimson-dyed skeleton clothed in a few rags of skin and meat.

Ignoring the commotion, Raven had scrambled down from the wag and run to his nephew's side. The Holy Child turned to him, tears streaming down his great pallid moon of a face, and collapsed into the older man's arms.

Doc tucked away his LeMat, took up his swordstick from where he'd leaned it against the wag, and brushed at his coat. "Well, gentlemen," he said, "it appears our work here is done."

RYAN DROVE THE WAG south as fast as he could. He was no longer concerned about running with lights on. With Nezahualcoyótl eaten alive by his followers, the Holy Child was in complete control of the Chichimec horde. Which meant in practice his uncle Raven was. Raven had no further appetite for war, and likely enough none of the Chichimecs did, either.

The old man had asked Ryan, just before the reunited companions left, what they could do. Their own homeland still faced devastation from the storms. There were fewer mouths to feed, to be sure, but that would only put off the day of reckoning.

"I have no idea," Ryan admitted. If they rescued Tenorio, he'd at least agree to trade with the Chichimecs, maybe even send them aid. Whether he could do enough was beyond Ryan's knowledge, and he was damned thankful it was also not his problem.

If Hector won, well, the Chichimecs would be on

their own lookout. And Ryan and company would be beyond worrying about it.

They had recovered Ryan's SSG rifle, as well as Jak's and J.B.'s weps, including the BAR lent them by Tenorio. The items had been stashed in a back room of the late Nezahualcoyótl's hut, apparently as trophies. The M-60 was missing and nobody admitted having any idea where it was; no doubt one of the raiders who had kidnapped J.B. and Jak had "lost" it as too damned heavy to tote back to the ville on foot.

Ryan had halfway hoped to find a plundered talkie or two. Now that they hadn't, he didn't regret it. Hector would no doubt have the radio freaks monitored.

One thing they had made Raven promise, which he had been glad to do: nobody was to leave the Chichimec-held ville before dawn. Hector would be assuming that all the outlanders, save the two women he held captive, had long since bought the farm. Ryan didn't want anything disabusing him of that notion before a 180-grain, copper-jacketed bullet tunneled through the back of his skull.

They made for the main city camp, which as far as they or the Chichimecs knew, remained undisturbed and blissfully unaware anything was amiss. Ryan surmised Hector would try to secure the city, or at least a firm foothold, and then challenge the scavvies to pry *him* out, rather than risk an all-out battle in the open between the encamped forces. Even at his most manic, Ryan judged, Hector had to know the scavvies would whip his boys in a stand-up fight, outnumbered as they were.

Of course, Ryan understood he had piled surmise upon supposition, as Doc might put it. It might be bull-shit on bullshit. Well, it was still his best guess, and his best play. If he was wrong, they'd all be taking a trip a lot farther south than anticipated….

All the same, he slowed and killed the lights when they started to approach the two camps. He drove up to just shy of the crest of what he judged to be the last rise before coming in sight of the scavvies camp and stopped. Leaving the Armorer where he was, in the gun mount with his automatic rifle, Ryan and Jak exited the wag and crawled up to the top for a look.

"Strike," Ryan said, scanning the camp with his monocular. The fires had been allowed to gutter low, but he could see forms sleeping peacefully with blasters stacked nearby. A yawning sentry wandered among them with a long FN FAL slung at waist height by a sling.

So as not to rouse the valley camp, slumbering a half mile or so off to the west, Ryan ran down on the scavvies with lights out, flashing them once as they approached the outskirts to alert the sentries and to let them know nobody was trying to sneak up on them. All the same the scavvie sentries were pointing their weapons at the wag when it rolled in among them. Only when they recognized the occupants did they relax.

It helped that they had taken time to wash up quickly before departing the ville—not just Jak and J.B. but Ryan, whose head wound had broken open, although the blood had run down over his patch rather than into his good eye so that he was unaware of it. As anxious as

Ryan was to rescue Krysty and Mildred, Felicidad Mendoza had said they were to be sacrificed, and that meant that nothing would happen to them before sunup at the very earliest. According to J.B., sunrise was still two and a half hours away when they rolled out of the ville under gathering clouds.

The scavvies were startled to see the companions appearing out of the north. The first thing Ryan told them was to spread the word not to show any lights or unusual activity. Only when the puzzled but agreeable scavvies had begun to comply did he and his friends start to tell the tale.

It took a lot more jawing—and time—than he was comfortable with to get them to comprehend all that had gone on, much less believe it. Fortunately no voices were raised and the wakened scavvies mostly kept to their bedrolls as requested. They lacked most semblance of military discipline, but their lifestyle demanded a great deal of self-discipline. And after yesterday Ryan could do no wrong in any of their eyes.

He needed all that, not just respect but hero-worship, first to get them to accept the incredible story, then to talk them out of mounting up right then, falling on the racked-out valley forces, and massacring them in their own beds.

"Not necessary," Ryan insisted. "They aren't that different from the Chichimecs. If we take out Hector, they won't fight with you on their own hook."

Colonel Obiedo, the nominal tactical commander had been on the firing line with a blaster-wag and died of anaphylactic shock, stung to death by yellowjackets whose rage had been stirred and then directed by the Holy Child. Current war chief apart from Ryan himself was the ranking surviving Jaguar Knight, a gangly mustached young man named Rino Espinoza. Fortunately he spoke English, and he had the quick and tactical mind Ryan had come to associate with Tenorio's self-constituted elite commandos. Once he accepted the bizarre tale was true, he agreed with all Ryan's reasoning.

He also agreed that the city forces should, as stealthily as possible, march down and secure the shore end of the causeway. If, as Ryan guessed, Hector had captured it, four Jaguar Knights would lead the attack and take out the guards quietly if they could. If snooping and pooping failed, they still had grens left over and even a couple satchel charges. Whatever it took, they'd grab the causeway entrance and dig in around it to prevent Hector bringing any more troops into the city than he had already.

"Risky," J.B. pointed out in a quiet aside. "If a firefight breaks out, no way Hector isn't going to find out about it."

"What's he going to think?" Ryan asked. "He knows we're dead. The natural assumption is the scavvies've learned he grabbed the roadhead. He won't let that spoil his shivaree."

The Armorer shrugged eloquently. "Yeah, I know," Ryan admitted. "Still more assumptions. But if any of them are wrong, we're chilled anyhow. I'd rather die on my feet than my knees."

J.B. sighed. "Amen to that."

From the south came a series of booming cracks. Past the dark drowned towers of the city, the southern horizon glowed red like the mouth of a forge.

"Don't like the looks or sound of that," the Armorer said. "Sounds like very angry smokies. Mebbe angry enough to dump another three, four feet of hot ash and poison gas on our sorry heads."

As if to emphasize his words, the earth shivered beneath their feet, like the flank of a horse that's had a fly light on it. Ryan shrugged. "Least of our worries right now."

Espinoza emerged from a nearby tent. "Let's go," he said.

"Say what?" Ryan asked.

Five other men emerged from the tent, armed, with their faces blackened. Despite the war paint Ryan recognized the other surviving Jaguar Knights who had remained with the forces in the field rather than returning to town with their *alcade*.

"We're coming with you," Rino announced.

Ryan looked to J.B. "Be a tight fit in the wag," he said, "but I think these boys could've ridden with Trader."

It was the Armorer's seal of approval. "Reckon you're right," Ryan said. "But we've still got the problem of getting into the city."

"We got the sealing plates stowed. I checked. Cannies never found the compartment. We can make her airtight and run on the bottom."

"Lake's too deep for the snorkel."

"Don't have an air-breathing engine."

"Got air-breathing *us*. Too many, too long. And the problem of trying to get out under water once we get into the ville, since there ain't very many places we can drive up onto."

"Excuse me," Rino put in softly, "but what is the problem?"

"Transport into the city itself."

"Ah," he said. Then grinned. "Is no problem."

Chapter Twenty-Nine

Ernesto, Don Tenorio's serious young aide, died game.

He was skinny, lacked muscle tone, and couldn't see anything but a blur since his captors had smashed his eyeglasses. But once they slashed through the salvaged plastic clothesline that held his wrists and ankles, the very first thing he did was send one of Hector's pet priests of Huitzilopochtli rolling down the steep sides of the ancient step-pyramid in the city's midst with blood spewing from a broken nose, until a broken neck ended the pumping of his heart. Of course, it wasn't easy to tell, since, as with all Nezahualcoyótl's assistant priests, they drenched themselves in the blood of their sacrificial victims and never, ever washed it off. Needless to say, they all smelled as if they slept each night in the rectum of a week-dead elephant.

By equally lucky accident the naked aide landed a kick directly in the crotch of an Eagle Knight trying to grab him and doubled the big man over. Don Hector, dressed up in gleaming gold and feather headdress and vestments, stood by bellowing in rage at the disruption. It was left to Felicidad Mendoza, naked but for a loin-cloth, a plumed headdress only slightly less ornate than Hector's and a heavy gold necklace that didn't do anything to hide her magnificent breasts, to step up behind the thrashing young man and stun him with a rabbit punch.

He was still stunned when they caught his wrists and ankles, spread-eagled him atop the stone slab at the apex of the pyramid, and Don Hector, leaning over him with an obsidian knife, hacked his chest and his rib cage open and cut his heart out over his living body. Lucky him.

The valley serfs and sec men assembled around the base of the pyramid cheered dutifully as their *cacique* held the heart, still steaming and pulsing, above his plumed head in offering to the sun. The hundred or so scavvies who had been rounded up by the occupying force and herded out to view the ritual watched in sullen, smoldering silence. The sun wasn't itself putting in an appearance at Hector's self-coronation, being hidden entirely on the far side of a leaden overcast that was thickened and deepened by smoke from the volcanoes, which were in full booming eruption.

Don Hector, face, chest and finery liberally splashed with gore, tossed the heart into a charcoal brazier made out of an oil drum with a quarter cut out lengthwise. A cloud of reeking steam and smoke rolled out. The priests dragged the still-twitching body from the altar and pitched it down the backside of the pyramid. Hector gestured for the next sacrifice, one of the wounded captured in the infirmary, to be brought on.

It was Felicidad's turn to do the honors. Her eyes and lips shone as she stepped forward, knife in hand.

"KRYSTY?" MILDRED ASKED. "Krysty, are you all right?"

"No talk," snarled an Eagle Knight standing guard on the same step of the pyramid as Mildred.

"Go fuck yourself!" Mildred retorted. "You don't dare lay a finger on us, needle dick."

The Eagle Knight flushed deep red and started to raise his laser arm. Then he lowered it and turned away. The black woman was right. He didn't dare risk damaging the guests of honor at his *cacique*'s inaugural bash as Emperor of the Valley.

"Krysty?" she said to the white-clad woman.

The redhead turned to look over her shoulder at Mildred. The first thing Mildred saw was how pale Krysty's face was; the second, the way the sweat ran down it in gleaming sheets. The day was warm and unusually humid for the valley, under all these clouds, but neither that nor the climb two-thirds up the pyramid was enough to make her perspire that heavily. The emerald-green eyes were unnaturally bright. The physician worried her fever had come back.

Then Krysty smiled.

The pyramid trembled beneath the soles of Mildred's bare feet.

CUTTING OUT HEARTS with a stone knife wasn't as easy as it sounded. After he had done three and Felicidad had done three, Don Hector called a water break.

He went to the side of the pyramid top, where one of those picnic tables with a parasol sprouting from the middle of it had been erected. It wasn't exactly traditional, but who knew there wasn't going to be sun today? The *cacique* knew that he and his chosen consort would need breaks. Also he didn't want his extraspecial guest to pass out from sunstroke before he had watched all his loyal retainers, and his foreign female guests, offered to the gods.

Don Tenorio had to be fresh for when his turn came. The gods didn't want any wilted lettuce.

"You seem to have flooded the city with all your forces and some of your citizens," Tenorio said when Hector joined him under the parasol. As were Krysty and Mildred, the *alcade* was clad in a lightweight robe made out of salvaged bedsheets. He wasn't bound.

"Not all. Still, the ceremony is much more appropriate for the presence of an enthusiastic throng, don't you think? Your people are as yet unwilling to cooperate, so I was forced to import a throng."

"What if the Chichimecs choose to attack your domain?"

Hector laughed expansively. "I have no fears. I controlled the Chichimecs all along. Nezahualcoyótl was my agent from the outset. I sent him among them, first to confirm reports of the Holy Child, then to manipulate the child and, through him, all of them."

Tenorio stared at him. "Why?" he managed to ask above the synthetic cheering of the sec men and the growing noise of eruption.

"To achieve my destiny I needed a united valley. How better to attain that than manufacture a menace? I could at once crush my foes and demonstrate to the scattered peoples of the valley that only by pulling together under my protection could they be saved."

The *cacique* took a swig from a blue plastic sippy bottle bearing the logo of El Instituto Atlético Blue Demon, a legendary predark martial arts studio. He held it out to Tenorio.

"Water?"

THE STRUCTURAL STEEL BONES of the building groaned as the half skyscraper shook around them. The Jaguar Knights paused and glanced up as dust and flecks of insulation drifted down from the ceiling.

Ryan felt his face muscles go taut. He remembered reading in a book once about quake swarms. If he didn't know better, he'd swear things were building up to a major bone-shaker.

He looked back at Doc; the older man's eyes were wide.

He, Doc and three Jaguar Knights were exiting a stairwell onto the eighth floor of a building that once had more than twenty and now didn't run past eleven. It should put him on a level just a bit higher than the top of the pyramid three hundred yards away. Also this level had no windows intact on the side facing the plaza. It was primo sniper turf, and had been picked accordingly.

For that same reason Hector or his sec boss may have thought to secure it. They deployed into a line abreast with a Jaguar Knight armed with an MP-5 on Ryan's right, Doc with his LeMat to Ryan's left, and to his left the other two scavvies, one carrying a second

MP-5, the other a big SPAS 12-gauge riot scattergun that could fire either semiauto or pump action.

The level had been an office. Everything of obvious value had long since been salvaged. There were still a few desks, too bulky, heavy and common to be worth salvaging for anything but their metal, and fiberboard dividers, chest-high on Ryan and shoulder-high on most of the scavvie commandos, that still partitioned the big room into rows of workstations. The line moved forward quietly but quickly. The sun was up and, from the roar of the crowd outside, the party had begun.

They had crossed halfway to the warm breeze blowing in the wall-size opening where the glass had gone, that already smelled of hot blood and burned human flesh, when a figure popped up from behind a cubicle. Before even snake-fast Ryan could react, a brilliant ruby lance stabbed out.

AN UNEASY MURMUR ran through the audience, whose backs were to the men skulking in the shadows of the office building's ground floor. "Now I *really* don't like it," J.B. muttered. "These valley Mexes don't usually bother to notice your little old seismic disturbances unless the earth opens up at their feet or there's lava seepin' under the door or something."

"Tighten up," Jak whispered fiercely from the Armorer's right. J.B. glared at him. He just grinned back.

There had been a pair of sec men stationed in the lobby, who had been much preoccupied elbowing each other and grinning at the swell spectacle of people having their bodies carved open and their hearts yanked out. They now lay in spreading pools of blood with flies crawling on their eyeballs, grinning through second mouths. The Jaguar Knights understood the making and use of garrotes, a fine, strong wire strung between two wooden handles. A loop rolled over the victim's head from behind, a knee in the small of the back, the handles yanked to the sides with savage force. Properly done, the garrote didn't choke, it cut. The two jokers had had their throats severed to the spine before they'd known what had hit them.

J.B., Jak and the other three Jaguar Knights, including Rino Espinoza, were poised to drive through the crowd to try to rescue Krysty and Mildred when Ryan opened the ball. It would have been more feasible had they actually been able to work their way closer; they couldn't. J.B. and Jak were small enough not to stand out among the locals, but their pale skins would give them away at once. Since there weren't any guys out there wearing hoods, mingling was out of the question.

So all they could do was hunker down and wait. They and Ryan both had talkies, although whether they'd work or not was a crapshoot, what with all the structural steel around and the lightning that was beginning to crackle through the threatening clouds overhead. One way or another, when the time came they'd rush out and just hose their way through the crowd to the pyramid. Jak still carried the autoloading shotgun taken off the dead Chichimec and these Knights also packed two subguns and a scattergun among them. For his part, J.B.

reckoned his borrowed BAR would prove to be an excellent people mover.

In case it didn't work he had both his Uzi and his Smith & Wesson M-4000 shotgun strapped to the overstuffed rucksack on his back. They had made a quick trip by Tenorio's HQ to collect their effects, efficiently and without loss, murdering a skeleton crew of Hector's sec men in passing. The Armorer even had Mildred's ZKR 551 handblaster and her personal effects stuffed into the backpack.

A bang made J.B. jump. He realized it was a gren going off overhead and not the building coming down on their heads, and relaxed slightly. Then it hit him: it was a gren, going off overhead...

"Trouble," Jak whispered.

"No shit." There was nothing to do but wait until they got the signal to move.

Or until they decided the others had been taken out and it was up to them to do or die.

THE JAGUAR KNIGHT to Doc's left went flying backward, flung in a way no bullet could accomplish by the explosive jetting of flash-boiled blood from his chest. His MP-5 chattered deafeningly, stitching a ragged line in the acoustic tiles overhead.

The Eagle Knight had prudently dropped out of sight the instant he had fired. No targets presented themselves.

With stealth off the table, the four survivors pulled frag grens from their pockets or belts, yanked the pins and tossed the bombs. A ripple of bangs and flashes answered, followed by wild shrieks.

As soon as he let his gren fly, the Jag to Ryan's right crab-walked rapidly to the right side of the room and then ran forward with his machine pistol shouldered. The other just jumped up onto the workstations and began jumping from row to row over the tops of the dividers, his combat scattergun at his shoulder, as well.

The Eagle Knight sprang up, quick but unsteady on his bare muscular legs. Blood poured from the black pit where his right eye had been. He raised his right arm. The laser flared and cracked.

It drew a line of ionization harmlessly past the charging Jaguar Knight and blasted a chunk of tile flaming down from the ceiling. The Jag shot him right in the chest armor. Two pellets, low, punched neat little holes in his opposite number's six-pack stomach.

The half-blinded Eagle Knight staggered backward a step. The Jaguar Knight jumped down and fired another shot into the chest protector. Ryan, moving forward more cautiously with his Steyr ready, wondered if the Jag had panicked. If he shifted his aim a few degrees up or down, he'd chill the bastard *now*.

The Jaguar Knight blasted out three more quick shots, scouring the molded plastic away from the curved steel-ceramic plate, which was the real armor. Each shot hammered the Eagle Knight another step backward—the last into open air. As he vanished with a wild scream, Ryan understood.

A sec man popped up like a prairie dog, aiming an

M-1 carbine at the scattergunner. Doc happened to be right across the divider from him. The blast of the shorty shotgun barrel on his handblaster tore the front off the man's head and set fire to what was left. The man fell thrashing like a speared trout.

Then the other Jaguar Knight was at the last line of cubicles, firing quick bursts from the flank into whatever sec men were left functioning. Ryan ran forward to take up shooting position in the open-window wall. The building was shaking again, not stopping this time, and the sky outside seemed to be growing darker. He ignored it. He reached the edge, just had time to note with mingled fury and relief the unmistakable form of Krysty standing atop the pyramid and Mildred's shorter form upright beside her.

Then a flash lit the faces of the buildings to his left.

Chapter Thirty

The top of the pyramid was shaking as if about to fall right out from under the gathering at the very top. The rumbling from the volcanoes was much louder than the roar of the crowd. The priests' eyes were starting to roll inside their blood-caked faces, but Hector and Felicidad didn't seem to notice. Nothing was going to spoil the occasion for them.

A woman approached Mildred, who had been held ten feet back from Krysty as the redhead was escorted to take her turn on the altar. The woman was wearing only a loincloth and a gold headdress that was quite modest by the standards of what Hector and Felicidad were sporting, and of course a liberal coating of lots of other people's blood. Only when she came quite close, walking carefully to keep from sliding in the blood that covered the whole top of the pyramid and dripped away down the steps, did Mildred recognize María Garza, Don Tenorio's housekeeper.

She held an obsidian knife in her hand. Mildred felt her flesh shrink from the black blade, then realized she wasn't going to cut her.

"I see you know me," the tiny woman hissed in English. "Does it surprise you? You did not know I spoke your dog's tongue."

She moved behind Mildred and cut the ropes that bound her wrists. Mildred winced as she felt the superfine edge slice the skin of her left wrist.

"It was I who gave the *yerba mala* to your witch friend," María said, voice dripping with malevolence and joy. "I myself let Don Hector and his men into Tenorio's residence. The fool never suspected!"

She rose on tiptoe to speak into Mildred's ear. "And my reward will be…eternal life!"

"You got that wrong, bitch," Mildred said, and smashed her elbow into the woman's face.

The Eagle Knights holding Krysty by either elbow released her gingerly and stepped quickly to the sides. Her sentient hair was moving like a nest of serpents, and there seemed to be a crackling in the air around her that neither one liked. She was left alone, facing Hector with her head down and her wrists bound in front of her.

Felicidad stepped up behind her with a *macahuitl*. She drew the weapon down the back of the flimsy white robe, parting it. She pressed maliciously hard enough to draw a welling crimson line down the white skin of Krysty's back.

"You seem very calm, *señorita*," Felicidad said tauntingly. "Don't you realize what's happening to you?"

Then she fell back a step and gasped. Before her eyes the cut she had made on Krysty's back from nape to tailbone sealed itself like a zipper closing.

Krysty raised her head. Don Hector looked not into two green eyes, but blazing miniature suns.

MARÍA STAGGERED back. With surprising speed, Mildred whirled, grabbed her knife wrist, then stepped past her, twisting the arm up behind the traitor's bare back. She gave the arm a cruel yank. María squealed and dropped the volcanic glass knife.

Mildred expected at any instant to be blasted to barbecued back ribs by lasers, or chopped to bits, or clubbed unconscious, or any other bad thing she could think of. She didn't care. She was on a roll, with an unexpectedly golden opportunity to get at least *something* back for herself, for Krysty, for their murdered companions.

She slid her free arm around the local woman's throat, let go of her wrist, then with the hand freed up, seized the wrist of her own arm. She heaved her shoulders with all her strength.

María squealed shrilly, then her neck broke. It felt and sounded like the breaking of a tree limb. The traitor went limp in Mildred's arms.

As she let the deadweight go, Mildred realized no one was paying attention to her. All eyes were on Krysty.

SHE BEGAN TO STRAIN at the leather cords that bound her wrists. The muscles of her shoulders and back and arms seemed to swell to inhuman dimension. The shaking of the earth grew and grew.

The sky to the south lit with an orange flash.

The woman threw back her head and roared as her bonds parted.

Don Hector pissed down his legs.

Felicidad Mendoza was made of sterner stuff. With a wild cry, she leaped for Krysty's back, *macahuitl* upraised to split her skull.

The crack of the explosion that had opened a gaping hole in the side of Popocatépetl reached the plaza. Felicidad dropped the weapon and covered her ears against the terrific tsunami of noise.

Then the rolling overpressure hit.

THROUGH SHEER REFLEX Ryan dropped flat and hugged the floor when he saw the flash. That saved him.

There was a breathless moment, then the noise and the dynamic overpressure hit.

The blast wave blew right through the windowless floor, all but unimpeded. The Eagle Knight with the MP-5 was bowled out into space. Doc came rolling and sliding past Ryan.

The one-eyed man grabbed Doc's wrist as he was swept over the edge. Ryan winced as the older man's weight slammed his arm against the floor. Fortunately his vector was more down than out. He didn't pull Ryan after him, and the one-eyed man somehow held on.

Then the other Jaguar Knight was by his side. Together they hauled Doc, still clutching his LeMat, back to safety.

Ryan grabbed up his rifle. Kneeling, he raised it, put his eye to the scope. He dreaded what he would see.

THE BLAST WAVE knocked Mildred off her feet. She saw the picnic table with its ludicrously incongruous parasol go spinning away on that awful wind. Then she did a bellyflop in the blood.

Gagging and spitting, she raised her head. Everyone had been thrown down by the shock wave except Krysty, who stood with legs braced, terrible and tall. From the plaza below came screams of fear and pain.

When Mildred made her move, Tenorio had jumped to his feet, which saved him from being blown away with the table. Instead he was knocked down and rolled off the top step by the blast. He was away free and clear then. He could have just lain there, or gone scrambling down the side of the pyramid, and made good his escape.

Instead he clambered back onto the top block of the pyramid, slipping and sliding on the blood that covered it and streamed down its sides, and threw himself onto the broad back of Don Hector, who was just disengaging his own face with a squelch from the pooled congealing blood. He began to pummel his rival baron with both small hands.

An attack from a merely human foe snapped Hector back to manhood. Bracing himself on his huge arms, he rolled over, casting the smaller man from his back. He scrambled to his feet, skidding on the blood. He kicked Don Tenorio, who was trying gamely to rise. Ribs audibly cracked. The smaller man fell onto his side.

The earth was shaking violently now. Focused on his fallen enemy, the *cacique* raised a dripping foot to stomp him.

"Hector." The voice was like another eruption. Hector turned. *She* was standing directly behind him.

He tried to flee.

Her hair unreeled. Like a whip, it struck his head and wrapped around his face. Then it began to drag him back to her.

Felicidad had recovered. The obsidian-edged club again in hand, she lunged for Krysty. Mildred tackled her from behind.

"You're a game little bitch, I'll give you that," Mildred grunted, "but no way will I let you win."

Felicidad jabbed back over her shoulder with a thumb. Mildred yanked her head up enough to save her eye. The nail gouged a furrow in her cheek. Felicidad rolled onto her back and the two began to grapple. Mildred had the edge in size and absolute strength. The sec woman had muscles like bronze wire wrappings and was slippery as an eel. Biting, punching and spitting like cats, the two wrestled in the foul red muck.

Like tentacles, Krysty's sentient hair pulled Hector back into reach of her arms despite his frenzied struggles. She grabbed him at shoulder and hip.

Fingers digging in so brutally that the blood started around them, she yanked him up into the air above her head. She roared. As if in response, the very earth of the plaza split open at the pyramid base. A great sulfurous cloud of smoke rolled up, lit yellow by molten lava from below. Sec men and valley dwellers and luckless scavvies screamed as they fell into the hell maw.

For a moment longer the Krysty-thing held Hector

kicking feebly over her head. Felicidad and Mildred both froze in mid-death grapple, staring at the incredible sight. Blood streamed from Krysty's eyes and mouth and ears, Mildred saw to her horror. But the red-haired being paid no attention.

Instead she threw Don Hector as if he were a toy. He went sailing out and out into space, trailing a lung-rending scream as he flew. Thrashing and twisting, he actually cleared the pyramid base, dropped into the crack in the earth, fell into the lava, where he vanished with a final shriek and a plop of glowing yellow liquid stone.

Grinding and growling, the sides of the crevice closed in again until they shut like jaws with an impact that rocked the pyramid.

Felicidad wormed an arm free. She punched Mildred in the eye. Then she squirted out from under the bigger woman like a slick watermelon seed squeezed between two fingers. On all fours, she scrambled to her fallen *macahuitl*, snatched it up, then turned back to Mildred. Mad triumph blazed in her eyes.

"Now, you bitch," she shouted, "I'll—"

Red tendrils wrapped around the weapon, plucked it from her grasp, tossed it over the pyramid's edge.

"Girlfriend," Mildred said, picking herself up, "you're in a world of hurt."

Screeching like a panther, Felicidad Mendoza hurled herself at Mildred, hands curled into talons. The black woman met her with a perfect overhand right to the middle of her face.

Mildred almost came as she felt that perfect sculptured nose crunch and splay beneath her fist.

Felicidad staggered back, clutching at her ruined nose. She looked up at Mildred with something like wonder.

Mildred took a quick side step and launched a side kick that landed right between the sec woman's centerfold breasts. Felicidad went sailing off the top of the pyramid.

Mildred slipped and fell down.

She crawled quickly to the edge. Felicidad's blood-smeared cinnamon body was still bouncing down the side of the pyramid, step by step. "Didn't have quite the hang time of Krysty's toss," Mildred muttered, "but not bad for a home girl."

She stood then, her flesh suddenly crawling at the contact with all that clotting blood. "God *damn,* but this is nasty!" she exclaimed, trying to scoop the gunk off her.

A fresh tremor jerked her back to the here and now. She looked up. Krysty was standing tall and alone, her hair like a nimbus around her head. Lightning skeined the black clouds above her.

Behind her, Mildred saw a figure rise up. An Eagle Knight, raising his laser armlet.

"Krysty!" Mildred shrieked.

The Eagle Knight's head exploded.

A moment later the crack of a rifle shot arrived.

Krysty collapsed.

Chapter Thirty-One

A full-bore earthquake erupted. The building was rocked so violently by the tremors, Ryan had to go prone to keep from being thrown to the floor. As soon as he was down, he got the rifle up again and looked back through the scope just as Krysty caught the fleeing Hector with her hair.

"Ryan," Doc shouted, "should we not vacate these premises before they fall down around our ears?"

"Fireblast, no! Krysty may need help."

But she didn't. Ryan watched in amazement as the earth split open and she pitched Hector into the fumarole. He almost fired when Felicidad came at Mildred, but then Krysty disarmed her with her hair.

"I say," said Doc, who had pulled himself up alongside Ryan. "I do believe Krysty is faring fine without any help from us at all."

Mildred punched Felicidad and kicked her off the pyramid. Doc applauded. "Good show! Jolly good!"

Ryan realized Doc was speaking with a silly stagy English accent. He couldn't let himself be distracted now.

He saw the Eagle Knight rise to his knees. Even before the man raised his laser arm Ryan had the crosshairs fixed, the proper elevation and windage calculated on the fly. With something like relief that he was able to *do* something, Ryan squeezed off the shot.

When the rifle came back down, Ryan saw the headless torso fall, he wasn't surprised; he knew it was a good shot.

Then he saw his woman fall.

"My word, is she hit?" Doc asked.

"No! It's the Gaia power—you know how it tears her up when it comes over her and gives her superstrength. Fireblast, the way she was this time, she may be dead!"

His every fiber longed to bolt down, then across the plaza and up the steps to her side. But he knew there was something he had to do first. He made himself keep looking through that scope, scanning the top of the pyramid for enemies who might harm his woman.

He found two Eagle Knights showing signs of life. He put a rapid stop to that. All the rest had fled.

The earth was still shaking. The skyscraper they were in trembled like a frightened child. Ryan scarcely noticed. He got up, shouldered his pack, hefted the rifle.

"Come on, Doc."

THE PLAZA WAS a madhouse. The scavvies were slaughtering Hector's sec men. The hapless serfs trucked in from the valley to watch their *cacique* crown himself emperor didn't seem to know whether to fight the scavvies, their own oppressors, or one another. The wise had already taken to their heels.

For what good it would do them. The earthshocks

just kept coming. The city was being shaken to pieces around them. All the time volcanic bombs were dropping into the city like glowing-hot, wag-size hail.

Ryan had expected to see J.B. and Jak, if he ever saw them again, already atop the pyramid. Instead Doc called out and pointed them out, still laboring up the steps with two of the Jaguar Knights. Ryan realized they'd been delayed by having to blast their way through the frenzied struggling mob.

The path was clearer now, a good percentage of the rioters having been killed or simply run off. "A piece of cake," Doc pronounced. "Provided we are not knocked off our feet or smashed by a ton of airborne lava."

IT WAS A NIGHTMARE CLIMB. Fine sulfur-smelling ash had begun to fall like snow. It wanted to clog the mouth and nostrils and make it even harder to pull air into lungs that already felt as if red-hot iron skewers had been thrust through them. Somehow Ryan made it across the plaza and up the pyramid. Even more amazingly, Doc stayed with him the whole way.

At the top they found J.B., Jak and Mildred gathered around Krysty. The black woman had stretched her on the altar, which had less blood on it than the pyramid top itself. A deceased Eagle Knight's plastic breastplate served to prop her head. To one side the two Jaguar Knights crouched over Tenorio, tending his wounds.

Doc collapsed into the red muck. Only the sound of his wheezing let Ryan know he was still alive. Ryan managed to stagger through the sticky blood and fall to his knees beside the sacrificial stone. He seized Krysty's hand, which was limp and cold.

"Krysty, we're here."

She opened her eyes. Mildred had cleaned her up as best she could, which wasn't very, given all she had to work with was her hands. Krysty looked as if she were a child who'd gotten naughty with the red finger paint. But it was worlds better than the way she *had* looked, which probably would have struck Ryan dead on the spot.

"I'll be fine, lover," she said in a voice that, though hoarse, was all hers. She squeezed his hand. "Now that you're…here."

Her voice trailed off and she went limp again.

There came a screech of metal and concrete tormented beyond endurance. All heads turned.

A skyscraper fronting the plaza tottered. Then it fell against the building Krysty's would-be rescuers had occupied with an unbelievable crash. That building in turn squealed, shook and collapsed, sending columns of water a hundred feet in the air.

Ryan heaved himself to his feet. With a strength he didn't know he possessed, he scooped Krysty off the altar.

"We've got to got out of here now!" he shouted above the din of buildings falling like dominoes, of lives and dreams and futures being shaken to pieces.

"To where?" Mildred cried. Frustrated tears streamed down her cheeks.

J.B. put his arm around her shoulders. "Only one place," he said.

THE WATER WAS KNEE DEEP in the underground armory. Ryan had feared it would be fully flooded. Soon enough.

The lights were on, the generator still somehow thumping away, saving them from having to navigate by Doc's purloined flashlight. Ryan splashed through the water in the lead, carrying Krysty in arms that felt as though they belonged to somebody else. Next came J.B. and Mildred, helping a semiconscious Doc. Jak brought up the rear with his Python in hand. He had fired his Browning shotgun dry into a pack of screaming valley peons who had attacked them barehanded, breaking the stock over the head of the last one before the others fled.

Smoke filled the air from waist level up. Ryan didn't know if the building was burning or if it was fumes from outside. Part of the ceiling had fallen in. A Bridgeport mill had toppled, crushing a bandsaw.

"What a waste," J.B. said, shaking his head. "What a nukeshitting waste."

They reached the door with the warning, opened it, passed through to the door of the mat-trans. Jak pushed the level. For what seemed an eternity nothing happened.

"Oh, *damn*," Mildred said, sagging.

Then, groaning like an old man rising from bed, the door opened. The walls of the jump chamber were black armaglass. Like obsidian.

"Wait!" a voice cried from behind them. "I beg of you, wait!"

It was Tenorio, standing alone in the shattered work-shop's far door.

Jak took J.B.'s place, helping to support Doc. The Armorer gently lifted the unconscious Krysty from Ryan's arms. They fell to his side like lengths of dead meat. His friends moved into the black-walled chamber.

Tenorio limped forward. "You were not altogether candid with me, my friend," he said. "I thought you were evasive when pressed for details of your journey. But you seemed to be of good character and well disposed toward us. So it did not seem hospitable to press."

"We were," Ryan said. "Well-disposed, I mean. I'm...sorry. We lied."

Tenorio halted ten feet away. The water surged and sloshed around his bare shins to the heaving of the earth. Debris kept dropping from the ceiling in chunks. The air was clogged with dust as well as smoke.

"So the reports that hinted at some marvelous means of transportation—teleportation, of travel without crossing the distances intervening—were true."

Ryan nodded.

"We could do great things with such means at our disposal. We have...much rebuilding to do, as you know."

Ryan stared at him. He didn't know whether to laugh out loud at his foolishness or to weep in admiration of his determination.

"You're a man, Don Tenorio, I got to give you that. I don't know if you're a saint or a fool. But you're a man."

"That means you won't help us."

Ryan raised a hand. It still felt like a club. He let it fall again. "I wish I could. But it's a secret we can't afford to share."

Tenorio looked at him. The moment seemed to stretch toward infinity.

The earth gave a mighty spasm beneath them. Ryan was slammed against the side of the doorway. Tenorio swayed but kept his feet. A length of pipe six feet long and six inches thick fell behind him with a splash that drenched his back. He gave no sign of noticing.

"Ryan," J.B. called urgently.

"You have helped us, more than we dared expect," Tenorio said. "You saved us from the Chichimecs and from Hector's tyranny. More than that we cannot ask. We will stand on our own. Or fall on our own. That is as it should be."

He raised a hand. "Farewell, my friends. Remember us."

He turned and walked away.

"Ryan!" Mildred called. "This place is falling around our heads!"

Ryan backed into the chamber. He watched the small, lonely figure walk away from him, head held high. The earth lurched. A segment of ceiling dropped, obscuring him from view.

The one-eyed man stepped into the mat-trans chamber and closed the door.

"Wonder if he made it," J.B. murmured.

"No way," Jak said.

"I think he did," Mildred stated.

Ryan turned and looked down. Lights were pulsating in the chamber and the mist started to form. Krysty lay in the middle of the floor. He knelt beside her.

"We'll never know," he said.

He lay down beside the woman and gathered her in his arms to await the transition.

DANCING WITH THE DEVIL

Don Pendleton's Mack **BOLAN**®
Devil's Bargain

Alpha Deep Six. Wetwork specialists so covert, they were thought dead. Now this paramilitary group of black ops assassins and saboteurs has been resurrected in a conspiracy engineered somewhere in the darkest corners of military intelligence. Their mission: unleash Armageddon.

They've got America's most determined enemies ready to jump-start the nightmare, and the countdown has begun. Mack Bolan is squarely in charge and his orders are clear: abort the enemy's twisted dreams.

If Bolan survives, then it gets really personal. Because Alpha Deep Six has a hostage. A Stony Man operative...

Don't miss this special 100th episode, available January 2005 at your favorite retailer.

James Axler
Outlanders

EVIL ABYSS

An ancient kingdom harbors awesome secrets...

In the heart of Cambodia, a portal to the eternal mysteries of space and time lures both good and evil to its promise. Now, a deadly imbalance has not only brought havoc to the region, but it also threatens the efforts of the Cerberus warriors. To have control of the secrets locked deep within the sacred city is to possess the power to manipulate earth's vast energies...and in the wrong hands, to alter the past, present and future in unfathomable ways....

Available February 2005 at your favorite retail outlet.

Or order your copy now by sending your name, address, zip or postal code, along with a check or money order (please do not send cash) for $6.50 for each book ordered ($7.99 in Canada), plus 75¢ postage and handling ($1.00 in Canada), payable to Gold Eagle Books, to:

In the U.S.	In Canada
Gold Eagle Books	Gold Eagle Books
3010 Walden Avenue	P.O. Box 636
P.O. Box 9077	Fort Erie, Ontario
Buffalo, NY 14269-9077	L2A 5X3

Please specify book title with your order.
Canadian residents add applicable federal and provincial taxes.

GOUT32